Wrecking Ball

Adventures in Time, Love and War

S D Anugyan

Published by New Generation Publishing in 2016

www.newgeneration-publishing.com

New Generation Publishing

Also by S D Anugyan

<u>Fiction</u>

Secrets: An Oxford Tale

<u>Non-Fiction</u>

The Poisoned Dragon: Healing with Feng Shui
and Geomancy

<u>Poetry</u>

Troubadours

Here Are the Empire Builders!

www.sdanugyan.com

To each and every person

who has given me shelter

over the years.

I've seen that look before

Shining from star to star

Neil Young

Surfers ride for love and wipe out when it hits 'em

Soldiers kill for love and nobody admits it

Iggy Pop

Contents

1

Arriving

"If it's at 1805 you take the 43B on the Royal Parade, by the civic centre. If you miss that it's the 83, 84 or 86 opposite the civic centre at 1840, by TK-Max. Then it's the first stop on River View Drive. You got that? Kay will be there to meet you, whether you get the first, or second... You really should get a mobile phone."

Duncan grimaced as he put the phone down, then pushed his way out of the booth. He glanced at his watch's large white dial. It was possible he'd make the first bus, even at his speed.

Taxi drivers looked at him hopefully, with a sort of amused compassion, until he struggled past them and across the station road, dragging his two plastic pink and blue suitcases behind on their little wheels. Three boys, none older than twelve, shot past on skateboards, gleefully yelling insults, their rumbling wheels temporarily drowning his. He grunted, more from tired recognition than physical effort. In fifty years he had graduated from being a 'wimp' and 'swot' to a 'fatty' and 'lard-arse'. He wondered if that were progress.

In fairness to his detractors, he was something of a comical sight: five foot five, a girth of at least forty-two inches, and rapidly thinning black hair on top of a sweaty face that resembled a small pink beach ball upon which someone had drawn a moustache. To add to the effect, on this tranquil summer evening he was wearing a formal blue cotton shirt, and a brown wax coat that went almost to his ankles.

He struggled on, over the rise and towards Plymouth centre. The way was well-signposted. Still, he managed to wander off amidst the maze of featureless roads and grey monoliths, at times bordered by low walls with rusty stumps where once there had been railings. There were reassuring colours from a few shop windows so he knew he was headed in approximately the right direction. He stopped in his exertions on reaching a particularly imposing building that turned out to be a mall named after Sir

Francis Drake. Unless it were named after a duck, which seemed unlikely.

He stood in its shadow, looking up, attempting to regain his breath. Supermarkets often reminded him of Eastern temples. The Drake Centre was more like parts of different futuristic and prehistoric beasts that had been thrown together by an insane geneticist. He wondered what Drake would have made of being associated with such a creation. It towered over him, even more so as it was high up on the slope. He was diminished, with a long climb if he continued in the same direction, a sensation so familiar it felt like home. Every time somebody went in or out, insipid bursts of an electronically diluted song greeted his ears. 'Gonna take a sentimental journey… Got my bag, got my reservations…' Perhaps one day it had had some life in it.

Once he regained some of his breath, he began to retrace his steps as he seemed to be headed away from the centre, then decided the bombed-out skeletal church was not a good omen, and deigned to actually ask for directions. His well-spoken, quiet manner compensated for his appearance so that the effete lady in high heels and a Burberry coat was not too disturbed and was happy to send him on his way.

Of course, he swiftly managed to deviate *from* his course, into a street full of construction vehicles and scaffolding. Pausing to catch his breath once more, he wiped the sweat off his brow with the back of his sweaty hand, whilst gazing upwards at the workers reaping in overtime. He was about to pick up his cases and continue in a direction, any direction, when he saw a young lady – the only other pedestrian – walking his way.

She was six feet tall, with long bare legs and long dark hair, dressed in cut-off jeans, an olive-green halter and navy blue trainers. His heart, like a wild thing, leapt. He couldn't do anything to restrain it.

·"Hello," she said, as she passed between the scaffolding and him.

There was a kindness in her features – her shy glance, her delicate nose – and clumsily he was noticing this when it was too late to respond. He couldn't help watching her go. No matter how intelligent a man was, he could be reduced thus to a teenager; and the sight of a beautiful woman could define a day. He frowned, unsure that he was permitted to use the word 'beautiful' anymore. Wasn't that verboten? The builders had no such compunction and were behaving according to stereotype. Duncan wondered if she appreciated their coarseness. He returned, as he often did these days, to the single fact that he had no idea what women wanted other than that they didn't want him; and in that there was a twisted sort of freedom.

By the time he reached Royal Parade he had missed the first bus. Following his brother's directions, scrawled into his tiny notebook when he was on the phone, he crossed the busy road to the back-up bus stop. Once there he thrust the book back into the left cavernous pocket of his wax coat, then magically withdrew a metal camping bottle of water. This was one thing he had learned since his exile: always carry water. As he drank, he wiped his brow with his other hand.

The glass-and-metal shelter was only half-full. He found a perch at one end, and was idly watching those around when another young woman grabbed his attention. She was seeing a friend off on a bus.

"I'll see you on the comput-ahh," she said, accompanying her strange pronunciation with a bit of air-typing.

The pretty friend he hardly noticed as the doors sighed shut, and the bus pulled away. The girl in question though was oddly striking. She was fairly small and fairly plump, in a red dress with white polka dots. Her hair was jet black, her lips adorned with bright crimson lipstick. It was a look, he mused, that he hadn't ever seen on young people. Before he had time to contemplate her more, she had gone.

He got onto the bus at 1840 as directed, and sat at the back, leaving his lurid cases at the front.

They had been moving for about ten minutes when he came out of disparate contemplations to notice that the girl was now sitting a few seats in front of him, across the aisle. She must have got on when he had been lost in his so many thoughts. At ease now to consider her more, he observed her practical black leather shoes, her bare legs, then her attire once again. Amongst all those around, she really stood out. The 1940s look gave her grace; or, rather, brought out the grace that was innate.

She alighted on one of many featureless streets, and they continued on their way. Soon he was the only passenger left and they were meandering within a housing estate that he guessed was created in the fifties, spread like pale marmalade from one hill to another on the outer rim of the city. The driver called out to him

3

and the vehicle came to a halt. Despite the street's name, there was no river in sight.

He thanked the driver, bumping the cases into every available surface as he exited. When the bus disappeared around a corner further up the hill, he was alone until he saw a tall stately figure approach. She was wearing plimsolls, a dark skirt and a long beige cardigan. Her grey hair was tied up in a bun, and her large round wire-frame spectacles complemented rather than masked the amiability of her face.

"Duncan..." the woman said.

"Yes."

"It's Kay."

"Oh." His face lit up, and they hugged, a bit longer than English people usually hugged.

"How was your journey?"

"Fine."

"My macramé meeting was just round the corner," she explained as she led him and his cases to her car, "so it was no problem meeting each bus. But we can go straight home. Eliza knows if I don't return, you were on this one, which we both felt you would be. At least it isn't raining. It's a beautiful evening, isn't it."

"It is."

She frowned. Much of what he did tended to be a source of puzzlement, and the inevitable coming series of bewilderments had begun promptly.

"Why are you wearing that coat?" she asked, concerned. "You must be far too hot."

"There was no room left in the cases," he explained. "It's easier to carry this way. I managed to pack the hat though."

"It's new, isn't it?" She produced a set of keys from her cardigan pocket and pressed the switch. A small bright red Volkswagen beeped and flashed its lights in reply.

"Yes, it was raining in Cornwall last week, and I thought, as I was coming to Dartmoor eventually, it could prove useful. I only had an old anorak. I might have made a mistake, the weather changes so much."

She opened the boot and stood aside for him to put the cases in.

"You should put your coat in as well," she said.

"Good idea." He looked relieved as he placed it on top of the cases.

He stood back as she closed the boot, glancing at him with a smile. His blue shirt was crumpled, and had in the past probably always sported a tie. His black trousers had the ghosts of creases remaining.

They drove northwards up through the winding, quietening roads, the landscape lit gently by the setting sun; both silent for a while, both affected by the subdued spell of the evening. When they eventually emerged onto a long straight stretch of road, Duncan started catching glimpses of the gilded moor.

"George is making the dinner," Kay spoke. "It's ravioli tonight, if that's okay."

"Of course."

"Vegetarian. Sorry that we don't eat much meat."

"I don't either much these days, now I know what they put in it. Besides, I have stayed with you before you know, Kay."

"I know," she smiled whilst changing gear and building up speed, "But it's been a while, and a lot has happened."

"Of course," she said, after a brief pause during which she wondered what would be safe territory, "we both want to hear about your adventures in the Caribbean later. But first, how was Cornwall?"

It wasn't that safe territory. He knew she wanted to know if he had visited his daughter in West Penwith, or chickened out. He had chickened out.

The previous night, in a fishing village close to where she lived, he had been kept awake by the restlessness of the birds on the rooves. On parting the curtains he caught a glimpse of a black-backed gull swooping down upon smaller gulls' nests. He felt he'd witnessed what he should not have thanks to the street-light and – haunted by huge dark predatory wings – he returned to bed, only to wake soon after with a further dark revelation about his life, the unconscious insidious motivations of those he had always believed his friends. Like his parents, they had always declared his best interests at heart but their motivations had always been selfish. The solution to any such angst these days, now that he was one of the mocked, was to seek refuge in the shy corners of time and the world. Thus, leaving the guest house, he had gone for a twilight swim, the small waders puzzled by his presence. The water was cold and deliriously invigorating. He liked that he was alone. During the day he avoided the beaches, perceiving the visitors as daytime maggots crawling over the shoreline, whilst admitting that to them he was probably a lumbering seal, as unfortunately clumsy in the sea as on land. That morning he preferred merely to float, caressed by the icy fingers of weeds. As the sun rose over The Lizard, a glow of comprehension accompanying its rays, he knew he had to go to Dartmoor early, tail between his legs, his mission a failure. He dried off and returned to the B&B to pack up his things.

"I didn't see Jasmine," he said honestly. "But it was beautiful and cold after the Bahamas."

"Oh."

They were turning west over the moor that was once Clearbrooke Airfield. The sun was blinding them slightly, and Kay slowed down. There were people walking dogs, some attempting to fly kites in the soft breeze, and motley ponies wandering about. Above was the silver half-disc of the waxing moon, suspended in blue infinity. To the north could be seen the rusty tors of the moor proper.

They were skirting the village, its sign to their left, when she noticed him grimace and smile. "What?" she queried chirpily.

"Oh…it's a further reminder how little we know about the past…the village name." She surmised that this was quite an admission from an historian. She had always admired his humility, when it emerged. "To call a place 'Crapstone'," he continued, "and be entirely *sangfroid* about it…is very English."

"As a people, I think we are quite comfortable with the unknown," she remarked.

As they trundled along the little track that led to the house, she glanced at him with her direct blue eyes and noticed him holding his jaw.

"Are you all right, Duncan?"

"I have toothache or something. It's only occasional." He looked at her as if he'd been caught out, promptly letting go of his jaw.

"We have a dentist in Tavy I'd recommend." She realised that when on the road, as he had been for some time now, regular dentistry was one of the many things likely to be left on the wayside.

The house's name 'White Spring' was as obscure in its meaning as that of the village as far as Duncan was concerned, though his brother had explained it once. There was a connection to the Findhorn Community in North Scotland, to Glastonbury or some other place imbued with mystical significance; that much Duncan did remember. The wooden gates *were* white, and had been left open by George in anticipation of their arrival.

Alerted by the smooth crunching of the tires on gravel, the man himself, wiping his hands on a pale blue towel, emerged from the Georgian (and how often had he been teased on that) house, dressed in a Laura Ashley pinny over a black sweatshirt and brown corduroy trousers. He was as tall and thin as Kay, with a similar genial grin, lively grey eyes, a thick moustache and nearly full head of hair, neither of which were losing much of their sandy colour. There was an agility to his movements, a clear sense of him always having been a practical man. In this and other obvious ways he appeared very much the opposite of Duncan who, most people agreed, had got the short end of the stick.

George tossed the towel over his shoulder and strode forward as Kay killed the engine, and Duncan clambered onto the gravel. They shook hands firmly, whilst performing a two-second hug, the accepted protocol for many years now.

"Good to see you, Duncan," George's grey eyes twinkled kindly.

"You too. Thanks." The gratitude was a general one, which George vaguely understood.

There was a bit of a kerfuffle as George wanted to bring both suitcases, Duncan insisting on at least carrying one, during which time Kay had shut the gate, taken the coat and disappeared into the house.

"She's preparing the annexe for you," George said, his hands still on both cases, his eyes on Duncan. "You know how she is. She won't let you even see the place until it's ready. You gave us such short notice, our friends are arriving later and will be in the guest room."

In the face of such incriminatory subtext, Duncan had to let go of the second case.

"Please close the boot," George said as he led the way.

Duncan waited in the kitchen while his brother took the luggage through to the annexe. He could have gone to the sitting room across the hall, but the kitchen was one of the few rooms where shoes were permitted and he needed to have them on when going through the garden. Five minutes passed. He examined the fresh ravioli waiting to go in the pot, a salad of many colours, and garlic bread wrapped in tin foil. He was restless and considering going to the living room or the annexe – both of which had particular

7

consequences – when he saw, through the latticed double-glazing, two people opening the gate. It was two women, possibly mother and daughter, carrying a collection box. Uncertain, he went to meet them at the front door.

He was taken by their similarity as they stood in front of him on the doorstep: their languid expressions, long straight mousey hair hanging like threadbare curtains each side of their faces, and four large ears that poked out like naughty hiding children. They were different mainly in the twenty or so years separating them, temporal variations of each other. After pondering them a while, Duncan realised he hadn't heard a word the mother had said and had no idea even what charity they were collecting for. They in turn were becoming rapidly perturbed by the plump stranger's silence.

He was now in a dilemma. He didn't approve of charity. In his high-handed way he believed it to be a form of social bullying, and questionable in its financing. But what if he were wrong? What if most of the money went to a good cause? There were also the good intentions of the collectors to consider. He was occasionally generous simply because he wished the person in front of him to feel gratified. He wasn't sure about these two, they scared him a little, wraiths from the moor. Maybe they'd just had hard lives and were trying to do some good. He should find out what their charity was, that might sway his decision. Scrunching his eyes to read the box didn't help and in fact was the final straw for the two women, dismayed by the portly man who wouldn't say anything but now had started pulling faces. They fled.

Surprised by this turn of events, Duncan returned to the kitchen. His head was in disarray. What had he done? If he had just given them money, he would have kept them happy but at the cost of his own principles. In his dithering, his principles were intact but the consequences could be dire. Social convention would mark him severely. Even worse, George and Kay could become stigmatised. Local charities had the power of self-righteous gossip at their command. What *should* he have done? His thoughts ran rampant, and once again – as so often – feelings of powerlessness swept over.

"Your rooms are ready, Your Highness," George called out as he returned to the house just as he noticed in the fading light the front door open and, beyond, the gate as well.

Alerted, he entered the kitchen and at first saw nothing but could hear a rasping sound. Kay, just behind him, went the other side of the island and saw Duncan on his back, desperately attempting to breathe, his face a deep crimson.

"Good job we're prepared after last time," she said, opening a drawer and producing a white paper bag.

She knelt down while George lifted Duncan into a sitting position. She put the bag over his mouth and spoke tenderly to him.

A short time later he was seated more comfortably in the sitting room. He had allowed her to put Rescue Remedy under his tongue, which tasted strongly of its brandy solution, and accepted the camomile tea. He was secretly more grateful when George brought him extra brandy. Once he had calmed down sufficiently to tell his story, Kay said to George, "That must have been the Anderson sisters. I'll go and see them tomorrow."

She took Duncan – once his face had returned from crimson to pink – to the annexe while George finished preparing the late dinner. It was now dark outside, the garden path lit by solar-lights along its meandering perimeter. The annexe was a converted shed, located snugly between the house and a high hedge. There was a comfortable office on entering, with a computer and various books and CDs. It had been Kay's workspace when she had her own business. To the right was a small bathroom and the bedroom was through to the left, a neatly-made bed and the two suitcases next to it clearly visible.

"It looks very nice," commented Duncan weakly. She always took good care of people.

"You can use the computer if you like. It has internet."

"Thank you."

"Ahh. I'll just go get you some more towels."

Left alone, he perused the shelves. The music was obviously Kay's taste: Dido, Emmylou Harris, Kate Bush, Suzanne Vega... More of a blues and jazz man at least ostensibly, he knew little of the artists. He chose one at random and slipped it into the CD player.

Over at the house, Kay was delayed returning by a phone call from the other guests who were making better time than expected. They had eaten but would join them at the table. She was then occupied giving advice to George, and laying two extra places. Consequently, Duncan was well-settled in before she made it back with the towels.

Some of the contents of his suitcases were strewn over the bed. He was seated at the desk facing the dark garden. He had had a shower without drying himself properly, using the white towel now wrapped around his waist. He was like a big pink baby, listening to Dido and looking confused

"Are you all right?" she asked, turning to him after stepping into the bathroom and carefully putting the extra towels on the rail.

"Yes, I'm just... I don't understand." He nodded at the CD player. "One minute she says she wants to be a hunter and go on adventures alone, then the next she's complaining that her lover has left her and the bed's too empty. What *does* she want?"

Kay was about to leave when she noticed what he had thrown on the bed.

"Did you pack any clothes?"

"Ehh...yes." He followed her gaze. "I just haven't unpacked them yet."

"That's a lot of books."

"Is it?"

"Dinner will be in five minutes," she laughed.

"Great." He had eaten a granola bar while she was gone.

"Oh. And Heinrich and Naomi will be here very soon."

In the kitchen, as she helped George drain the ravioli, he asked how Duncan was.

"Fine," she said through all the steam. "Except I've never seen anyone baffled by Dido before."

He was about to comment when headlights outside alerted them to the new arrivals. Kay went to greet them and to open the gate fully.

When Duncan got to the house he met the predictable, general confusion of suitcases going up the stairs and people coming down. Introductions were made, and dinner promptly served.

The two couples had met during a conference on 'Peace in the New Age' at the Findhorn Community. Despite their forty years' difference, they had hit it off immediately. Kay at the time put it down to unknown past lives, whereas George simply stood with them in the night air by the tranquil bay during this observation, and smiled wryly whilst smoking his pipe. A gentle breeze from the east took the aromatic fumes, scattering them over the quiet waters, that lay like a quivering dark mirror between the large forest on the other side, and the small fishing village on theirs.

Neither Heinrich nor Naomi held any opinion as to the connection, perfectly content to go with the flow. If compelled to suggest a reason, the former may have commented that Kay and George were good listeners and had English politeness honed to such a fine art they wouldn't interrupt his rants. Even that would have been over-stating things, with a trace of irony intrinsic to the young man's nature. Indeed, if one built a fully stereotypical German male, then had the means to transform it to its complete opposite, the end product could very well be something like Heinrich. He was thin, with a long, clean-shaven face, a short mane of thick black hair, and thick black-rimmed spectacles through which he observed the world with perspicacious blue eyes and perpetual, silently bubbling amusement.

Naomi was not so much the straight man – that was everyone else – as the appreciative audience quietly, and sympathetically, chuckling. She was of medium height, with brown curly hair and soft doe-eyes. Every inch of her exuded warmth. The phrase 'all heart' would have needed invention if it hadn't existed by the time of her arrival in the world. Kay had once ventured that Naomi alone in humanity could be lacking a Jungian shadow. There had been sudden silence when she suggested this to the other three, till Heinrich commented that Kay should try leaving the top off the toothpaste sometime. But even he was mostly silent.

At dinner he was on good form. Seated next to Naomi, and opposite Duncan, he was describing their journey.

"Then when we drove off the ferry, we saw all these signs, 'Please do this,' 'Please do that,' 'Sorry for any delay,' 'Thank you for your patience,' and we realised: *that's* the secret to speaking perfect English! Just put 'please sorry thank you' in any sentence and you've got it right."

"And 'welcome'," put in Naomi.

"Yes! And 'excuse me'."

"That was the policeman at Border Control."

"The authorities are not always like that," said Kay bitterly.

"Kay's referring to a problem a friend of hers, Charlotte, had coming from Manchester," said George.

"A button in her jeans set off the alarm, so she was shoved into a plastic bubble and searched aggressively under her bra, in her pants, everywhere. She'd been abused as a child so this was unbearable for her. The gum-chewing bimbo dismissed her tears, saying 'I'm just doing my job.'"

"When she went to Customer Services, distraught, they simply said, 'Our protocol's changed'," George smiled thinly.

Heinrich and Naomi listened seriously to the account.

"The names may change," said Heinrich, "but the behaviour doesn't. 'I was just doing my job' doesn't cut it anymore, whether doing it for God, country or your mortgage."

Duncan had been silent for a long time, but was listening to every word whilst enjoying the ravioli immensely. "Most people are ignorant of history," he said now, looking up at them, "that is how they can repeat this kind of behaviour without feeling ashamed. The cliché is true. Or they're fooled by the change of names, as you said."

"They believe they're working for the common good," said George.

"The Japanese and the Germans believed the same in the Second War. We've had plenty of recent examples too. Besides, the English were not exactly without a sense of moral self-justification when they took over the world."

"Did you give lectures in this?" Heinrich asked.

"Not really. I'm stuck in the Middle Ages."

"You're under-representing yourself again, Duncan," George said quietly. "You even gave lectures on common historical trends to the public. You're in no way limited in scope."

"We attended one of his lectures," said Kay eagerly. "Duncan was very good, very authoritative. He was exploring the idea that genetic imperatives find their way into the collective by any means necessary. For example, whilst the Anglo-Saxons were repelling Vikings at Stanford Bridge, the Normans were invading on the south coast. The English needed the Norse blood so it was destined to come in. Though Duncan wouldn't use the word 'destiny', would you...?"

"Oh I'm comfortable with the word."

"You just wouldn't use it!" George cried.

"Then can you call, for instance, the Nazis' Final Solution, a 'false destiny'?" asked Heinrich.

"I...wouldn't use the word," Duncan admitted.

"It's ironic then," said Naomi, glancing shyly at Heinrich, "because we think it was destiny for us to meet."

"How did you meet?" Duncan ventured to ask. He had been curious about them.

12

"I was camping at Bodensee," said Naomi. "Heinrich's parents ran an inn there."

"I was the lackey!" Then he became serious. "My beloved is now under-representing *her*self. She was researching an organisation that protected Jews during the war."

"Including my grandparents," she said softly.

"Who were sheltered by my grandparents."

A silence fell over the table. George and Kay, who had heard the story before, never failed to be moved even by its sparse details.

"I suspect, Duncan, you will insist on an obvious logical explanation here." Mischief had returned to Heinrich's features.

"I wouldn't diminish something like this," said Duncan.

"A usually undisclosed part of the story," Kay said, "is that Naomi was officially researching local folklore for her thesis."

"There was some subterfuge there," grinned Heinrich, lifting his white wine to his lips.

"After meeting Heinrich," Naomi said to Duncan, "the thesis was delayed by a year."

"That's not surprising," Duncan said.

"She now had a real goblin to study," quipped Heinrich.

Conversation turned to Duncan's experiences in the Caribbean. He told them that the divide between the haves and have nots was so extreme there it was like a parody of Britain and America; then he became surly and uncommunicative, pretending to focus on the Italian ice cream once it was served. He left early but politely, saying he was tired. After standing, pushing his chair back to the table, and assuring Kay he had all that he needed, he was gone.

"Have we made an English faux pas?" asked Heinrich once a momentary silence had passed.

Their hosts dismissed this with shakes of their heads.

"He doesn't like talking about the Bahamas," said George.

Kay disagreed. "I don't think it's that, George. Have you not noticed that whenever a romantic story enters conversations with him, he gets more and more withdrawn before leaving the room? He did that last time."

"I thought I saw him react," Naomi said, looking at her. "Our story is quite romantic." Heinrich merely nodded in agreement.

"He had two serious break-ups within three years," said George. "He was oblivious to any mid-life crisis, then later went for broke."

"His wife left him," Kay expounded, "after she found out about his affair with a student. The girl Evelyn, who was in her early twenties, left him soon after. The university found out and he lost his job. There are still all sorts of legalities going back and forth. Meanwhile, his son in Norfolk won't talk to him, and he's too terrified to even say hi to his daughter in Cornwall."

"Jasmine actually wants to talk to him, but can't get hold of him," put in George. "He doesn't do email – though he did have a university address – nor does he have a mobile phone."

"He's assumed that as Rowan has sided with his mother so firmly, Jasmine has as well."

"Ow." Naomi, noticing a grin of new-found admiration on Heinrich's face, had struck him on the shoulder.

"You shouldn't approve," she said.

"No," he protested, "it's just...*Duncan*?!"

"He put on more weight in the last two years," said Kay. "He's become even more of a roly-poly but women always liked him, and he was a hit with the students. Evelyn I believe was something of a siren. In the picture I saw she's certainly quite beautiful."

"Yup," said George, "now there was a woman worth getting out of bed for. What?"

"He got hauled up in front of the university authorities," Kay continued, the only one ignoring him, "then in what must have been a slow news week the press got hold of the story. They interviewed some of his colleagues and the final, public depiction was of a man so dried-up, boring and repressed it was doubtful he was having sex with anyone, including his wife, and other students."

"Ha," Heinrich grinned, "First he's put on trial for having sex, then for not having sex."

"Normally the sympathy would go with the one cheated on, but Rose walked away with nearly everything, including their friends' sympathies. As well as material things, he lost his career and reputation which seemed to hit him the hardest. He's been travelling like a teenager on an extended gap year for a while."

"The only one unhurt, I assume," Naomi pointed out, "is Evelyn."

"I don't know what the extent of her feelings towards him were."

"It's his own fault," said George. "He should have kept it in his pants."

"No," she said firmly, "don't judge. Rose was always so reserved, who can say what the state of their marriage was, she certainly never let on to us. I'm very worried about him. He doesn't know where he's going or what he's doing. He's surviving

14

on his meagre share of the house which can't go on forever, especially if he keeps travelling to all those islands. He's got an odd sense of budgeting which means he won't do things like take taxis but will fly to the Caribbean on a whim."

"That's for some historical research he's not telling us about."

"That won't keep him warm and dry. He went to Malta, Cyprus and the Bahamas. Also Ibiza though that might have been a mistake. I think we've got to keep an eye on him while he's here. He always gets into trouble of one sort or another."

"Yes! I proclaim we should follow him wherever he goes, and whoever has the best story of Duncan's misadventures after two weeks, wins the prize."

"No! That's not what I meant!" She knew his mischief was a pretext, that he was acting out of concern for his brother, but her role was to object.

"What's the prize?" asked Heinrich.

"A bottle of single malt."

"Sold!"

"No!" screamed Kay.

"Does anyone mind if I smoke my pipe?" asked George, reaching for it on the sideboard.

They all knew, and had never told him, that he usually smoked only when happily surrounded by friends, so would always concede.

"I'll go make the coffee," said Kay, resigned, and not just to the smoke.

They were singing 'Roll Out the Barrel' in the next apartment for the third time since leaving Plymouth. He had always thought there was a sadness underlying the song, and never enjoyed it quite as much as his peers. 'There's a garden...what a garden...' It was full of yearning like 'The White Cliffs of Dover' or many of the other songs for which the English had particular affection; when they weren't being merely humorous. The boisterous compartment was obviously filled with servicemen and, judging by the accompaniment, servicewomen. The mobilisation of women on such a large scale was one of the aspects of life here which had fascinated him on arrival to the shores of this muddy island. For all its talk of emancipation, America had a bit of catching up to do.

His own, more sedate, compartment was filled with languid smoke rather than sound over the carriage's rattling. To his left,

15

two soldiers in khaki and a man in tweed and a trilby were puffing away whilst conducting an earnest but subdued conversation regarding the wheat crop that year. At least that's what he thought the topic was, he found their accents so difficult to penetrate. The soldiers were clutching their Lee Enfields, upright on the vibrating floor, the civilian a walking stick. He smiled at the observation, then turned his attention to the vision by the window.

Being diagonally across, and her back to the engine, she was as far as possible from him, which he considered a loss for she was quite a lady; not quintessentially English, he would argue, but quintessentially female. With a sage-green dress and thin black jacket draped over her shoulders, a veil half-covering her pale smiling face, and flame-red hair bursting forth from under a large lime-green felt hat, she could slip comfortably between the pages of an American detective novel. He looked at her ruby lips, as she focused on the misty countryside rather than her fellow travellers. The lipstick looked real. Her stockings were new and unladdered, the clothes well-maintained though obviously self-tailored, the fabric on her dress subtly worn in parts, her shoes practical and flat. Any excess of sartorial elegance would have been obscene at such a time. That she had worked hard to look her best, felt patriotic.

"Do you have a popsy back home, sir?" He was startled by the private next to him, addressing him with something of a leer on his wide face with its sticking-out ears. He wasn't fooled by the geniality of the man's features; the hardness lurking within made facing either end of his rifle a dismal prospect.

Caught out, he instantly and invisibly sought solace in his rank. The withdrawal was unnecessary, he quickly realised, as he had effectively bought everyone's loyalty by handing out cigarettes when they first boarded, stabbing his out on the floor half-smoked early on. He still hadn't got used to the British brands which tasted bitter and deadly.

"I… Yes, I do," he said on recovery, fumbling for his wallet.

She was a Vargas girl to others' eyes, he knew. The picture was from a glam shoot done not primarily for career – she didn't actually need one since their engagement – but from a salacious pride. He had four others in his shaving kit, this the only one he felt secure showing in public.

He flashed the picture proudly to the men. There was a sudden silence.

"She's a corker," said the other soldier, thin, wiry, just a kid really.

"Yeah. She's quite a gal." He put the wallet back in his flying jacket.

Even the lady in green had attempted a brief discreet look, but the last occupant, two seats along from her, a middle-aged unsmiling woman in stiff tweed and a bonnet with dried heather squashed down on her head – funny how the women were on one side, the men on the other – was not so impressed. Both women had refused a cigarette earlier, but only the elder now refused to show even a glimmer of interest or be swayed by the American's charm. She was not fooled by the young pilot's casual demeanour, having seen too many of his countrymen break down and cry, whether for the loss of a friend in action or absence of a family. She secretly admired them for their candour, though would be uncomfortable if any of the men in her life indulged in such demonstrative behaviour.

She looked now at the young American, his jet black hair, slightly longer and more unruly than any she had seen on British airmen, and his handsome, unblemished features.

The pilot avoided her eyes, till she spoke out.

"You have an admirer."

Confused, he looked up at her uncertainly. She nodded to his right, where a small boy in the corridor was pressing his face against the glass gazing at him wide-eyed. He pushed the door open and stood up, peering down at the boy. There was a younger lad standing near. They were both wearing shorts and neatly pressed shirts.

"Are you all right there, sonny?" He addressed the child as he had once been addressed by his elders. He felt it gave him a part to play with gravitas.

"Are you a pilot?" the boy asked shyly.

"Yes, I am."

The boy, so much in awe, went quiet. His brother came to the rescue.

"Eric wants to be a pilot."

"Do you, Eric?"

"Yes." Then bravely he asked, "What kind of planes do you fly?"

"Many different ones."

"Spitfires?"

"I have, yes, but other great planes too, like Hurricanes, Mustangs... Soon I might be flying Typhoons again. Have you heard of them?" His audience seemed out of their depth, so he added, "Sometimes they're called *Bombphoons!*"

"Wow."

"Yes, wow. Now tell me, Eric, if you want to be a pilot, do you study hard at school?" He asked the question kindly but the lad seemed a little dismayed. "Have you just been to Plymouth?" he changed the subject helpfully.

"Mother came to see us," was the tacit answer.

"Granny's on the train," put in his brother. "We're staying with her."

"Oh I see." He never failed to be moved by the stories of evacuees, the disarray of heart and home. "Here." He reached into his pocket and drew out a chocolate bar. Ritualistically, he always put one under his pillow whenever he had a new bunk, which was often; but it seemed to have more symbolic purpose here. "Make sure you share it with your Granny."

The boys, delighted, ran off down the corridor. Pulling the door shut, he returned to his seat, pleased as always to play the hero.

He glanced out at the leafy banks, bright foxgloves showing bravely through the grey sunlight, harbingers of the reams of fireweed he looked forward to later in the summer, so redolent of favoured parts of his own country. They approached a little English station wrapped in the mist, and the train slowed down. Unsure, he caught the large-eared soldier's attention. "Yelverton," nodded the latter.

He pulled his kit bag down from the rack. By the general inaction from the others, he inferred he was the only one leaving. "See you fellahs." Then, the train stopped, the station's name was shouted outside. The beautiful red-haired woman leant forward and opened the door, stepping neatly onto the platform. His departure was less elegant but he made it out, knocking the civilian's legs with his bag, the irritated man then pulling the door quickly shut after him. As the train departed with accelerating tempo, the musical faction next door had moved onto 'The Thing-Ummy-Bob', delivered chaotically amongst peals of laughter.

He turned, smiling, to view his situation, another lonely platform in the middle of a foreign countryside. A few people, mostly military, had left by the exit, and five, including what looked like a prison guard, were crossing the bridge for another train. The only other person on the platform was the red-haired woman, who had passed under the bridge and was standing a good fifty yards away. He could see her in the mist, obscured further by the train's steam as the locomotive whistled and disappeared into the yawning maws of a tunnel.

What was she doing there? There were no other destinations from this platform as far as he knew. He watched as she reached into her bag and withdrew a cigarette case. He had superb vision and he could see, even in this ground-level cloud, that the case was silver. Faintly, as in the far-off distance, there was a sense of rejection, that she hadn't accepted a smoke from him; then this was overcome entirely by the mystery of her actions. There was an immense silence left from the train's departure. Watching her light up, her eyes hidden under the veil, he became aware of birdsong around, as if waking from a dream, and someone talking.

"Captain Donnel?"

He turned, like a man moving in water, and saw a diminutive RAF corporal standing in front of him, neat and rigid in his scratchy uniform.

"Yes. Hi there."

They saluted.

"I'm your driver, sir. Corporal King. I was told to meet you. Sorry about the weather."

Before Donnel could do anything, King had thrown the kit bag over his shoulder and was leading him to his ride.

He seemed to be the only one not walking to the airbase. It felt unfair, sitting in the back of a large staff car, as they passed various people in uniform headed in the same direction, including a few American sailors. The Brits often treated him well, and with warmth, as much as they could with their scarce resources. One of the first to be posted after Pearl Harbor, he had felt initially daunted by sudden immersion into a country at war; then his disposition had swiftly shifted to appreciation for the native resilience and humour.

"How was your journey, sir?" the corporal asked over his shoulder, as he drove slowly, carefully.

"No problem. I couldn't see much of the countryside in the mist though."

"Yes, sorry about the weather, sir," King repeated. "Americans are often shocked at the state of Plymouth."

"I passed through Coventry, London, and a few more of your cities last year, so I'm used to it."

King went silent, for which his passenger was grateful, before the garrulous driver added proudly, "We built the airfield from what was left of Plymouth after the raids."

Donnel looked out at the perimeter fence as they drove alongside, an occasional glimpse of a hangar or a stationary plane just visible beyond. The obscure shapes they passed were embalmed in white, the only evidence of movement the sound of a Merlin engine being turned over. He recognised the twin propellers of a Whirlwind looming closely. He knew flying here was often hampered by the lack of visibility, as with many of the British airfields.

"Where are you taking me?" he asked.

"It's the old Station Headquarters, sir. Ravenscroft. I think the officers were too comfy to move entirely to the new HQ on the airfield. Won't be long now."

Ravenscroft was a Gothic-style mansion to the south west of the airfield. He guessed it to be Victorian. Following King's directions, he went in to be met by three RAF officers on their way out.

"Another bloody Yank?!" exclaimed a squadron leader, cheerfully slapping him on the shoulder before he had time to salute.

"Sorry about that, sir. We heard you needed a hand."

"Good to have you on board, son."

Donnel wasn't fooled by the joviality. The man had the demeanour and eyes of one much older, but was about the same age as him. As with numerous other pilots who had survived the summer of 1940, the Englishman's wounds were not of the physical kind.

"I think Spiffy's waiting for you upstairs," one of the other men said.

The trio disappeared, laughing. The house also contained the officers' mess and quarters, and there was the scent of beer on their breath.

Group Captain Derek Smythington was seated at his tiny desk, back to the bay window, when Donnel was shown in. He saluted as formally as he could. Smythington stood up to return the gesture, with a gleam in his eye, as if it were all a joke. He had a lively, restless attitude even as he sat down.

"Please take a seat, Captain."

Donnel didn't know what to expect. His orders had been to simply report to the commanding officer rather than the adjutant, and take it from there. This had shortly followed his promotion. He didn't know if there were a connection.

"Do you prefer I call you 'Captain'?"

"People tend to use my first name, sir. Jackie, or Jack."

"'Jackie' will suffice. I don't think we have many of those around."

"Yes, sir."

Donnel had known many in a similar position surrender to the greyness of bureaucracy; losing any sense of being in touch with those under them, sitting at a desk while entire squadrons came and went. Smythington was different. Despite being a good ten years older, and shorter, than Donnel, he had thicker black hair and an intelligent piercing brightness in his grey eyes contrasting with his five o'clock shadow. The system was currently attempting to surround him with paper, which he was valiantly keeping to both sides of the desk in order to be in command of whatever situations presented themselves in front.

Donnel's arrival as it turned out had resulted in more excessive paperwork with little substance. If Donnel weren't clearly such a happy-go-lucky character, the meeting would have had a more sombre tone. The group captain considered him silently for a moment, his grey eyes twinkling, a sadness far off in their depths.

"I don't know what to do with you," he confided.

"Sir?"

Smythington tapped the sheets of paper in front of him.

"All I've been told is that you're here to help with a new Rebecca unit for fighters. Is that true?"

"That's more than I've been told, sir."

"You are familiar with BABS?"

"Not really, sir."

"I can't say I am either frankly. Beacon systems never came into play when I was doing sorties. More used to flying by the seat of my pants myself. I've also been shot at by our own gunners because the IFFs don't always work. It always comes back to the human being at the end of the day.

"Look, I can only second guess as to why you're here. This isn't the first time a passenger has arrived without his luggage. I have no new tech, and no clear instructions as to what to do with you, other than keep you on ice for the time being. If the chance comes, will you be up for shipping patrol or something of that ilk?"

"Of course, sir. I don't want to be sitting on my petunia all day."

"It counters my orders but to hell with that. You flew Typhoons at Tangmere before Holmsley South, so you've had experience. The bad news is we have no room for you. You're welcome to join us at meals and for drinks, but we'll have to accommodate you in one of the Nissens on the airfield."

"That's fine, sir. I'm quite used to that."

Smythington stood, looking out through the window into the mist.

"Perhaps there is no new Rebecca," he said, musing, "and you're here to show us how to fly in pea soup." He thrust the window open and leant out, shouting, "Corporal King! I'm about to send Captain Donnel back down to you, if you're not too busy chatting up every pretty WAAF within ten miles. Take him to see Sergeant Billings."

There was a cheerful affirmation just audible before he shut the window.

"Not that he has any chance. They call them 'pilot's cockpits', you know...the WAAFs...which insults both sexes. It's the ground crews who keep the planes in the air. There are maybe thirty people supporting every pilot. War messes up perspective.

"Let's get you sorted."

When Donnel had returned to the staff car, and was getting in, there was a flurry of activity. An American jeep arrived with customary abruptness, pulling right up to the house steps, stones shooting out from under the wheels. Two naval officers got out, not even noticing him, their eyes directed at Ravenscroft's imposing walls. The driver remained in his seat. Simultaneously, a Hillman Minx pulled up gently from the other direction. After switching off the engine, a WAAF sergeant emerged from the driver's side. She was slim, with long, wavy, untied brown hair under her hat. The bag which she hoisted over her shoulder was an elegant barathea bag matching her blue-grey uniform. She too was looking up at the house when a wing commander with a classic walrus moustache walked out, oblivious to the Americans' presence and charging right past them. She smiled at him in greeting, to be met with outrage.

"Have you forgotten how to salute, Sergeant?!" he roared.

"No, sir, sorry, sir." She quickly and nervously performed the belated gesture.

"I don't know where they get you people from," he garrumphed as he went on his way, without saluting.

Donnel by now was in his seat, and the naval officers a good distance from the scene, but he could see their amusement. He wondered if they had caught the irony in that for all his bluster, the officer had made no comment about the woman's hair.

As they pulled away leisurely from the house into the mist, he looked back. The officers had gone in, the woman following.

"She's new here, sir," said King over his shoulder.

"The WAAF?"

"Yes. I heard she was coming. She's a liaison or something, I'm not sure what. Because of all you lot arriving I guess. It looks like she can handle a car all right." He started chuckling. "Where I was before, near Leicester...I heard a Wellington got delivered. A woman got out. The welcoming committee kept waiting for the pilot. It took them a while to realise it was her." There was that welcome gap of silence again, before King added as an afterthought, "Funny how she didn't salute though."

In the time it took to get to the guardhouse at the west gate, Donnel had learned about King's experiences at bases all over the UK. His involvement with rounding up the crew of a downed German bomber in Surrey three years earlier, was rendered with vivid detail but not, it appeared, with exaggeration. ("They apologised for bombing the wrong town!") Not once did he go into details regarding his family, other than mentioning a young son in passing, and that omission made it all the more poignant.

It didn't take long for the accommodation to be sorted. The most southerly hut behind the Bellman hangar, down along the western perimeter, was empty, he was informed.

It was an eerie walk along the peri-track, trees hanging dark and forlorn, several Nissen huts he passed devoid of life, and the hangar to his left looming over it all, like a lord of the underworld. A car went by on the adjacent road, headlights pushing through the mist. It sounded like an Austin Tilly. Its engine's fading roar was the only sound until he became aware of singing.

He walked instinctively towards its source, over the damp grass, when he came across the most extraordinary individual he was to meet for the duration of his short and eventful life.

23

The man had dark black, round unshaven features and a large mouth. He was lying on his back, wearing USAAF khaki trousers and a dishevelled US Army jacket. He appeared to be a private but nothing of his dress seemed reliable, so even that was questionable. He had no hat. The words of the song were incoherent but were interrupted anyway once he became aware of Donnel's approach. He sat up abruptly, which was as much of an effort as he was prepared to make.

"Are you Private Hawker?" Donnel asked, astonished.

"Ah could be," Private Hawker said in such a way as to make Donnel smile for some reason. There was wariness there, but also amusement. Indeed, Hawker smiled back with a generous flashing of white teeth.

"I'm going in Hut 8. Sergeant Billing told me to ask you to get me sorted."

"That fellah. Did he say anythin' else?"

"That I was to 'kick your *arse* '."

"Okay. That's him alright." Hawker got to his feet, nodding. "I'll show you your 'accommodation' then get you some of their pox-ridden blankets."

His vernacular was intriguing. He sounded educated, East Coast probably, but with twangs of the South. Something told Donnel he never completed his education.

"Are you from New York?"

"I am, yes." He was surprised. "You, sir?"

"I was born in Frisco."

"Iss meant to be nice, sir."

"It is. And call me 'Jackie' please."

"Benjamin. Ben. Nice to meet ya."

"How are you coping with the English weather, Ben?" Donnel asked as they walked towards the hut.

"Iss okay."

"I miss the sun myself."

"The mist is saying, 'enough of the foolishness of summer, go in, behave yourself, be silent.'"

Donnel was speechless as Hawker led him inside.

When Flight Lieutenant Trevor Smith arrived at Hut 8, it had been dark for almost an hour. Even before he entered he was in a mild state of shock and peevishness. The sight before him threw him even more. The hut with its half-dozen bunks, was empty of personnel but for two men, one of whom was heating up a pan of water on the stove, a cigarette dangling from his mouth. The other was lying on a top bunk, reciting poetry. They both appeared to be American, but the uniforms were confusing, particularly in the dim light.

"Hi there," said Donnel. "You must be Smith. You're in time for coffee. The real stuff. None of your limey ditch-water." He now removed the cigarette with his free hand and flicked the ash to the floor. "Ben has recited what he knows of Thoreau, and is now wandering through Brooklyn with Whitman."

Hawker went quiet and sat up to look at the newcomer. He noticed immediately that the RAF officer was slightly dishevelled, and even fragile. His hat was at an angle, a button missing from his jacket, his fair hair tussled. Only the moustache remained exactly where it should be.

Donnel's technique for handling British reserve was to bombard it with affability, so he persisted.

"I'm Jackie Donnel, your roomie. This is Ben. He runs things around here so I recommend we keep on his good side. Don't ask me where he kips. I guess in the trees. Coffee?"

"There's only two of us here?" Smith exclaimed, moving into the room. He had a pronounced limp, and there was clearly some pain as he moved. "The other two huts seem to be packed with your countrymen."

"I know. And I'm not allowed to talk to them, nor they to me. Their CO came over especially to inform me of that."

"Asshole," said Hawker, almost to himself.

"They're Navy," Smith said, tossing his bag onto a bed.

"I don't think that's it. Coffee?"

"You look hungry," commented Hawker.

"I am. Flipping hungry. They'd stopped serving at the mess. Got a drink in me before coming here. I'm whacked. Fortunately Spiffy told me to nip over the fence rather than walk all the way up to the gate. Saved me a lot of bother. That coffee looks good."

"I can get you beans," Ben proclaimed then was gone.

"Really? He can do that?"

"I'm beginning to think he can do anything."

"What uniform is he wearing?"

"Don't ask me," Donnel said, pouring the coffee into three tin cups. "No milk, I'm afraid," he said, handing Smith one.

"Still ambrosia for me, old chum." They knocked their cups together. "Good to meet you. You're a pilot, I take it."

"As charged."

"Spiffy told me you'd be here. He didn't tell me you'd be the only one here. And...Ben?"

"He was with other troops at the camp in...Gunnislake?"

"Yes, it's near here."

"But he didn't get on with the others. They called him a coconut."

"A what?"

"Coconut. Dark on the outside, white on the in. He went to university in New York before they kicked him out too. At least I think that's what happened. I don't always understand him. After the trouble in Gunnislake, they demoted him and put him on General Duties at the white camp at Beer Something-or-other. He managed to piss them off too. They figured they could keep him in General Duties here, looking after his fellow countrymen but under the watchful eye of you Brits. You don't seem to have the same issues. Mixed squadrons work really well."

"Try telling that to the Scots and the English."

"True. All because of a little squabble three hundred years ago."

"I'd say that a bit quieter in future, Jackie. Best don't say it at all."

Hawker returned with half a loaf of bread and a tin of beans.

"I couldn't get no butter," he declared, swiftly taking over the stove duties.

"That's...thank you, Ben." Smith was impressed.

"Iss okay."

After Smith had eaten, the three men settled in for the evening. There were two wooden chairs which the Americans pulled closer to the stove. Smith sat on a bed, after also pulling it nearer. Hawker was smoking the Black Cats Donnel had been glad to surrender, especially after Hawker had given him a whole box of Camels. He tossed a packet over to Smith.

"Ben gave me a load," he said.

"Ah still have my sources," smiled Hawker.

"Well look what I've got, chaps," said Smith, producing a quarter bottle of Scotch.

"Hell, yeah," Donnel approved.

As they drank out of their tin cups amidst a thickening cloud of smoke, the officers compared their day's journeys. Smith, it turned out, had the worst of it marginally by the end. Overcrowded trains, the bombed-out town centres, the tired faces, were ubiquitous but his arrival had been markedly different from Donnel's.

He had been one of the ground crew assigned to 210 Squadron at RAF Hamworthy in Dorset, till receiving orders to transfer from duties on Catalina craft there to the Walrus Amphibians at Clearbrooke; or, as his team stated on hearing the news, 'from the beauty to the beast'. Catalinas had extra credence added to their grace ever since one had spotted the Bismarck, leading to the powerful German ship's ultimate defeat. The Walrus had no such celebrity status, so Smith kept quiet about having requested the transfer himself.

As luck would have it, there were two officers driving to the nearby airfield at Roborough who were happy to give him a lift. The two men had had their meal at the mess, accompanied with several drinks, before they left. Smith sat in the back of the car, clutching his kit bag, feeling hungry whilst listening to the banter from the front seats. He was not present as far as they were concerned while they brazenly compared stories about battling the Hun. They were a few years younger than him, probably only about twenty. He lacked the willpower to interrupt their flow of youthful pride by informing them he too was once a pilot. Their conversation – overheard in snippets over the noise of the car – moved onto full disclosure regarding the physical attributes of a WAAF one of them had slept with. At least it was meant to be full disclosure. The story seemed to testify more to the pilot's credentials than the girl's. That she had given in to his advances apparently spoke well of his moral fibre and poorly of hers. Smith fell back into his seat, grateful he couldn't hear any more.

It was twilight when they turned north from Plymouth. A tangible sense of anticipation pervaded the car as they headed into wilder territory.

"I trust you know where you're going!" he said to be friendly, leaning forward.

The mist was everywhere and there were no signposts.

"What?!" asked the other passenger, turning.

He repeated his comment, feeling stupid.

"Oh we know," was the reply, then the two men talked quietly amongst themselves and laughed. Smith sat back, musing sadly that a need for secrecy had permeated even private conversations. He was feeling more and more that life was something for other people, he was excluded. Maybe he had actually died.

They turned off the main road and went up a little track. The masked headlights revealed a gate with an MOD notice of No Entry. They stopped.

"This is a short cut across the airfield," he was told by the driver while the other man got out to open the gate.

"To Clearbrooke?"

"Of course."

"Thank you."

"Don't mention it."

After they had driven through the gate, they didn't stop as the two men would return that way promptly. They crawled along carefully, on sidelights because, Smith was told, the short cut wasn't exactly legal. He had a few glimpses of buildings in the dark mist, and was puzzled by the lack of lights.

"They must have had one of their power cuts again," said the driver.

"Typical Clearbrooke," said the other.

They had gone a bare hundred yards when coming to a stop next to the shape of a Hawker Hurricane.

"That building straight ahead is the HQ. They'll get you sorted."

"I was told to report to the CO."

"That's the place."

He stepped out into the mist with his kit bag, thanked the men effusively, and found himself in the midst of an eerily quiet airfield, the dwindling tail lights and purr of their engine the only signs of life. Then he was alone.

He glanced at the Hurricane, almost reassured, and walked in the direction they'd indicated. The building seemed quite small, the more so the closer he got to it.

It wasn't that late. Where was everybody?

He moved along the wall till finding the doorway. The door swung open easily.

"Hello?" The echo of his voice was that of an entirely empty room.

He must have had the wrong building. He could see another nearby, and went to it. The mist was clinging to his skin like drowning fingers.

This time, the doorway didn't even exist. There was no door, not even a window.

He touched the wall. It was made of wood. He pushed and the wall moved.

28

He rapped hard with his knuckles, and the empty sonorous sound within told him what he needed to know.

Dropping his kit bag, he started frantically looking for other buildings, anything. In his panic, he found himself by the Hurricane, or another one. He couldn't be sure it was the same.

He reached up to touch the propeller roughly.

The blade was made of balsa wood, the tip of which broke off in his hand.

"It was a dummy airfield," he told the men glumly, staring into his whisky. "To fool Jerry. They switch lights on during a raid so the bombs go there instead of Roborough or Clearbrooke."

"I've never heard of these things," admitted Donnel.

"Nor I." He looked over at the others. He probably shouldn't have told them about it. If he hadn't been tired, a little drunk and pissed off, he wouldn't have.

"How did you get here?"

"The bastards came back after ten minutes. They weren't that cruel. Their idea of a prank. They knew the guys in the Ops Room on the airfield, and that they were at the other end, so wouldn't bother them if they kept quiet. I was dependent on them giving me a lift, so didn't say what I really felt. I think they knew from my silence, especially when I got out at Ravenscroft. Hope I never see their faces again."

"If they want entertainment they should go to the movies more often."

"Then nipping over the fence to get here, I tore my jacket. Lost a button. I'll go look for it in the morning."

He was feeling a bit sheepish: his admission of being fooled so easily, then actually disclosing the presence of the ghost airfield to two foreigners, allies or not. Overall he felt much better, having got the evening off his chest.

"Ben will get one for you, I'm sure. Ben?"

The only answer was an incomprehensible mutter, then a brief snore, Hawker having crawled onto a bunk and gone unconscious.

Donnel and Smith laughed. Smith felt assured by the knowledge he hadn't given enough details of his journey to disclose the exact location of the decoy.

This was before he learned that Donnel had a reputation for leading flights home in all manner of weather.

2

Meeting

Smith, in shirt-sleeves, rejoiced silently in the early morning sun. It was redolent of those times when he had climbed through the clouds to burst into, become part of, the heavens. He bathed his face in the warmth as he dragged on his cigarette, washing the acrid taste down with the even more acrid taste of black coffee. Three spoons of sugar had done little to help. Behind him, Donnel and Hawker were darting around, buckets clanging feverishly as they emptied latrines and cleaned up after the pre-dawn departure of their neighbours. He was having nothing to do with it, it was too good a morning. Above him birds were chattering to each other in the trees. He could feel the moisture radiating from the surfaces of the leaves. Ahead of him the uncut grass glistened with dew, and further, beyond the perimeter fence coming up the road, were two women carrying a milk pail between them.

They seemed not to notice him at first, focused more on the show going on behind him. Then the tall thin sergeant turned, and met his gaze. Their eyes locked softly. She was about his age, her crisp uniform complementing her large crystal-blue eyes, soft round cheeks, and wavy blonde hair tied back elegantly with elastic.

"I pray to God that's milk you've got there!" he called out. "This coffee tastes like tar."

The WAAFs slowed down and approached the fence after a brief, tacit consultation with each other.

Smith threw his cigarette to the ground, stamped it out and went forward to meet them as they put down their pail. He didn't allow his obvious limp to slow him down, pushing any pain to the back of his mind.

The smaller woman, an ACW1, peered at him with shadowed eyes against the sun. She had brown hair held in place with a kerbigrip and a longer face than her friend. There was empathy there too. She reminded him of an animal poised for defence but with a preference to being stroked kindly. She looked up at him, smiling, still with the shadowed eyes.

"You got any tea?" She was a Londoner, he guessed, unsure from which part.

"We have everything." He glanced back at the hut. "Come to our ante-room and we'll get a brew-up. I do apologise for not having shaved or dressed properly, but it is the height of luxury inside, I assure you."

The sergeant was contemplating him with her wide eyes. He had all the manner of a fly-by-night boy – and she was so tired of *them* – but it felt like an act, it wasn't the real man. She would like to discover who that was.

"It doesn't look very luxurious," she commented, laughing sweetly.

"Stating the bleedin' obvious today, are we, Joyce?" her friend teased.

"Oh it's Buckingham Palace inside," he insisted. "Okay, maybe not, but we're doing dashed well. We even have room service. Of a sort. We just don't have milk for some reason."

"Ah! Company." Donnel had arrived eagerly, slightly breathless.

"I'm trying to persuade these young ladies to join us for breakfast. And not just because they've brought milk."

"It's for the WAAF mess up the road," the sergeant informed them cheerily. "We're doing a favour."

"How far is it?"

"Far enough from you lot," the aircraftwoman now spoke up.

"Oh we're very trustworthy, m'lady," Donnel insisted.

"Of course you are," she laughed sceptically, looking up at him.

"Will you please do us the honour of joining us for our morning repast," said Donnel, directly to her. "We have eggs."

She was relaxing, pleased, but, "The fence..." she said, eyeing its barbs.

"Here." Donnel took his jacket off and threw it over the top wire. "Old combat trick. Now if you put your foot on a lower strand..."

She put her hands on his shoulders gently, while he reached under her arms. She may have been small but had a fullness restrained under her uniform. With his help she floated gracefully to the other side.

"Angels one!" she laughed.

"If there's a sentry, we've never seen one," Smith said to placate the sergeant who was looking anxiously up and down the track.

She handed him the pail, then with his assistance joined her friend.

"I'm not as elegant as Sandra," she said, straightening her hat and brushing herself down.

"I disagree." She was like gossamer on the breeze, he had thought, though he would never say it. His weak leg had offered no protest. "I'm Trevor Smith by the way. Trev. This is Jackie Donnel."

"I'm Joyce, and this is Sandra."

She was still looking hesitant about proceeding. Sandra, picking up on this, said, "Come on, Joyce. Let's have a shufty. See how the other half live."

Joyce was about to comment that it was probably the wrong half, when she was distracted by Hawker's approach.

"Voilà the third musketeer," Donnel proclaimed. "Ben, come and meet our guests."

Hawker was striding forward, his sartorial chaos at odds with his upright stance and direct gaze.

He shook hands with the women. "There's plenty of food," he said. "Come on."

Donnel and Sandra lingered outside, the victims of some unknown force.

"I don't want t'be rude or anythin'," she said to him, "but you're an officer." He had no idea what to make of the statement, so waited for her to elucidate. "You were helping him," she added emphatically.

"You don't think I should?" He took out his cigarettes and held out the pack.

"It ain't that... It's just...'e's a plonk like me...I think. And 'e's black... Other white Americans I've met..."

"I see." He lit her cigarette, then his, drawing in the smoke, then letting it out, their own private cloud. "I never even considered that. He needed help, that was all. I have nothing else to do. Plus he's sort of in charge around here.

"Sorry it's an American cigarette," he said, watching her coolly draw in the smoke then add to the cloud.

"It's fine!" She liked that he was so considerate to others, and felt she was talking to an equal despite the difference in their ranks.

"So you're not on a mission." English accents were intriguing to him, and hers held a singular mystique, the way she oscillated between roughness and delicacy. It was as if one moment she was ready for a punch-up, the next to make love to the world.

"They don't know what to do with me," he said.

She fell silent, in sympathy, and focused on her cigarette, and the smoke, drifting to the trees.

By the time they joined the others, Joyce was in a chair by the stove, leaning forward in her shirt-sleeves, cigarette in one hand, a cup of coffee in the other. She was still wearing her hat. Hawker was sitting upright in the other chair next to her, Smith at the stove pouring hot water into a tea-pot.

"We wondered if you were persuading Jackie to get you some nylons," Joyce laughed.

"Is that our contribution to your noble culture?" Donnel asked.

"Hey, you guys don't have to wear soddin' twilights and blackouts." Sandra had noticed how two bunks were drawn diagonally across the floor to be nearer to the stove. She sat down on one promptly, tossing her hat aside with relief.

"I'm sure that's true, whatever the heck they are." He sat on the other bunk. Unlike Sandra, he had to lean forward to avoid scraping his head on the top bed.

She had stamped her cigarette out on the floor, and was unbuttoning her jacket. It wasn't hot so early in the day, but with the stove it was warmer than outside the metal walls. He couldn't help confirming with a glance what he'd suspected, that she had large breasts underneath the uniform. The rising sun was casting its rays through the sole, eastern, window; and both women appeared to advantage, their light blue shirts shining wonderfully amidst the dull tones of the hut.

"It *is* quite comfy, I've got to admit," Joyce said, peering around approvingly. "Why are you here though?"

"Everything's full right now," Smith answered.

"There's room at the WAAF quarters. You should move up there," Sandra said facetiously.

"As tempting as that sounds, I quite like it here. I suspect we've got the best cook on the airfield."

"Thass my cue," said Hawker, standing, reaching up to a top bunk where there was a veritable larder, and bringing out a handful of eggs.

"Shell-eggs?!" exclaimed Joyce, impressed.

"This is farmland," said Donnel, "in case you hadn't noticed."

"Joyce and I live in our own little world," Sandra laughed.

There was a lull in the conversation as Smith poured out tea for her and himself, topped up everybody else's coffee and got out of Hawker's way.

"Have you two girls known each other long?" he asked, as he sat in the vacated chair.

"We were plotters together," said Joyce. "The beauty chorus right at the heart of things, in Bomb Alley."

"And you managed to both get posted here?"

"Not at first…"

Smith caught the look between them. "You can tell us. It's sub rosa here."

"What does that mean?" asked Sandra sharply. "None of us are Navy."

He laughed gently. "It's an old medieval term. They would put a rose on the ceiling above meetings, which meant nothing they discussed was to leave that room."

"Oh." She tossed her hat further, to the end of the bed, and spread out, yawning. "You can tell them, Joyce."

Joyce glanced at her, wondering whether she meant it, then decided she did, even if she were exaggerating her nonchalance.

"This was three years ago, when things were really bad. Invasion was imminent and we were working round the clock, while around us an entire city was being demolished. I couldn't sleep at night for the dreams. They gave me Luminal to stop that. Half the girls I knew were on Benzedrine."

"I was on martinis," said Sandra, staring upwards to unknown skies.

"A lot of martinis, I think it's fair to say!"

"No argument 'ere."

"You've got to understand, it was much worse…   At Clearbrooke we haven't been attacked once. Every day there felt like our last. I was a good girl myself …"

"But you wish you weren't!"

"I didn't really party like the others but I could certainly sympathise. Anyway, I was in the dress circle handing a report to the CO, when suddenly there was commotion below. Even in the midst of air raids, a decorum was maintained. However, when new info was coming in by the minute, plotters had to scramble on the

34

table to get pieces moved. At times it was a bit of a scrum. This was one of those times, with a difference.

"When the CO and I looked down, there was Sandra, half-way across the table, asleep. Her face was pressed to the table, her backside sticking in the air. She was still holding onto her rake."

"I got tired waiting."

"The CO – not a nice man really – "

"Bastard."

" – He bellowed blue thunder but it was unnecessary. The whole incident couldn't have lasted more than twenty seconds before Sandra was dragged away."

"I went quietly."

The men were all chuckling at the story. Donnel looked at Smith and Joyce, how comfortable they looked in the chairs next to each other, like an old married couple. Then there was Sandra, supine and relaxed. And Hawker, greatly entertained, as he neared completion with his work at the stove, the enticing smells seducing them all.

"She was demoted, sent from one place to another, then eventually here, to what was considered the sticks."

"Been downwardly mobile ever since. Gave up on the Boards and everythin'."

"What rank were you, may I ask?" Donnel wasn't sure how insensitive he was being but was too curious to hold back.

"We were both corporals," Joyce said. "We became friends when we were billeted together earlier. We drank and flirted all around London for months."

"Be honest, Joyce," Sandra commented. "You call any conversation with a good-looking man, flirting."

"Are you flirting now?" Smith asked candidly.

There was silence, then: "Is she going red?" Sandra chuckled, without looking round.

"Slightly."

Joyce's embarrassment was relieved by Hawker handing out plates with scrambled eggs, fried bread and sausages, to general amazement. He sat down next to Donnel as they all started eating.

"This is like heaven," said Joyce.

Sandra had sat up to partake with obvious pleasure, washing the food down with gulps of tea. "It doesn't look like much in 'ere, but I'm startin' to see what you mean. Ta, Ben."

"Did you ask for a transfer to Clearbrooke?" Smith asked Joyce.

"Yes. Yes, I did." She stopped eating for a moment, surprised that he'd worked it out. Her closeness to her friend must have been more evident than she realised. "It took a year to come through, but I wasn't doing much."

"What do you do now?"

"I work at the squadron office. Clerical."

"Ahh." It struck him that she too had been demoted in a way. "And you, Sandra?"

"Parachute packing. Mostly."

"I owe my life to one of you."

"Really?"

"Probably to one of you plotters too," he said to Joyce. "Funny we use the terms angels one, angels two etcetera, because I often felt it was like angels guiding us up there. Particularly when a woman's voice came on, saying 'Keep your angels.' It was reassuring." He noticed their rapt attention, and knew they wanted his story which he shrugged off with a short explanation. "I was coming back from a sortie last year and had to bale out after a squirt from a 109. It was at angels ten! It's how I got this gammy leg." He resumed eating.

"Are you going back to flying now?" Joyce sounded concerned.

The others waited while he swallowed, washing it down with a swig of tea.

"I'm back to my first love, engineering. My degree was interrupted by the war, but they're cutting a lot of corners these days, and figured I can't do any harm here. I'll be with the ground crews." It too was ostensibly a demotion. He didn't see it that way particularly as he had fought for it. "They're not rushing things, want to break me in gently. I'm even allowed a few days to just wander around, meet folks."

His stoicism was too marked. It wasn't only Joyce who could see that this was a man still in pain, whom the doctors had advised to take it easy.

"Look on the bright side," Sandra said, putting her plate on the floor and stretching out again with a yawn, head nestled in her hands. "You may be a ground wallah now but you're still paid more than us."

"If we're into comparisons, Ben and Jackie are both paid more than me, I believe."

"Let's not get into that," Donnel protested, who had been following the conversation with fascination, whilst stuffing his face.

"Yeah," said Hawker. "Dunno if I *am* being paid."

Sandra persisted. "It's still a man's world. We 'ad some Russian visitors at Leighton Buzzard – God, I 'ope they bombed *that* place – and they were shocked we weren't paid the same."

"They scare me as much as the Germans," said Joyce. "I wouldn't put it past them to build concentration camps."

"You can't say that! They're our allies. Our enemy's enemy, and all that."

"I know, but…"

"Maybe," Donnel said, "the challenge is to discover what each country is really good at, what its true nature is, then do everything possible to encourage that."

"Right now, Germans seem good at killing people. Even that kids' book 'Struwwelpeter' gave me nightmares," Sandra muttered. "Mind you, their propaganda leaflets make good bog paper, I'll give 'em that."

"Maybe they'll be the best at building cars or something… Music! All those famous composers! But whatever it is, whatever it is ultimately, it can't just be killing people. No country deserves that as their ultimate destiny."

"We can't afford the luxury of philosophy right now," said Smith firmly, echoing Sandra. "I knew immediately what we were fighting the day I saw the sky blanketed out by Heinkels. There is a madness that has taken over the world, and we have to stop it, whatever it takes. I'm sure we're all agreed on that."

"Absolutely," Donnel said, the others all nodding in agreement.

"Drat." Joyce was looking at her watch. "I'm only working a half-day, but need to get back to our quarters first. Not least to deliver the milk. Breakfast was marvellous though, thank you."

"And you, Sandra?" Smith asked.

"I'm not really on stand-off, though I was up at first light. There's a Rodeo goin' out this morning. They notice eventually if I wander off for too long."

The women didn't want to risk leaving via the gate, so went back over the fence with Hawker who was heading to the sergeants' mess at Crapstone for some reason. They left not only with profuse thanks, but the arrangement to join the men for dinner in the hut that evening, Sandra commenting it was clearly the venue of choice.

Thinking Smith should check in properly with the adjutant, Donnel went with him on an amble across the airfield. Progress was gradual as Smith could only manage a slow pace, even with the aid of his scruffy-looking stick. This was frustrating for Donnel as he liked to move fast in life.

"You ended up in the drink, when you were shot down," he said, to fill time.

"Yes."

Smith's tone invited enquiry, but as they were going past the Bellman hangar, a sound in the distance made Donnel pause.

"That must be them," said Smith.

"Yes!" At the north-east of the runway, movement could be discerned. The chorus of growls made Donnel smile. "Typhoons," he said.

All around, ground crews were standing upright to observe. The whole airfield seemed in abeyance, motionless in the hot still air. The roaring increased. The machines charged down the runway and into the air one after the other. Cheers and waves erupted all around. Donnel and Smith watched as the aircraft climbed into formation.

"You'd think you'd get jaded," said Donnel. "But I never do."

Smith knew what he meant. As they ambled on, he glanced at the men working on an Avro Anson by the hangar, knowing he'd be meeting them all soon. There was a green goddess fire engine parked nearby, obviously awaiting attention.

"It's that moment," Donnel continued, "like an accidental surge into beauty, transcendence, the 'lonely impulse of delight'."

"I'm very glad to get back on the ground," Smith countered. He was wondering how hot Donnel was prepared to get in his leather jacket from the rising heat. They were both wearing sunglasses, but Donnel seemed more attached to his overall image.

"No, you're right, Jackie. I loved it. Till that day."

"When you were shot down."

"A bit of a scrap over the Channel. We were outnumbered which wasn't unusual in those days. Bogeys everywhere. I didn't know I'd been hit myself. I was more focused on the flames engulfing the engine." He punctuated the end of each sentence with a sharp intake of breath, struggling with his injury.

"What was your crate?"

"A Hurricane. Loved it. Beautiful machine. Not considered as sexy as the Spitfire, but it's loyal, steadfast."

"No argument here."

"Unfortunately it's also made of canvas." He fell silent, recalling the day vividly. "The 109s were more than a match. You might be right about the Jerries making cars.

"When I bailed out, the shock of that, on top of the shrapnel wounds which I wasn't yet aware of, the jolt of the harness... It was like I was in another world, confused and helpless. I saw the 109 do a 180... I'd heard stories about Jerry fanning chutes with their wings to cause the pilots to drop, so I was expecting the worst... We're still under sub rosa, aren't we?"

"I'm assuming so."

"Because I haven't told anyone else this outside the debrief. The 109 came right at me, I was braced for it, when he circled. I could see the man looking at me, and that he had a tache just like mine. Then I realised: he didn't return to kill me... Nor was it simply that he wanted to make sure I was all right. He wanted to *connect*.

"He was gone in a flash, but the encounter was as big a shock as the destruction of my plane, because now there was a personal connection. Prior to then, I had simply been knocking down machines. I didn't say this even at the debrief, but I think they guessed. I couldn't kill another German after that. I remembered the look of the pilot, and kept thinking how easily it could have been me. If by chance I had been born in Germany, what sort of circumstances could have led to me flying 109s? Now I don't know if I could kill anybody. I know we have to, and I will play my part. I just feel I can do that better on the ground.

"I trod water for two hours or so before a Walrus appeared. I had my Mae West on, which was odd in hindsight because that very morning I had considered *not* wearing it. You know what a pain they can be in a cockpit, one can hardly bloody move. It had been 50-50 whether I put it on or not. That life can depend on a moment like that, makes everything seem so fragile.

"I'd been spotted before by my boys... They'd obviously alerted base..."

"So you had your squadron, Mae West *and* a Walrus working for you."

"I know everyone takes the mickey out of Walruses. They're...ungainly."

"To put it mildly."

"But when I saw it arrive and land on the water, and come towards me... It was the most beautiful thing I'd ever seen. Love isn't only about appearances, is it!?"

They picked up pace and were still laughing when they got to the admin buildings.

Sandra was in the middle of a diatribe about conscientious objectors when the visitors arrived. "The last war was a load of bollocks, we all know that, but this time the conchies can kiss my arse..."

The WAAF sergeant who stepped in now was the one Donnel had seen the previous day outside Ravenscroft, except now she had her hair tied back. Someone must have had a word. Accompanying her was a squadron leader. That she was clearly leading, created a confusion of protocol and nobody moved. Not allowing anyone time to react to their arrival anyway, she launched straight into the conversation with a smile.

"It can be argued," she said, "that this is all the same war. Peacetime is simply preparing for the next stage of conflict."

Silence hung in the air, as they all appraised the situation, Donnel the only one getting to his feet. The four sitting were on a variety of newly acquired seats, including two deck chairs. They had drinks and cigarettes in their hands, smoke floating amongst them in the low light. Empty dinner plates were stacked on the floor by the stove. Donnel spoke for everybody.

"Now that you've effectively disarmed us, how can we help you guys? Or is this just a social call?"

"Social business," the squadron leader said with a grin. "Evening, Trev," he added, winking at Smith.

"Hello, Dave." The two had met at the mess the night before. "Everybody, this is Squadron Leader Proudon."

He was tall – even taller than Smith – very thin, clean-shaven and with neat blond hair. His brown eyes were the darkest thing about him, and even they shone with a nervous humour as he explained his presence. "Sergeant Drummond has been asked to act as liaison between American and British personnel – smooth out any wrinkles, as they say – and I'm showing her around."

"I hope you didn't write that guide us Yanks all had to read, Sergeant," Donnel teased.

"Why? I thought it quite accurate. We do make terrible coffee." She looked shyly around the room. "That was issued in

Washington." He could tell she wasn't used to putting herself out to people, her role one she would not have chosen. She tucked her hat under her arm. "And call me Maggie, please."

Introductions were made, and she and Proudon sat next to each other on the nearest bunk, despite Smith and Donnel offering their chairs. Proudon looked fairly comical, his head sticking up past the top bed, still with his hat on.

"You have come at a fortuitous time," Donnel said, the only one still standing "We're celebrating that Ben found Trev's lost button by the fence, we have the best quarters on the base – thanks to our collective effort – and 414 arrived in their Mustangs now that the fog's cleared."

"He ran outside like a little kid when he heard the engines," Smith said. "I thought they were Spits."

"A subtly different sound of beauty."

"Did you get to meet the squadron?" asked Maggie.

"Hell, yeah. Hey Maggie, if you weren't on duty, I'd offer you a gin and tonic."

"That's the delight of my job," Maggie said warmly. "There's little to distinguish between being on or off, so I will gladly accept."

"You refused a drink next door," commented Proudon with a thin smile.

"This is our last port of call," she said.

He was the officer but seemed to defer to her constantly. Donnel wasn't alone in wondering why she wasn't of higher rank, although not the only woman present to whom that applied. Joyce was also officer material. Sandra he considered too unique to satisfy the system. Besides, climbing the ladder by doing the Boards, saluting the right men in the right way, would be like compromising her principles – not that she would admit to having any.

"Is there anything you have to tell us, Maggie?" asked Joyce as Donnel poured drinks for the newcomers and refilled everyone else's glasses.

"Actually, no, just to let everyone know I am available, and if anyone has any suggestions…"

"A civvy dance would be nice. Dining-In-Nights just don't curl my toes," put in Sandra eagerly.

"Eh yes…actually, I was thinking…"

"A summer ball," said Smith, " that would be whizzo."

"The officers had one," said Sandra glumly. "There should be one for the plonks, the ground wallahs and everyone else who keeps getting missed out. Even Yankee layabouts."

Hawker spoke for the first time, staring into his glass.

" '*Centre of equal daughters, equal sons*
'*All, all alike endear'd...*'"

"He does this," said Donnel, returning to his seat. "Someone must have replaced his internal organs with books."

"You are no slouch yourself, *old boy*," Hawker grinned broadly, looking up.

"I know the poem," Maggie said, eyeing Hawker thoughtfully. "It's Whitman, isn't it?"

"'America'," he said, leaving the others uncertain whether that was a title, an allusion, or both. "I strongly feel we need to develop a society where everyone has opportunity, and the dispossessed are given succour."

Joyce looked at him curiously. His range of vernacular was more varied than Sandra's, and would take some getting used to.

"They're talking about it here," said Sandra. "What to do about the poor and unemployed once the war ends. Of course, they're assuming it will end. Meantime, I'm happy to be getting free medical and clothes."

"The war will end," Donnel said firmly. "We're going to win."

"Are you sure?" asked Proudon.

"We all are."

He looked around. It was hard to determine everyone's feelings on the matter. They were talking in the context of fresh news of the advance of Japanese forces, allayed only partially by the advance of U.S. Forces into Italy.

"There's an old general in 'War and Peace'," he elucidated. "I think his name was Katusov. He frustrates those around him by rarely doing anything. He allows the Cossacks to go out and do some fighting, merely to let off steam, not because he thinks it will make a difference. The thing is, he is old enough to understand that the outcome of a war is decided deep down, in the collective will, and that France has already lost. In a similar fashion, the Axis powers belong to an old, out-dated state of mind; and they have united the whole world against them in a new way."

"Yeah!" Sandra cried out. "Hitler may go on about racial purity, but he's forced everyone to travel more, and have sex with foreigners. It's a world party! And it's also given Americans something to do."

"In the same way, " Donnel smiled, "that Katusov knew it wasn't about stratagems and skirmishes, though they have their part, it's not merely about weapons and aircraft now."

"Shit. We've already won," she added soberly.

Proudon seemed the only one unconvinced.

"I wish I had your certainty," he said to no one in particular.

"I'm going to look at the stars," Hawker said, standing up and leaving.

"It *was* a beautiful sunset," Maggie stated, also getting up, glass in hand. "I'd like to see the sky too. I'll be back soon," she said to Proudon, who was uncertain whether to follow her.

Hawker was standing only a few yards away in the gloom, staring straight up above the trees. The stars were brilliant. Hearing her approach, he looked round, surprised.

"Mind if I join you?"

"The heavens are free," he said.

Torn between the two attractions, that which was above and that straight in front of him, the latter was the victor. He offered her a cigarette before taking one himself.

"Thank you."

She leant close to him as he lit a match. He was aware of her delicate skin, light orange from the flame, her gentle eyes.

"Did you study poetry at university, Ben?" She could smell the cloying scent of trees in bloom, behind the cigarette smoke.

"Yes. In New York. For a short time." He wasn't sure what to say to her, she was so refined. The temptation was to lie, which he resisted. He was going to be himself.

"I did a bit of American poetry, but not much. I was more drawn to classics, the old classics like Homer. I think I like mythical contexts."

"My hope lies in the future."

"Yes. I understand." A slight breeze caught a stray wisp of hair, pulling it in front of her eyes. He could see it against her porcelain skin. In contrast, to her he had almost disappeared into the darkness, a presence.

"Sandra," she said, altering the conversation. "She seems angry. Have you noticed that?"

"Yeah. I don't know why."

"It's because of the cinema," said Smith's voice.

43

They turned round to see Smith limping towards them. He was just visible under the stars, a few lights of buildings twinkling behind. His pain was more intense in the night time, and he was using the stick to help manage.

"Sorry. I couldn't help overhearing." Their attitude showed no offence was committed, and he continued. "Joyce told me. Jerry bombed a cinema in Sussex recently, killing families, children…"

"Was there anyone she knew?" Maggie asked grimly.

"No. But it was a cinema she had gone to as a child. She had fond memories of it. Also a school at Guildford was machine-gunned last year. That got to her personally too."

"Innocence demised," said Hawker.

"That's one way to put it."

"Jackie may be right," said Maggie. "The collective will is that people who bomb children cannot win a war."

"Do you think we ourselves haven't been killing children? No man who releases bombs from up far can know that for sure. I'm just grateful I always knew what I was aiming at."

"Look," said Hawker, pointing up. "There's Regulus, and Leo."

"Oh!" cried Maggie softly in delight. "Did you study the stars?"

"I tried to, when in New York, but I couldn't see them usually. The southern skies were better," he mumbled.

She glanced at him in the dark as Smith shuffled closer to see where Hawker was looking, and the three of them fell silent under the canopy of light, the red glowing tips of cigarettes by their sides, to be forgotten momentarily, then drawn to their lips in slow random rhythm.

"To some," said Duncan, "the Christmas truce implies that at heart all anyone wants is peace, that armed conflict can best be channelled creatively into an amicable game of football."

"I take it you don't entirely agree with that synopsis," Heinrich grinned from across the table.

"Granted, the impulse to be friendly is a natural one. There were further attempts at truces, for instance, such as in 1916, but by then the generals had ordered snipers to snuff out any attempts at kindness from the other side."

"Which implies that the violence has to be sustained by an infrastructure."

"Always."

"Surely *that* implies kindness can also be sustained," Naomi, who had been listening rapt, wide-eyed, head leaning on her husband's shoulder, spoke for the first time since the lecture had begun.

"It does, but paradoxically it is often adverse circumstances which show what a person is really made of. It's easy to be nice when surrounded by nice people."

"War can make monsters out of anyone," said Heinrich.

"I remember in one of Duncan's lectures," Kay said, eyes alive with interest, "he mentioned the theory that claimed the growing detachment from the consequences of killing began in the twentieth century with the British naval blockade of the First War. They starved up to a million German people with that strategy."

"Yes, I find it interesting," Duncan said, "that Churchill – a soldier at heart – was one of the few who objected to the blockade, understanding later how it soured the Treaty of Versailles. He was also astutely uncomfortable with the bombing of civilians in the next war."

"Death was not an abstract concept for him," Heinrich observed quietly.

"He wasn't removed enough," Naomi echoed with unusual bitterness.

"Desensitisation has always been present," Duncan continued. "The illusion of glamorous battle, coated with words of patriotism or romance, idealism the most ruthless motivator of all."

"Nowadays we just muzzle reporters," George came in now, waving his wine glass in the air with an ironic toast. "Hence, a missile strike can seem less barbaric than a public beheading."

"There are many ways to remove people's sense of involvement. I interviewed a Belgian ex-soldier once. He was conscripted despite his health problems, thanks to a sadistic doctor, and ended up in an anti-tank regiment. When the Soviets invaded Czechoslovakia, he was with the other men lined up along the German border the next night as part of the NATO defensive. They were fully expecting tanks to roll across at any moment.

"Basically they were a suicide squad. Their job was to dig holes and lie in them, waiting for any approaching tank to go over, crawl up the rear and shove explosives down a vent. They each had a few seconds in which to identify the tank, where to put the explosives and do so, before being shot by another tank behind.

"He told me, they were all beside themselves with fear, and were injected with drugs to keep them in their holes, waiting for death. Without the drugs they would have probably all run."

"Elvis Presley's addictions began from his time in the Army," Heinrich pointed out.

"I think," Naomi spoke softly to Duncan, "you have just emphasised the point that war is not natural."

"I suppose I have."

"Me," said George, "I just have to stub my toe to remind myself of the reality of pain. I am under no illusion about my capacity to feel. It would take more than an artificial dichotomy to get me to fight. I find it extraordinary that people use labels like 'Christian' or 'Jew'…"

"Or 'New Age'!" Kay interjected.

"…or 'New Age', as if that can sum up a person."

"Do you find that you have a jaded view of humanity, having studied so much of its past?" Heinrich asked Duncan whilst running his fingers through Naomi's hair.

"A bit," Duncan admitted. "I think it's a fault, a peril of academia to know too much, more than is useful. When we watched 'Marple' last night, my old tendency would have been to dismiss its rosy view of the forties. Now I cannot help but wonder if the nostalgic view might not be an accurate, transcendent view of the past, like a benign echo – and all we historians deal with is echoes. Yet I only have the opposite of benevolence, which is maybe a twisted version of the truth. There is no antonym for nostalgia."

"'Antonym' means…" Kay began.

"It's the same in German," Naomi smiled.

"Speaking of the admirable Miss Marple," Heinrich proclaimed, slapping the table, "what shall our entertainment be tonight?"

"I vote for 'Fawlty Towers'," said George. "You told me once how much you like it, and we haven't watched an episode for a while."

Heinrich and Naomi both beamed at the prospect, and everyone leapt into action to clear the table.

"I love English humour," Heinrich said to Duncan while they were picking up condiments together. "You rejoice in failures, like Basil…Dunkirk, or the German POW who escaped. When I visited London in the nineties, the BBC were celebrating India kicking you lot out fifty years previously. I love it." He smiled fondly, reminiscing of that early exposure to Britain; encapsulated by delight and disbelief of the ambiguity of the English language, that 'a couple' might not always be 'two'.

In the kitchen, Kay was loading the dishwasher. When Duncan handed her some spoons, she looked at him compassionately. "Your tooth is really hurting, isn't it?" He had eaten very little.

"Yes," he said with some helplessness, standing rigidly.

"It's a good job we got you that appointment tomorrow."

"Yes. I'll take some more painkillers now."

"With all that alcohol?" she exclaimed, as she straightened up. "Is that wise?"

"They work better that way. Kay, I…eh…I won't be joining you guys. I'll just go and read. Thank you for dinner."

"Thank you for helping."

In the annexe, when she went to check on him a bit later, he wasn't reading but throwing books around his bedroom.

"Duncan?"

"I can't find my cards," he grumbled. "I must have left them in Cornwall. Solitaire relaxes me."

"Here." She gestured for him to join her at the computer. "In the 'Games' folder." With a few clicks she showed him the programme. "You can use this."

He sat down, amazed. "Thank you, Kay."

"You don't have to keep thanking me, Duncan," she laughed. "We're family. Goodnight." She kissed him on the forehead before leaving him to his game.

The following morning promised to be a beautiful one. He turned up unusually early for breakfast, then after coffee, toast and eggs, headed off to Yelverton to 'get a few bits and bobs, but just for the walk really'. George was still in the office, and the others hadn't got up by the time he left.

It was only a few dozen yards to the edge of the airfield. After crossing the road he stepped onto the moorland, accompanied by the song of a blackbird, and was pushing his way through the trees that lined the road, when he noticed foundations of small buildings. There were a few of them, at least three, adjacent to the road. They must have been huts of some sort.

He was suddenly struck by the awareness that people had met here, they had discussed things, events had transpired, none of which would make it to the history books. As an historian, this was not an unusual state of mind for him at a site, but it was the immediacy of the feeling which was new. Whatever had happened here had happened just yesterday. What did they know about it? The more he considered it, the more he was overwhelmed by the feeling of everything being present. There was no distance, he was standing there now, and these other unknown people were as well.

Shaking the impression off, he resumed his passage across the airfield, past more mysterious lumps of concrete, pathways, structures and artificial mounds.

The sun was well above the horizon, and he started to regain himself. He was dressed in bermuda shorts and a short-sleeved blue-and-white striped linen shirt. On his head was a beige baseball cap with the unexplained number of 55 on its label, on his feet some comfortable navy-blue sneakers. Kay had forced him to go shopping with her in Plymouth to be better-equipped for the summer. The Ibuprofen was working well, he was experiencing no pain, and even the sight of clouds rolling over from the moor did nothing to dispel his mood.

In such a celebratory state, he bought a bag of doughnuts at the post office, and was headed back home when the clouds overtook. In perfect timing, the Ibuprofen ran out of juice, and the deep throbbing pain in his jaw returned. He felt his skin chill. He sat down on a grassy knoll. It was a horrible pain and it was resuming its vitriolic abuse upon his cranium with manic glee. His body wasn't up to much these days, and now even his head was under attack. Recently he spent so much time between pain-killers and pain, in a world neither alive nor deceased, he wondered where he belonged. He surveyed the greying moor, the gorse bushes bright yellow with dampening promise, the sheep and ponies wandering contentedly. He noticed a large rock nearby. It was little more than a foot in diameter, jagged and unpredictable in its protrusions. There was no obvious roundness, warmth or consistency in its features, but it seemed perfectly in place despite its singularity. He liked it. He started speaking to it.

"It's not just my view of the past that has changed," he sighed, glancing in the direction of the huts. "Once I considered everyone who disagreed with me a fool, now I find I am in constant disagreement with myself."

On returning to White Spring, he presented the bag of doughnuts to Kay, who reacted much as an equestrian would to a bouquet of ragwort.

"Don't you think, considering the fact you're going to the dentist, this might not be the most appropriate thing ?"

"I just thought we could have them for tea," he said defensively, clutching his jaw.

"Did you see Heinrich and Naomi?"

"No, I didn't." He put the bag down on the kitchen island.

"They set off not long after you."

"Oh."

At the dentist, he was delivered the bad news. The molar giving him pain demanded root canal treatment. As he was peripatetic, and the success of the treatment was uncertain, the best course might be to have the tooth out. This he agreed to, but the news got worse. His teeth and gums generally were suffering from three years of neglect, and another molar wasn't far behind the main offending one in state of decay. They gave him a prescription for antibiotics to calm the infection before his next appointment.

When arranging the appointment, and after paying for the session, he inquired after the costs for the extraction. He left, reading the shiny brochure with the prices clearly defined. By the time he'd got his prescription from the chemist, and paid for that, he had decided he was going to stop with the one extraction and take his chances thereon, for a while anyway. He had to start watching his pennies, as dentistry demanded quite a few.

He'd been told not to drink alcohol whilst on the antibiotics, so decided to go to a pub, the first one he came across. He wasn't due to meet Kay for half-an-hour. The blonde Aussie girl who served him obviously thought beauty a sufficient end and was consequently rude to him, because she could afford to be. She was nice to everyone else for some reason.

He sat quietly at a table by himself. The pain was returning so he downed some Paracetamols with the Dartmoor ale, and was trying to focus on the instructions that came with the penicillin but kept getting distracted by the loud conversation two tables away. It was three middle-aged men agreeing vociferously about the shortcomings of the government, and a woman simpering and delivering sporadic high-pitched laughs.

After ten minutes of this, with the throbbing pain, and his general state of mind, Duncan had had enough and loudly proclaimed the men complete and utter morons, the woman in this case merely being the chorus. The stunned silence from their table did little to caution him, at first. Even the central figure, a lithe, muscular and tightly-coiled individual with unkempt black locks and grizzled face, didn't faze him despite the venomous gaze. Duncan was used to academia where words were words, and childish insults were par for the course.

He understood their silence to be a continued interest in his point of view. "You're blaming the government for raising prices on alcohol and tobacco, and for banning smoking in pubs. If drinkers – and, I assume, smokers – such as yourselves took some responsibility, by doing everything in moderation, we wouldn't have the collective health crisis we have now, and it wouldn't be costing so much in medical and social care. It is because of your behaviour the rest of us have to face increased taxes, and now extortionate rates for an occasional drink or cigarette. Even smoking in public areas may have remained acceptable if it hadn't been so excessive."

He smiled at his audience. If he had been with his peers, someone may have provided a counterview – which even now he was expecting eagerly – such as that smoking, drinking and over-eating were merely symptoms of a people heavily divided by wealth. The psychology of collective social inferiority was not something of which he was aware. Neither was his current audience. In the absence of intelligent repartee, they were left with violence as the only honest exchange. The expression of the muscular man in the blue flannel shirt now gave Duncan pause for thought, even before the man stood up.

"Excuse me." Not wishing to leave a glass half-full, Duncan hastily gulped down his beer, gathered his things, and departed.

Moving along the jostling Tavistock High Street, he glanced backwards to see his fears well-founded. The man wasn't far behind, the other two men accompanying their leader, all three pairs of eyes locked on Duncan.

The shops at best offered only temporary shelter, and were like caves with no back doors.

He darted into the entrance to the Pannier Market out of desperation. To his relief, it was quite busy, with numerous traders plying their wares.

Seeing an appropriate niche, a stall with piles of DVDs – none of which were of interest to him normally but currently offered several hiding nooks – he swiftly pushed himself in and found a bottom shelf suddenly deserving, he felt, of immediate attention.

Indeed, as the proprietor was nowhere to be seen – perhaps chatting to someone at an adjacent stall – Duncan sat on the floor and made himself as comfortable as possible.

Within a minute he caught a glimpse of black curly locks passing by the stall, and he slumped further, his heart racing.

Another two minutes passed, and he risked another look. A young couple perusing the DVDs on the table were surprised to see him, then recovered and resumed their search.

Peering over the plastic cases, he scanned the surroundings.

None of his pursuers were evident. His ploy must have worked. With so many entrances and exits, they'd assumed he'd gone elsewhere.

He couldn't be sure yet though. He should wait a bit longer.

At this point, another series of dilemmas presented themselves.

First, he could see the toilets at the far end of the covered market, and was made aware of a pressing need to visit them. However, he had a shy bladder, and didn't like using public toilets when other people were present. Once he had been told this was a psychological hangover from boarding school. He'd never been interested enough to get to the root of it. Normally he would wait and watch for a lull in traffic, but his well-being was at threat from another source, complicating the situation.

For he was also aware of a drop in blood sugar. The beer hadn't sustained him for long. The accompanying tension, nervousness and sudden fatigue meant he needed to eat something quickly. He'd passed a stall selling baked goods on his way in. But was it safe to emerge?

He rose a bit higher to examine the threat level, and was distracted by a young woman walking down the aisle. She looked very much like the one who had reduced him to a teenager a few days before by the building site in Plymouth. Young, tall, dark hair, elegant in a long mauve tie-dye skirt and sandals, she was such a vision, the assault on his confused heart was becoming too much. Trapped in a maelstrom of conflicting desires and needs, he sank back onto the floor.

The good news was that the pain in his jaw had gone.

"Why are you lurking in the Romantic Comedy section?"

A maternal blonde woman, looked down at him curiously and kindly.

"Ehh yes, I'd like these please." He grabbed a couple of DVDs from the bottom shelf and stood up, looking around anxiously.

51

"That will be six pounds please." His prompt payment allayed any fears she might have about the situation, though she couldn't help glancing in his direction as he left the market distractedly. She felt she'd stumbled into one of her movies, maybe a Hitchcock.

The car was by the leisure centre. Duncan managed to cross the road with no sign of his pursuers, and make his way alongside the river. He wondered if he could find a sheltered spot in which he could relieve himself.

There were too many people around. He was dimly aware of the beauty of the singing river, the trees swaying overhead, birds flitting, but any appreciation was drowned by his pressing need that had by now jostled into first place. Briefly, that need lost its position when he caught a glimpse of a chequered shirt the other side of the car park. He ducked down, weaving amongst the vehicles.

The first Kay knew of his arrival was the passenger door being flung open, him clambering in, and putting his seat belt on.

"Hi, Duncan. How did it go?" She started the engine.

"Fine. I have to go back."

"Okay. Oh you got some DVDs. That's nice. I thought we could pop into the supermarket, get some food for lunch."

"Do they have toilets there?"

"It's a supermarket. Of course. There are toilets in the square. You must have gone right past them." She couldn't muster the energy to be puzzled as they exited. He was glancing around nervously. If she inquired after every exhibition of odd behaviour, it would ultimately be both exhausting and self-defeating. He could rarely explain himself fully.

"I missed 'Woman's Hour'," he said randomly and sulkily after a pause.

Her effervescent smile lit up her features. "You can hear it online. Funny how there's no 'Men's Hour'."

"They'd only talk about tits and cars," he grumbled.

They were on the edge of the town and entering the Morrisons car park when she said, also seemingly at random: "Are you going to call Jasmine soon?"

"I…I don't know. Why would she want to talk to me?" he said, disappearing into his seat as if to illustrate his discomfort.

"She's your daughter! You have a grandson!"

She punctuated her exclamation by pulling into a space. He was out the door and in quest for the toilets before she had put the parking brake on.

"You're pretty much all she does talk about," she said to the empty seat.

Dinner had a Moroccan theme, with couscous, hummus, a hot soya-meat sauce and various salads. The wine was Italian, which Duncan couldn't touch now he was on the antibiotics.

They were examining the DVDs he had bought. He wished he could disappear into his seat again. He was the only one by now who didn't know their titles.

"They're second-hand," said Kay, taking a sip of wine, "so the cases were a bit dirty until I cleaned them with disinfectant."

"Two with Kirsten Dunst," Heinrich grinned. "Is that your type, Duncan?"

"America does have a plethora of beautiful women," said Naomi.

"It's an economic product," Duncan said, feeling drawn into the conversation despite himself. He sat up straight.

"Pardon?"

"Your English is getting *really* good," Heinrich teased her.

"Do you think only America is capable of producing so many beautiful people, all these film stars in particular?" Duncan launched. "No, it is the natural consequence of a country rich in resources. It can simply afford to produce its dreams on celluloid and impose them on everyone else."

"Mmm." Heinrich looked doubtful. "Other countries are rich in resources – Germany, say – but not so many people are interested in *their* dreams. More like bloody nightmares, what." This last, delivered in exaggerated pucker English, more for Naomi's benefit. He smiled at her winningly.

"India might be a better example," said George, "in terms of media output."

"Thank you, George. Yes, Bollywood still doesn't compete with Hollywood in terms of global domination."

"I glean a subtext in Duncan's assertion," Kay said.

"That is quite an accusation!" Heinrich exclaimed.

"You are correct as always," Duncan said, glancing at Kay whilst pushing food around on his plate. "I often think we in the so-called developed countries forget the importance of Nature. I for example am as guilty as anyone of such a neglect. I read about Nature in books. I think our cerebral emphasis is a ghost of the industrial revolution, resulting in a pretence that we have power over the world."

"Which we only do in the short term," said Naomi.

"Precisely."

"Not a ghost, a zeitgeist," said Heinrich.

"Which haunts us particularly now like a hangover from the materialism of the 1950s, a materialism which was necessary at the time in order to rebuild."

"The pretence that more financial wealth creates more happiness," said Kay. "Which may be true up to a point, but once you go beyond that, all sorts of neuroses develop. We, we're fine mainly because of George selling his business, and I'm grateful for that. We don't need more."

"Thank God for that," George raised his glass, "or the Divine Goddess or Odin or whoever."

"Probably Ganesh," commented Heinrich.

"Or the interest rates."

"You look very thoughtful, Duncan," Naomi observed.

"My mind is still on present day materialism. The rubbish that people will buy, the acceptance that anything is better. Their desires are impoverished, and desire is intelligence."

"If that were true," said George, "teenagers would all be geniuses."

"You're thinking of sex…"

"And music players, and DVDs, and beaches, and drugs…"

"…which are all fixations of impoverished desire."

"They should be permitted a good time," Naomi protested softly.

"George may be right," said Heinrich. "Teenagers are distracted by their desires, as are we all to some extent. But they could do with more focus. Their intelligence would be better applied…"

Duncan was suspicious. "Do you believe that?"

"No…eh…I was drawing you out. Caught!" Heinrich held out his hands in a gesture of surrender.

"I didn't think so. Our education system has a narrow definition of intelligence, a definition I myself have been willingly trapped by all my life, because it suited me. I repeat, desire is intelligence. We become experts in our fields because we desire to

do so, and that is a reflection of something deep within ourselves –
even if it is the need to conform, which it is in some cases."

"And you, Duncan, how did you become an historian?" Naomi
asked gently.

He caught George's eye and the brothers laughed.

"We used to play with airplane models," George explained,
"and make up stories about them. I used to love the German World
War Two planes because of the engineering – even as a kid – their
designs made sense to me; but I also had a fondness for flying
boats like the Catalina, because *they could float on water*! At that
age, such a feat seemed extraordinary.

"Then one day we were playing out one of our scenarios, when
an uncle was visiting."

"Uncle Geoff," said Duncan.

"He had served during the war in some unnamed department,
and he asked us about the Catalina's role. We explained it was
doing reconnaissance, because it was a Catalina that had
discovered the Bismarck, bringing the might of the British Navy
upon it, and thus defeating one of the most powerful ships ever to
sail 'the seven seas'. He went very quiet and told us that wasn't
what happened.

"Apparently the decoders in Bletchley Park had known for a
while exactly where the Bismarck was, but didn't want to reveal to
the Germans that they were listening, *and* understanding. So the
Catalina was sent in that direction to 'accidentally discover' the
battleship and report back. Of course, the plane was seen by the
ship, who then reported that they had been spotted, as was the plan,
before being sunk."

"You English are very cunning," Heinrich said.

"We're a nation of actors and liars."

"You mean you're skilled at diplomacy."

"Uncle Geoff went very quiet after telling us this, then left the
room. We both think he had told us something he shouldn't have
at the time, though now the story is a matter of public record. But
that's how the seed was sown. It was a seminal period for both of
us, my interest in engineering starting around then. I loved
German planes in particular. Duncan and I take turns with the
story. It's your turn next, Dunc."

"Is that what got you into history, Duncan?" Naomi asked, as if
doubting his brother's depiction of events.

Duncan nodded. "I was fascinated by this revelation. It was like there was this whole other world underneath the obvious one."

"Did you have a good history teacher at school?"

Naomi had hit the mark.

"He was the *only* good teacher."

"You always exaggerate that side of things," George muttered admonishingly, spooning some couscous into his mouth.

What with the chronic pain in his jaw and everything else going on in his life, Duncan had had enough.

"'*Exaggerate?*'" he cried out. "You weren't the one at ten years old, beaten bloody in the rugby changing rooms by some sociopathic elder. Not only did no one come to my assistance," he turned to his audience for comprehension, "but as I lay sobbing my guts out, blood and tears dripping onto the concrete floor, one boy came to me, questioning me carefully, not to see if I was all right – he wanted to make sure I wouldn't tell any teachers. Even if I had, they would have shrugged it off as boys being boys, a necessary toughening up for the big bad world. This wasn't education, I see that now, it was conditioning, a collective bullying to ensure the individual keeps in line as they grow older. Not one of the staff there, apart from Mr Burgess, seemed to even like children. It was systematic abuse."

He was still in that changing room. He stood up. "And those parents who pay for expensive schools, are merely paying for a shinier veneer on cruelty."

"Duncan..." said Kay.

But he went to his rooms to drink brandy, munch on a doughnut and play solitaire.

"It sounds brutal," said Naomi eventually to George who, used to his brother's outbursts, had continued eating.

"George fitted in a lot better," Kay said. "It was a mixed boarding school, but that didn't seem to make much difference to Duncan. He was picked on a lot by the other boys. His confidence with girls suffered considerably. His general confidence, I guess."

"The school was in Scotland," George said after washing food down his gullet with a swig of wine, "and Duncan has avoided the country his whole adult life. Which is hardly fair as the pupils and staff were as much English as Scottish. Though the boy who beat him up that time was Scottish. Rather unsettlingly, he became a policeman, or a lawyer. I forget which.

"I only heard about the incident years later. Duncan kept the code of silence..."

"It sounds like he could do with some therapy," Heinrich commented.

"We tried to get him to Findhorn but he refused..." said Kay.

"Despite us telling him there were more Americans than Scots there," George added.

"He did join us for a Communication Workshop in Hastings."

"That took some courage," George acknowledged. He didn't remark that Duncan had been more interested in a lift to the famous battleground, and had given the appearance of having stumbled into the group by accident.

"The strange thing is...   Well, we're not supposed to betray confidence..."

"Dunc won't care."

"...but we're all family. It's strictly sub rosa, it doesn't leave this room..."

Heinrich and Naomi nodded.

"There was an exercise where we were all blindfolded and supposed to wander around the room; then as we bump into each other, we simply touch, and become aware of everyone's physical presence."

"Yes, we did that in the Experience Week," Heinrich said.

"Then you'll know that eventually everyone is in the same area, touching everyone else lightly. It's designed to break down our fear of tactility, and help us become aware of our senses other than the visual, how things *appear*. But Duncan never turned up! We didn't know this until the end of the exercise, when the focalisers told us to take our blindfolds off, and Duncan was in a corner, touching the walls. The focalisers spoke with him a bit about fear of intimacy, but he had a glazed expression, like he was far away somewhere. There was an elephant in the car with us later..."

"And it was only a Fiat!" exclaimed George.

"...None of us wanted to broach the subject. He was married to Rose, and even then I wondered about their relationship."

"Sounds like he's completely stuck," said Naomi.

"Actually," said George, about to reach for more salad, then deciding against it. "I always have the feeling Duncan has gone further than any of us, just in the wrong direction."

"With his experiences at school, that is hardly surprising."

George nodded. "I often wondered when he told me about the attack in the changing rooms, 'What would I have done if I had been there?' I never got the answer to that. I like to think I would have defended my little brother, but he's right, the pressure to conform is immense. It makes cowards of us all.

"The whole effort of every individual is to avoid the black dog, keep ahead of it at all costs, by working hard, keeping the spouse happy..." His eyes glinted at Kay, assuring her, if any assurance were needed, that she was not implicated. "...keeping authorities off your back...it takes effort. There is also a fear element, to keep us running... Duncan is one of those who can't keep running anymore, and by not so doing, is opening himself to experiences we all wish to avoid. Yet through his courage he is the only one likely to find that the whirlpool delivers him to another, more fragrant shore. Speaking of which, can I smoke my pipe yet?"

The others were too taken aback by his loquaciousness to respond effectively, till Kay snapped, "No, you can't, you know that. We haven't had pudding."

3

Intriguing

Naomi was walking back alone from Yelverton early the following day, when she espied Duncan headed towards her. It was another crisp, sunny morning with white clouds tumbling playfully overhead. That they had been blessed with such good weather since arriving in England, was just one of the numerous things that conspired to keep her in high spirits. Seeing Duncan, looking like an overgrown schoolboy in his new shorts, baseball cap and walking boots, was an additional factor. She had found herself growing very fond of him; he was a fascinating character, keeping their evenings particularly lively with his chatter and insights. She loved Kay and George, but without Duncan there would have been a certain homogeneity in their meetings. There was no chance of that now.

Most of what Naomi conveyed in life was silence, and in that silence was a warmth that most people could feel, and usually reciprocate. It was difficult not to love her. Aware of that ability, she rarely felt it necessary to expound with words, and thus was intent on simply radiating Duncan with her smile; and, if he chose to respond verbally, she would do so in kind.

To her surprise, as they neared each other, and he was in receipt of her full onslaught – for she really was very fond of him – he gave her but the wisp of an effete English smile, and went on his way. She stopped abruptly and looked after his departing back. This was unprecedented. Had she done something to offend him? The previous evening he had left dinner in a huff, but he did that most evenings. It was part of the entertainment and he had always acted as if nothing had happened the next day.

He continued his march across the airfield, and she continued to watch, amazed, as he sat down on a little knoll of grass and started talking to a rock.

He didn't stay long with the rock, he found he didn't have much to say to it.

Instead, he wandered over the airfield, noting idly the various concrete blocks, remnants of an esoteric archaeology, his mind in another matrix. The problem, he thought, was like solitaire: if you choose the wrong card at the beginning, all choices afterwards are doomed. The inexorable march of history, even personal history, was biased. How could anyone hope to resolve things in linearity?

He returned to the rock.

"I married for love," he told it. "At least I thought I did. How can a young person know what love is? Yet perhaps they can, because if I am truly honest, I had doubts even at the start. It's just, everything seemed right: she was an academic like me, she was attractive, and found me so, our friends approved the match... Getting married was what everyone did. Then the children are born, sexual attraction isn't so much of a factor, and you wonder what it's all about. At least I did.

"I think I only knew how lost I had been the moment I heard Evelyn reading 'The Franklin's Tale' in the original English, and I was lost again, in a new, more authentic way. The songs, the cadences, the lulls in each line transported me. I had missed that flame so much; the flame I thought I'd had with Rose, and now believed I'd really found with Evelyn. Unlike in the movies, beautiful women are rarely single, but here I had found someone, as in a movie. My arousal, every time I thought of her, told me unequivocally for the first time that my marriage was in trouble, there was no flame there even of respect. Little did I know the new flame would burn only for so short a while. Then the whole hoo-ha started, another story."

He paused, reflecting on this. The rock waited for him to continue. "It was like a group therapy thing I did with George and Kay once. We were blindfolded and supposed to blunder about in the room till we found each other, and feel each other up. I still don't know the point of that, but I'd understood we had to leave the encounter to chance. *Apparently* we were meant to actively seek each other out. Having misunderstood, I never chanced across anyone, and ended up alone in a corner. Afterwards, they kept reading things into that, how I was avoiding contact etcetera etcetera; and *that* remained the prevailing story, which I could do little to dissuade. They didn't want to know the truth, they just wanted confirmation of the story."

He got to his feet and looked out across the airfield, more effectively camouflaged by time than it had been by man when operational.

"The real story is rarely written down," he said.

"He walked right past me as if we'd never met," Naomi exclaimed to Kay in the kitchen.

"Ahh. There's a reason for that," Kay smiled assuringly whilst sorting out the bread Naomi had brought. She had never seen her put out like this before.

"Was he upset?"

"No more than he usually is, and not with you. He has face blindness."

"*What...?*"

"He didn't know until about four years ago. People generally didn't know much, now they think up to two per cent of people have some form. His is quite mild but he finds it hard to recognise people out of context unless they're wearing familiar clothes or something to identify them. He'll have no trouble with Heinrich because of the glasses. As I change mine quite regularly, and don't always wear them, I usually tell him who I am when we meet elsewhere. You should do the same, he'll be very grateful."

"Mein Gött." She pulled herself up on one of the stools, as Kay started firing up the espresso machine. "I can't imagine what that's like."

"He has to wing it every time, he told me once. If someone talks to him out of the blue, he'll be polite and subtly tease it out of them who they are, if their voice hasn't told him already."

"It's like having one's role removed."

"Yes, but in the university he had a clearly defined role, so it wasn't a problem. People were always where they were supposed to be. Since his ignominious departure, nothing is so clear-cut anymore for him. He constantly has to make things up on the spot. I suggested he should just be nice to everyone but he decided that took too much effort, so he just generally scowls all the time unless someone greets him."

"In which case he'll smile politely."

"Precisely."

"Sounds like he's got a lot to scowl about," Heinrich, stepping into the kitchen, George just behind him. "He's lost his job, his home, his reputation, and zero kilogrammes..."

"At some point," George said, "he'll have to ask himself if the doughnuts or the diabetes came first."

"That…was worthy of a German."

"Where did you two come from?" Kay demanded.

"We were in the garden," George said. "Hey, you've put the machine on, wizzo."

"He told us he has hypoglycaemia," Heinrich continued. "Does he have any other problems?"

"I think his not recognising Naomi on the moor is enough," Kay smiled as she selected cups for everyone.

"Ha, so that's what happened."

"He was also talking to a rock," Naomi said, shrugging her shoulders, bemused.

This last gave even Heinrich pause. "If you think that will win you the whisky…"

"Because I really love whisky."

"*That* was worthy of an Englishman."

"He has been very well-behaved this time," said Kay. "He hasn't got into trouble once."

"That we know about," said George. "Here he is now."

Heinrich waved to Duncan unheeded through the kitchen window as he opened and shut the gate hurriedly, then came breathless into the house, his face pink with effort. He was undaunted by the kitchen gathering, and addressed only Kay.

"The solitaire game. On the computer. It has something called an 'Undo' function, doesn't it?"

"Yes," she said hesitantly.

"I thought so."

And he was gone before she had time to invite him for coffee.

George shrugged. "You've heard of mad scientists," he said to the guests. "Well, we have a mad historian."

"I don't understand," said George, seated opposite his brother in the annexe, his elbows on his knees, as he considered the floor. Duncan was by the desk, facing him keenly.

Kay had sent her husband to summon Duncan for lunch. Gleaning that he was involved with something, they had all conspired to leave him alone for a few hours.

"I explained it as fully as I am able," Duncan said.

"It won't work," George protested, looking up. "Nobody will accept it."

"If I publish it as my own translation, add a bit of pseudo-medieval jargon to put up a smokescreen, then people can accept it on any level they like."

"'Translate'? You mean, from Latin?"

"No." Duncan was getting impatient. "I'll say it's from medieval French that was translated beforehand from the original Latin. I'll also mess with the timeline, put in events that didn't occur till later."

"Look, I still don't know if you're saying this document is genuine or not."

"Don't you?"

It was George's turn to get impatient.

"Cut the crap, Dunc. Does this document exist or not?"

"What do you think?"

"I think it's nonsense. It sounds like a Monty Python skit. It's not possible."

"That's the problem, George. You're always confined to the possible."

"What is that supposed to mean?"

"No offence, I've been pretty much trapped myself. I'm just saying..."

"You're saying I have no imagination."

"Well, it's what Dad always liked about you."

"You keep him out of this!"

"Why? You always had the same opinions."

Kay, who had been approaching the annexe to find out about the delay, was in time to hear the latter exchanges; and to break up the fight that had escalated to the men slapping each other, and falling to the ground whilst tugging each other's ears. After pulling the brothers apart and forcing them to their feet, she was obviously torn between the desire to laugh and the need to admonish. "You ought to be ashamed of yourselves," she said predictably.

When she led them back to the house, Heinrich and Naomi saw immediately when they entered the dining room that something had occurred. Kay was managing to maintain her serious face, and the two men – with their red faces, tussled hair and looks of shame – looked more like brothers than they had for a long time.

"What happened?" Naomi asked directly over the salad bowl.

"Just a slight disagreement between Lettuce and Lovage," Kay replied, going to her seat. "Sometimes I suspect none of us ever actually grow up."

As the meal commenced, Heinrich couldn't resist stirring a metaphorical, rather than a literal, pot.

"What were your parents like?" he asked both George and Duncan.

George looked up from his plate, subdued. "When one wasn't miserable, the other would step in to take their place. It wasn't that happy a childhood for either of us."

Duncan grunted. In his opinion, the Golden Boy had no right to claim discordance. Their father had been a successful engineer, and George inherited the business. If Mother had ever had an opinion – about anything – she never voiced it, but concentrated on a silent betrayal. They had married for love.

Kay watched them carefully. Duncan was a man of deep currents, nothing could ever be fixed directly, you had to let the waters go where they would. In contrast, George was a great believer in WD40 when things didn't move and should, Superglue when they did and shouldn't. It was one of his and Kay's rare arguments in their twenties, when he mused aloud whether the same principle could not be applied to children. She had objected to his tone, and wondered that what she had at first taken for humour in her lover, might not always be so. Even now she wasn't always sure.

Duncan was emerging spontaneously from his depths. "What's everyone up to this afternoon?" he grinned.

"Heinrich is accompanying me to the dance class this evening," said kay, "but that's about it as far as plans are concerned."

"He can dance?"

"He's the best!" Naomi exclaimed. "Unfortunately I'm not."

"Poetry in motion," Heinrich said proudly, then to Naomi, "and you, schnooki, are poetry in life."

"It's good you weren't here the last time, Heinrich," George said, eyes twinkling. "There was an embarrassing incident. She went rushing out of the house, late, then came right back, yelling, 'I forgot my knickers!'"

"Ha!" Duncan exclaimed boisterously in the midst of all the laughter. "Thank God it wasn't Scottish country dancing!"

The laughter dropped dead on the spot as they all looked at him.

"You know, Scottish country dancing..." he flustered, wondering about their reaction. Then he understood, and his face became bright red. "Oh...oh...my God...I didn't mean...I just meant, all the high kicks, and the..."

George reached out and put a hand on his brother's shoulder reassuringly. "It's okay, Dunc, we get it. No need to dig yourself in any deeper..."

"Anyway, you three seem to be wandering all over the airfield these days," Kay smiled kindly, "George and I thought we'd like to do the same this afternoon. He's meeting a friend at the pub, so we can drop him off there."

"We're up for that," Naomi said, checking silently with her partner. "Duncan?"

"Eh...sure...my social calendar is free." He was poking his tofu burger dubiously with a fork. "It's not as if I've got any work."

"That's because you're Homo ludens," she said cheerfully.

"What?" Her ploy had succeeded, and he was out of his slump.

"'Ludens' is 'play'..."

"Yes, I know, but..."

"It's a theory from a man called Huizinga that we are a species whose natural tendency is to play, and that we should acknowledge that instead of being so serious all the time. I was suggesting that you embody that truth."

"I like that," said George.

"That's because your whole life you've been playing with giant Meccano sets," Kay teased.

"Language," mused Duncan, turning his attention to the left-over couscous salad from the previous night. "It's so deep-set in us, it becomes the hard wiring."

"So it is decided," said Heinrich brightly. "This afternoon's playground is the airfield."

"Yes," said George. "I've got to admit, I tend to just drive over it. It's a place to get somewhere else, and that's it as far as I am concerned."

The unpredictability of English weather manifested once more as they left the house and wandered up the lane towards what had once been the station's entrance. The sun was visible only through a monochromatic haze of white cloud, and there was a disconcerting frozen quality to the humid heat, brought by sudden short-lived breezes. "It's like the weather is neither one thing nor another," commented Naomi. Even the oaks and the sycamores either side of the road had an inappropriately autumnal look to their leaves.

Duncan was looking at the concrete foundations he had noticed before hidden behind the gorse when Kay asked him about his tooth. They were a few yards behind the others.

"It's much better," he answered. "The antibiotics seem to be working."

She said nothing, her mind on the dull pain in her chest that she had just that day decided to see a doctor about. She could spend her life cultivating eternal youth, physically and in spirit; but as the years increased so did her certainty – as it does with us all – that the assassin would strike, no telling when, how or from where.

"Tch. George!" she called out.

She had noticed a proliferation of rubbish being blown about gently under the trees. He turned and joined her, handing her a plastic shopping bag, and retaining one for his own use.

"He does the recyclables," she explained, "I pick up the other stuff. We don't like seeing this around, and animals can choke on the plastic."

Duncan froze, contemplating the scene: the rustling crisp packets, the din of blind consumerism, the ruin of many a cinema outing and purveyor of alien colours in streets and hedges.

Suddenly he sprang into action, picking up as much of the offending detritus as he could, Kay smiling gratefully as Heinrich and Naomi joined in.

"We'll leave it all here," George said, once they had finished, "and pick it up on our way back."

At the old airfield entrance, now simply a road leading towards Yelverton across the moor, they halted in the muggy heat to look at the map on a board.

"It's an interesting shape that the runways make," George commented. "It could be a stick figure of someone marching."

"More like they're dancing," Naomi observed.

"Yes...you're right actually. What do you think, Duncan?" he grinned mischievously at his brother. "Any hidden patterns?"

Kay looked on anxiously, but George's taunt – whatever its source – was clearly amicable, and Duncan had understood it as such. He came to examine the map more closely.

"It looks like a gyre to me," he said, "if we're going to be assigning shapes to clouds."

"A *gyre*?"

The two men started talking between each other animatedly in the language of brothers, and Kay, understanding little, went on to join the other two who had gone on ahead.

"They're all right now," Heinrich observed.

"Yes, it's like this every time. They have one stupid blow-up, then they act like they're the best of friends and always were."

"It's the same with Heinrich and his brother," said Naomi.

"I find it hard to believe you'd blow up at anybody, Heinrich."

"Family has a way of getting under your skin."

"It sure does." Kay, coming from an unusually large family in middle-class Surrey, had grown up contending with three sisters and, to a lesser extent, one brother. She had often wondered what any of them had in common and, now that she was older, she had the answer of 'too much'. Also, memories of her mother's rigidity made her paranoid of her own. "Their father was very mean to Duncan," she said, diverting thoughts from her own background, "and I think George has some guilt about that. He was the practical one, you see, and Duncan as a child appeared to be practically useless – in his father's eyes."

"And when he became a history teacher?" asked Naomi.

"Even then. His father couldn't see the necessity of such a profession. He thought the world was being ruined by intellectuals."

"He wouldn't have liked me, as an academic."

"Probably not." She didn't mention that her father-in-law had also been anti-Semitic, though his ire drifted in his latter years, becoming more focused on the unemployed as the root of society's problems.

They were walking on the grass alongside the road, and were passed by a car. Simultaneously, coming in the opposite direction were two hikers with backpacks on the other side of the road; who were alerted to a cyclist coming from behind by the ringing of a bell. The hikers quickly got onto the verge. The cyclist, dressed casually in jeans and a white t-shirt, whisked past, long brown hair flowing behind.

"Asshole!" yelled one of the hikers, in a strong American accent. He was a burly chap with a thick black beard. His girlfriend was also quite stocky, with long straight blonde hair and a granite-jaw.

As surprised as Kay and her friends were with this outburst, they were even more so at the cyclists' hearing, as were the hikers. He slowed down immediately and returned to the scene.

"I'm sorry. Did you say something?" he asked the American.

"You didn't say 'thank you!'" the girl explained loudly.

"Why should I have? You shouldn't have been walking in the road."

"Oh this isn't a free country then?" argued the man.

"It's a country that appreciates common sense, something *your* country obviously still has to learn."

"At least we've learnt how to hold on to our manners!"

"I see no evidence of that."

"You didn't say 'thank you'," the girl repeated.

"If I said 'thank you' to every idiot I met, I'd have no breath for cycling."

The argument continued pointlessly. George and Duncan caught up with the others, who had been standing mesmerised by the ridiculous scene.

Heinrich couldn't resist. "However did they win the war?"

Naomi burst out laughing, and the group, broken from the spell, were free to continue their journey. On glancing back, Kay saw the debaters also continuing their separate journeys, with no obvious physical damage.

"It's like walking past invisible buildings," Naomi commented, looking around.

"It's funny," said Kay, "we come through here several times a week, by car or bicycle or on foot, and we've never really thought about it much, have we, George?"

"No, we haven't," he agreed. "We notice the wildlife, the horses, the plants, but otherwise we're probably always too focused on where we're going, the lure of the pub, or the feeling of nearing home, to be much bothered by anything else."

As they meandered towards Yelverton, Duncan found himself wandering off, at least in his mind. The others were alternating from admiring the newborn ponies, to enjoying the kite-flying, and the natural beauties of the moor, while he started noting the clothes everyone was wearing. It was taken for granted, the attire of daily wear, even the high fashion of the rich and famous. Yet now, looking at the range of clothing around him, worn by a people at play, he was struck by its impermanence. No era's fashion ever repeated itself seriously. The inexorable tides of style reflected the impermanence of the moment. It was all so beautiful if one could perceive each present with clear vision; and how men and women acted, responded, to their time was a reflection of their own capacity to love. He looked down at his red canvas trainers and bermuda shorts. Even he, with his jocular sartorial approach, was very much a person of his time.

"Duncan? Are you coming?" George asked from a few yards away as the others moved off. "Come on, what are you thinking about?"

"Just that I'm grateful not to be wearing chainmail," Duncan said.

"On a day like this? I'm not surprised. Come on."

His name was David Allen. Both he and George were old enough to remember the comedian of the same name, and had been impressed as teenagers with his dry wit and charm, how he always managed to stay the perceptive side of inebriation. As a doctor who, like George, had retired early, this Dave Allen never drank excessively nor smoked. In the past, he tolerated George's pipe with only an occasional flippant remark. Now he never bothered.

The issue never came up anyway, as the two of them went inside The Rock once David arrived, and the others left the debris from their cream teas, Duncan calling out valiantly, "We'll pick up the trash!"

They sat with their pints of Dartmoor ale at a corner table.

"So that's your brother," said Dave.

"Yes."

"What was he going on about exactly when I arrived?"

"He was pontificating that the fourteenth century church under Richard the Second forbade all magical thinking, 'ergo' Christianity and science are actually the same religion."

"Ha." Dave smiled pensively. "That *is* amusing as a concept." But he looked uncomfortable, as if from another, foreign thought, and they both concentrated on their drinks.

He was a tall thin man, with a full head of gingery hair, and nervous blue eyes. Whatever accent he had once had when growing up in the north of Scotland, was all but gone, and could only faintly be heard on occasion as a lilt in the careful way he enunciated. It was as if each expressed thought came only after lengthy deliberation.

"And what was that comment about the trash?" he asked, putting his drink down.

"I told you before. Kay and I take it upon ourselves to clear up corners of the moor now and again."

"Ah yes. Good for you. A bit of community spirit. We need more of that."

"I hope we don't need another world war to bring it out. You'd think we'd have learnt by now."

"Ahh, mankind..." Dave said wistfully, then, "What?" George had clearly reacted.

"Oh, it's... Duncan must be getting to me, I'm questioning the simplest things. I just wondered why there's a gender in there: 'mankind'. It doesn't exist in French, *'l'humanité'*..."

"Isn't that feminine?"

"Ahh...touché."

"So how is it with your guests?" Dave changed the subject.

"Good. Really good. I've always liked them, had an immediate fondness for them when we met, as did Kay. Heinrich makes me laugh. It's not even that he's that witty, it's not an English cleverclogs humour. He's also a mathematician, so we have a pragmatic side in common. Though he does go on about the poetry of it a bit much."

"Where does he work?"

"He helps his parents with their inn in Germany. He seems quite satisfied with menial jobs. I get the impression his degree was an automatic thing for him to do, and is now more of an entertainment for him than anything else. Art and literature he takes much more seriously."

"A bit of a conundrum there. He'd do well to follow your example."

"I doubt that will happen. I also suspect he's more led by Naomi, and what she wants to do, than he is by his own desires. She *is* his desire."

"You met them at that Findhorn community, didn't you?"

"Yes."

"Do you think you'll go back there?"

"Only if Kay wishes to go, which she might."

"*She* is your desire."

"Ah. You're probably right."

"You never seemed that sold on the New Age approach to things."

He was pushing the obvious here. Jill, Dave's wife, had initially met Kay at the Gaia Fair one summer on Newton Abbot racecourse, when both husbands had been tagging along. They had espied each other as potential allies, gone off to the beer tent, and remained friends ever since, whereas the women met only now and again at special events.

"Not so much anymore. One time – a long time ago – Kay and I had visited friends from Findhorn at their longhouse on the Cornish border. They had other friends there, a couple of whom were smoking pot. Seeing this, I happily lit up my pipe, only to have the lot of them admonish me for polluting the atmosphere, whereas we'd been subjected to their fumes for a good half-hour. I just saw the hypocrisy in that moment. Which seems to underlie any collective idealism."

"It might not be fair to generalise."

"No, and I don't, but it revealed a side to the alternative community I'm always aware of now."

"Duncan's not a New Ager, is he?"

George hesitated, buying time with a sip. He was picking up on his friend's obstinacy, a simple refusal to accommodate anyone's opinions that did not validate his own. It was subtle but irritating, and reminded George what he did like about his wife's predilections and friends. It also reminded him uncomfortably of himself. He may have favoured the nuts-and-bolts approach, but inevitably there was a price for nuts and bolts. After a few more sips he was back on track, and put the glass down.

"Old Ager more like. He takes his history seriously. His fascination with courtly love in the middle ages – you know, knights and damsels in distress and all that – drew him deeply into his studies as an undergrad. He was always a hopeless romantic. Emphasis on the 'hopeless'. His wife was a stunner. He made an ass of himself wooing her, but she eventually relented. They did have a lot in common."

"She sounds impressive. Does he talk with you at all about what he's going through?"

George considered, then smiled. "He once said 'talking with men about emotional stuff is like talking to a pack of dogs'."

"He may have a point. Admit it, we've both been checking out the barmaid with the long legs and short skirt; and we're happily married men."

George nodded, acknowledging that he'd been caught.

"I did look up what I could about prosopagnosia, as you asked," Dave said. "Although I doubt I found anything you couldn't online."

"I thought you might have some fresh insights..."

"Not really. Harvard seems to be the main place for it, they've done considerable research. But I did get in touch with an old buddy, a psychiatrist, and he told me something interesting. It appears there is mounting evidence that face blindness may be connected to a depletion of oxytocin. It's a hormone associated with feelings of love."

"So I recall. Then what is the conclusion?"

"I don't think there is one yet. But I could speculate in a fanciful way that feeling unloved might be one of the things leading to prosopagnosia."

"Interesting." George leant backwards into his chair, thinking.

"Though what interests *me*, is the way the condition removes the ability to recognise patterns..."

"That's just it though," George now leant forward emphatically, "Duncan sees patterns everywhere. He's been on a quest to places a group of knights visited in the middle ages."

"I thought you said he just came back from the Bahamas."

"Well, places he *believes* they visited..." George was suddenly trapped between what he could reveal comfortably to his friend, and what he had sworn to Duncan not to reveal to anybody yet. There was a very fine line between the two.

"That's related to the patterns," he said, having decided. "Duncan claims there's a secret landscape beneath the geography of New Providence, the central island. But I've looked. There's nothing there. Just modern roads and some tacky American architecture. Anyone who sees a pattern in that lot has to be imagining it."

"How does that connect to medieval knights?"

"Look, this is strictly between us, it doesn't go further than this table." He was looking around furtively to see if anyone could hear, then felt ridiculous doing so.

"I swear, I won't even tell my cat."

"He's found an old document...or he's written one..."

"'Written an old document'?"

"We all start acting a bit crazy around him," George said breathlessly. "I can't tell what he's telling me. Either the document exists, or he's written a text drawn from several sources, or he's making the whole thing up. He's infuriatingly ambiguous about things sometimes.

"The gist of it is, there was a group of knights... Knights Templar...conspiracy nuts go on about them a lot... These knights were secret even to their Grand Order, a secret group within a group...and they were on a mission..."

By the time George had indulged in another pint, and divulged in a rambling manner a few of his brother's secrets, and was stumbling back home, Kay was walking with the phone to the annexe. She knocked on the open door and looked in to find Duncan in a tizzy at the computer.

"It's unbelievable!" he cried out to her. "Even if I go back, and undo the card sequence, I can still end up stuck. Yet it is fascinating how the choice of one particular card at the beginning affects all the others sequentially, making a success *or* a dog's breakfast of it. Completely randomly! It's not skill, it's luck. Yet how come, even with this extraordinary ability to go back in time, this gift of hindsight, things can still end disastrously? Sometimes the odds are stacked against us in such a way, we have no chance from the very beginning... Drat it."

Silently, she withdrew. On reaching the back door she spoke into the phone.

"Jasmine? It's not a good time. He's in one of his states... No, about Patience, which he is not exhibiting very much of right now."

She laughed at the reply.

"Okay, Jasmine, we'll keep trying. Lovely to catch up. Speak to you soon."

Thus, with the gentle conspiracy of so many women putting the world to rights, she entered the house, and started to prepare dinner.

"Do you want another go, Jackie?" the flight lieutenant asked.

"No thanks, Jim," Donnel replied, "I prefer to sit behind a pair of Brownings up in the sky." He didn't want to admit the Lee Enfield had kicked like a mule and after only ten rounds he was feeling it in his shoulder. How soldiers put up with this self-inflicted injury, he had no idea.

"You didn't do too badly," the man smiled.

The sounds of guns of various descriptions and size rebounded off the hills, accompanied with smells of cordite drifting across the cool Dartmoor air. Paradoxically, the scene of various Army and

Air Force teams competing had an aura of peace about it. It wasn't just that the matches were friendly, but perhaps also because they were ultimately on the same team, held by the all-encompassing serenity of the moor.

This last contemplation of Donnel's was interrupted by the roar of low-flying engines overhead. Many of those on the ground let out a cheer, but there were also cries of "You bastards! Crash, why dontcha?!" and so on, as the planes diminished in the grey sky.

"If you can't keep it together now, what would you do if they were the enemy, you ponces?" demanded one team leader viciously.

"That's 276 on their way back," commented the flight lieutenant.

"And showing off," said Donnel.

"Looks like they're all there though, that's the thing."

Their conversation trailed off as the English officer focused on the team's current performance, and Donnel had his attention seized by a commotion further along, and down the slope to his right. There was a group of soldiers at the pistol range, mostly men and some women; but one of the women wasn't Army, she was Air Force. Her light blue shirt stood out against all the khaki, her hair untamed once again beneath her cap. It was Maggie Drummond. She was perfectly poised, calm, as she blazed away at a target twenty yards away with a pistol. She knew what she was doing.

There were shouts from the men and cheers from the women as she emptied the magazine. Smiling, trying not to show how pleased she was, she accepted the hugs and pats on the back from the ATS girls, some of whom were taunting the men.

Donnel made his way down the slope. Their eyes met.

"Done well obviously."

She nodded, glad to see him, but also there was an uncertainty there. Perhaps he had intruded. As things turned out, if he were where he should not have been, he was hardly alone in that.

He watched as she took the magazine out of the pistol. He noticed that it was a Colt 1911, US Navy issue.

"A gift," she explained, noting his gaze.

"Are you on the team?"

"Not really." She glanced around at the celebrating women. The men, prepared to forget their defeat in the name of festivity, were starting to celebrate with them, laughing at their own humiliation. Cigarettes were being passed around and someone had produced a hip flask.

"I was in the vicinity and the girls asked me to help settle a bet."

"Are they as good as you?"

"Better sometimes. It's the benefit of moving in privileged circles before the war. Firearms and aristocracy go together."

"You have a varied role around here."

"Well, it beats card-indexing," she said with a meaningful, though abstruse, look. "I was in a women's gun club in America," she added.

"Ahh. That makes sense," he said ambiguously. "It seems the smaller the weapon, the worse I am at using it. I can't hit a target with a pistol at ten yards. I've tried..."

"Please, hide this," she said suddenly and unexpectedly, moving close to him, shoving the pistol into his hands. "My jacket's in the car. Try and cover me."

Swiftly he slid the weapon under his jacket pocket, whilst looking around to see three Army officers headed towards their ebullient group.

"Heads up, guys," he warned the others, as he and Maggie moved further down the slope, away from them. He took care that she remained on the other side of him from the officers who were still some distance away. Before they rounded the hill and were out of sight, he glanced back to see the shooters tidying up as the officers descended. The women seemed the most unfazed. Was that evidence of good breeding? Donnel wondered.

They made their way through hundreds of British troops going in various directions on the lower track, their puttees splattered with mud. A Queen Mary pushed by, carrying a tank under tarpaulin, its wheels spraying everyone in the vicinity with more mud. Still shielding her, he got the worst of it.

He recognised her car nestled amongst the trucks and jeeps.

"How did you get here?" she asked, visibly more relaxed, after retrieving her jacket, putting it on and fastening the buttons. It was as if, after letting her guard down, she needed to put on armour to feel secure.

"With the team in a truck. They won't miss me, if I can get a ride with you..."

"It's the least I can do."

After they got in, he handed her the gun. She took it in her long slender fingers, and held it for a moment, thoughtfully, nervous again. "You didn't see this," she said decidedly, opening a compartment in the car door, and sliding the weapon in where it fitted neatly. "You didn't see anything. I should have been more discreet. Hubris always gets the better of me."

"No problem."

They left the camp unhindered except for the sheer amount of traffic. This hardly lessened on the road between Okehampton and Tavistock, where there was a constant stream of traffic both ways. To the east the rising ground of the moor reminded Donnel in some way of a prehistoric beast lurking in the background. Its presence was always felt, especially now with the low layer of black cloud lit in gold-yellow flecks by the sun, which had emerged in its last moments before reaching the horizon.

Maggie was a careful driver and didn't overtake, preferring to pull back from the rambunctious GIs in the back of a truck. "I don't know if they're leering at me, or jeering at you for being the passenger," she joked.

Along a straight stretch, an American jeep filled with officers came right behind, then pushed past, weaving into the distance.

"It's like something's up," Donnel commented. "Maybe we're getting closer to the big push."

Maggie ignored this, smiling at the departing jeep. "I was impressed the first time I saw the way Americans just charged across the grass. It was an oddly liberating experience. Me, I'm stuck in this clumsy heap."

"Oh it's not so bad," Donnel grinned. "It's nice, isn't it."

"What is?"

"This…co-operation."

She smiled at him with what could have been kindly condescension.

"Right up until Pearl Harbor happened," she said, "Standard Oil was refuelling U-Boats in New Jersey."

"Are you saying…?" He couldn't finish.

"I'm merely suggesting that our two countries weren't necessarily always so cosy."

"Things are very different now," he protested. He felt his world view under threat.

"I would say, yes, since a few months ago things have improved considerably. Even the Army and Navy are talking to each other."

"What circles do you move in?" Once again with her, as was often the case with the English, he suspected the preference for discretion – almost fetishistic – to be naturally flowering into national secrecy. Secrecy and honesty might not always be antonyms, he pondered.

"You saw my circle back there," she laughed finally, interrupting his thoughts. "My other circle is you chaps."

"Us...you mean...at the hut?" It suddenly dawned on him, and he was pleased. He had no idea she felt that way about them.

"Of course. Everything else is just my job."

"Well, Sergeant Drummond," he said, leaning back, "your absence was noted at last night's soirée."

"I had things to do."

"We even have a gramophone now."

"That sounds good. Can you teach me the jitterbug?"

"If you teach me the waltz."

Their lightness was brought to an end by a sudden melancholy on her part.

"The Germans," she said after a while. "And the Japanese. They dance, they do the waltz, everything we do..."

"Presumably."

"Yet they fight like people who do not know love."

They were entering Tavistock alone. No other vehicles, military or civilian, were in sight till they reached the centre.

Donnel eyed the people walking about. "It looks like a friendly town," he commented. She made no reply as they rattled through the streets. When they emerged the other side of the town, and were pushing up the leafy hill to Clearbrooke, they became stuck behind another army truck, British this time, and she pulled back.

"You're a really good shot," he remarked, eager to keep chatting. "After the war you should compete or something."

She glanced at him wistfully. "I often wonder if, once you become really good at something, the best thing is not to just quit it and go onto something else."

At the top of the hill, as they approached the airfield, a white plane with US Navy markings lifted up in front of them, glinting as it turned towards the setting sun.

"Catalina. Looks like top brass to me," Donnel commented. "Wonder what they're up to." He received no reply, and they remained in silence until getting to the main gate.

He reached for his ID only for them to be waved through.

"You're a popular girl," he remarked.

Only her smile – a constant, subtle default when she was not lighting up a room with her broader smile – said anything, until she turned off the road abruptly and they bumped over the grass towards the huts. "I learned from the best," she laughed.

There were cheers from the various representatives of the US Navy as they rattled past them; whether for her audacity, being a woman or being an audacious woman, wasn't clear.

They parked next to their own hut – Donnel was pleased to consider it as such, meaning it belonged to their whole little group. As they got out, Maggie was peering over to the Bellman hangar.

"Is that Trevor?" She was indicating a Walrus currently engaging the attentions of a team of men, one of whom was crouched on the top wing.

"Yes, it is. You really have excellent eyesight."

"Said the pot to the kettle. Will he be all right up there? What's he doing?"

"He started today. A lot of salt water damage on those craft. The paintwork needs constant attention. He wanted to start with the basics, get into the swing of things. Guess he has to prove himself."

"Better not let Joyce know. She'll give him a tongue-lashing."

"As delightful as that sounds, she's been sent to Roborough today for some meeting."

"So who's at home?" she asked.

"Let's go and find out," he said as they stepped towards the door. "You missed my curried beef last night, fortunately, so Ben's promised us another example of his culinary brilliance."

"Is there anything he can't do?"

"Find his uniform…"

Yet as they stepped into the low light of the hut, greeted with the smell of frying onions, they were both startled by the sight before them, so effectively and dramatically contradicting Donnel's assertion.

Hawker was standing talking to Sandra, who was in one of the deck chairs, with a mug of tea in one hand, a cigarette in the other. He was dressed as if for parade, in a neatly pressed USAAF airman's uniform. He had apparently just walked in.

"He even has a hat," Maggie gasped softly.

"Not as nice as mine," Donnel retorted quickly, no less in shock.

Hawker, conscious of their looks, put a brave face on it, saying, "I thought I heard your car."

A movement from one of the bunks at the back provided a distraction.

"Is that you, Dave?" Donnel said into the darkness. "Don't tell me you never left last night? I thought Intelligence never slept."

"Just catching a quick snooze," Proudon stood up, revealing his tall frame. "Hope you don't mind."

"Why would we? You know you're welcome here, D'Artagnan."

"And you look well-settled in, Sandra," Maggie said, moving into the room.

"I was off an hour ago."

The five of them were going about their various domestic duties, such as lighting cigarettes, when Donnel's face changed expression at something behind her, and Maggie looked around sharply to see a familiar shape filling the doorway. It was Wing Commander Gleeson, the officer who had admonished her before for not saluting. She didn't make the same mistake this time, trusting that the others would follow suit.

"What are you doing here, Sergeant?" he barked, pointing his black cane in her direction, ignoring her salute.

"My job, sir. Checking that our guests are comfortable."

"I see. And *I've* been checking up on you. By the way, I don't see how being a liaison permits you to drive all over the grass like the cowboys with whom you've been fraternising."

"Yes, sir."

He stood still, peering at her, while she and the others remained frozen. He seemed to be staring at her hair, which had remained loose since leaving the firing range, but he was unclear as to what the regulations were. Despite being the Senior Admin Officer, through machinations he had managed to limit dealings with women in his work. All the same, he sensed something was amiss. She looked too free for his liking, like a harlot he thought, a harlot without lipstick.

"I have been informed that there are women here," he said accusingly.

Puzzled, she looked round to see Sandra's empty chair and her cigarette floating lifeless in half-drunk tea.

"Only me, sir, as far as I know."

"Well..." He was uncertain, convinced that something was amiss but with no idea as to what. His eyes alighted on Hawker who was doing a remarkable show of standing stiffly. "You must be the replacement for that Hawker fellow."

"Yes, sir."

"Good to know. That bounder was useless. I'm sure he was up to something. Sergeant, a word with you outside, if I may."

Maggie delayed following him out just long enough to see Sandra peering out from under some blankets on a bottom bunk.

"I saw his shadow before he came in," she giggled.

Once a palely smiling Maggie had left, the four remaining burst into suppressed laughter.

"I think this calls for a real drink," proclaimed Donnel.

He got out the glasses and Hawker commenced cooking duties.

Outside, Maggie felt like a guilty schoolgirl as she walked a few steps behind the wing commander in the dampening air, the last of the sun feebly making its way through the trees. His car and driver were parked on the verge just north of where Runway One ended. He glanced back at her, as if to say, 'This is how it should be done.' A few steps further and then he stopped.

"Is there something of particular interest in my cane?" he demanded, waving it at her.

"No, sir, why…"

"'*Why* are you looking at it?' you mean."

"It's just that my father had such a cane, sir."

"I see." He grimaced at her, still suspicious. Everything she said appeared questionable. He wondered if her father really did have a cane. What was she up to?

She in turn was hoping for a glimpse of humanity in the man. He had served in the Royal Observer Corps precursor of the last war, she knew. Other survivors from that time she had met had been shaken to their core, their attitude to life profoundly altered. This didn't seem to be the case here, it was as if he had ossified in the trenches. His ridiculous moustache, his cold piggy eyes and port-addled cheeks were like a cartoon, denying any vulnerable spirit that once had been present. Then again, after all these years of service he was only a wing commander; for this at least she could summon some empathy.

"I don't trust you, Sergeant." He had got through the previous conflict largely through bull-headedness, and it was a strategy he frequently returned to at times of bewilderment or stress. "There's something going on. Your position here was uncalled for, there were others already covering your allotted tasks. I would like to know who arranged your arrival, and why. Your attitude has been in question from the start, and that you choose to associate with a motley band of foreigners says little for your judgement. You haven't heard the last of this, believe me. Where were you stationed before?"

She hesitated before replying. "Eastcote, sir."

His little eyes narrowed as if to discern another lie, then he turned and went to his car, twirling the cane like a baton.

Back in the hut, Sandra had remained supine on the bunk, tucked under the blanket still, and resting her head in her hand as she chatted merrily to the men, a fresh cigarette trailing ash onto the concrete floor. Maggie thought she resembled a film star in soft light. Hawker was still cooking, the other two in deck chairs, also with cigarettes. As the air was getting chilly, they were inclined to be near the stove.

"He'd put a drink in my hand, then sod off for a game of arrows with his mates. Honestly, English men are as unromantic as you can get."

"Come on now!" objected Proudon good humouredly.

"No offence." She paused to inhale more smoke. Breathing it out languidly, she turned over onto her back. "Why am I looking at a picture of a semi-naked woman?"

Maggie went to sit with the men, accepting a cigarette from Donnel.

Hawker glanced over at Sandra, smiling. "That's Jackie's bed you're on. She's his fiancée. Tallulah, meet Sandra. Sandra, meet Tallulah."

"Wowzer."

"That's a common response," Proudon observed.

Maggie got up to look. "That's quite a girl," she said, leaning over Sandra and examining the picture above her. She looked over to Donnel. "Whatever are you doing here?"

"Note we're not allowed pin-ups," Sandra moaned, taking several drags of her cigarette.

"Do you want them?" asked Maggie, returning to her seat.

"Probably not," she said sourly.

Donnel, embarrassed, was remaining silent.

"Would your mother approve?" Maggie asked him pointedly.

"Probably not," he admitted.

"Certainly not, I would say."

"She's very religious. My family is Roman Catholic. Tallulah isn't."

"And you? Do you practise?"

"Not really." He remained looking sheepish. "Tallulah was studying comparative religion before dropping out, but we're both...non-religious. Except we like the way Indians talk about the Great Spirit."

"An ex-Catholic is someone who doesn't believe in hell, but knows that he's going there," Hawker grinned.

"Come off it, man!" Donnel threw an empty packet of Camels at him, which he dodged effortlessly. "To tell the truth, there was much I loved about the church: the certainty of ritual, the mystery of authority... I still go to Mass sometimes. I feel comfortable there."

Maggie had noticed that Hawker was glancing over in Sandra's direction again. She could see a flicker of concern in his dark features.

"Don't worry, Sandra," she said, taking up his cause. "We're both as fetching as the future Mrs Donnel."

"Hear hear," said Proudon.

"It don't bother me," said Sandra, sitting up on the edge of the bed. "I'm not goin' ter get *my* kit off for a photo."

"By the way," Maggie asked, "how did you manage to hide so quickly before?"

"I saw the shadow of his big fat belly as the door was openin', then rabbited. Growin' up in Croydon...you learn to move fast, or you're toast. There were always stupid fights goin' on for reasons no one could remember. The Krauts are just the latest in a long line. What did 'e want you for anyhow?"

"He doesn't like my decorum," she said flatly.

"You're not vain enough, Maggie. They always used to say to us in boot camp, the vainer we were, the smarter, the better. Even when fighting a war we have to look good."

"That's ubiquitous," said Donnel. Then added to her blank stare. "We all have to be smart."

"If that's what wins a war then the Krauts have definitely lost, 'cos they look ridiculous in their goose-steppin' kinky boots." She swiftly turned her attention back to Maggie. "I bet it was a class thing."

"What do you mean?"

"Gleeson's not as posh as you. I bet that gets up 'is 'ooter."

Donnel shook his head. "Sometimes I can't understand a word you say."

"Me? You're the bloody foreigner."

"That's hardly fair!"

"'Fair'? You talk t'me about fair!"

"Will you two belt up," Proudon intervened.

"Yeah," put in Hawker as he stirred the sauce, "we're supposed to be fighting the Germans. This is worse than the baseball-rounders débâcle. The rules have to be agreed upon."

"What I want to know," Smith said, as he entered, "is why there are no drinks in your hands, and no music playing." He had just washed his hands, and now examined them for any remaining grease before going to his bunk and picking up a towel.

"I'll sort the music," Sandra said, getting to her feet eagerly.

"Jackie promised to teach me to jitterbug," Maggie announced.

"Oh I…" Sandra glanced up as she wound the gramophone by the far wall. They had arranged the beds in such a way, there was plenty of space around it. She looked suddenly sad as she chose a record. Donnel caught her look, and stepped towards her as 'The Boogie Woogie Bugle Boy' filled the air. "If I may," he said, holding out his hand.

She accepted somewhat begrudgingly, then started to relax as he took her through the initial steps. "Quick quick slow slow… Finger wagging is optional…"

Hawker meanwhile, seeing his chance, left the stove and went over to where Maggie was sitting. "I can show you," he bowed, and her eyes lit up.

He actually proved to be the superior teacher, with Donnel consistently looking over to check his own form. The two men remaining became the slightly envious audience, seated with their drinks, until Smith took it upon himself to be in charge of the gramophone.

The ladies were quick learners, and the jubilation continued till half-way through 'American Patrol' when the smell of burning was evident.

"Ah shoot," Hawker exclaimed, reluctantly letting go of Maggie and rushing over to the stove. "I guess we're having Cajun style again."

"I bet my mum wished she had that excuse!" Sandra parted with Donnel, laughing.

Maggie went to put a conciliatory hand on Hawker's shoulder, and kissed him on the cheek. "Thank you, Ben."

Donnel, observing, was sure he could perceive a blush on his friend's cheek. Sandra was heading towards the drinks. Her head was down, but she was happy. The tune ended, Smith changed needles, turned the record over, and she grimaced at the melancholy notes.

"Not that one," she protested, sinking into her chair, "that's worse than Vera soddin' Lynn. I don't want to read his bloody letter."

"I think we're about to eat anyway," Donnel, amused, said to Smith. This was confirmed by a nod from Hawker.

As they all settled down with their drinks and slightly charred bean stew, Donnel and Sandra were in adjacent deck chairs. "No fan of the British songbird then?" he asked.

Sandra had been succumbing to the glum temptress again, but she could hardly hold back the lightness she felt in his presence.

"I associate her with my first gas mask," she smiled, "bollocks-freezing winter, the throbbing of the Nazi bombers, damp concrete floors of over-crowded shelters with leaking roofs…and the skies above even more terrifying.

"We had just got a wireless for the first time, and she was always on it. I felt she was tauntin' us with promises of a better tomorrow. I was about to leave for training, and my last days at home were not exactly relaxing. I liked the spam we started gettin' though."

"I'm glad I never had to experience all that," he commiserated.

"Dad got a Morrison shelter. I don't know how he afforded it on two squid a week. Maybe it was his way of aspiring to a middle-class way of life. That was even more ridiculous. The Luftwaffe raining all bloody hell on us and there we were crouching under a glorified table. I was glad to leave, though I'm always worried about them even when they're in Kent."

"You found *us*, Sandra," Maggie said, then was immediately embarrassed. "This tomato sauce is really good, Ben," she changed the subject.

"Thank you. I know someone who grows *tomatoes* in the village." He used the English pronunciation which made her smile.

When Joyce arrived they were tucking into a steamed fruit pudding that Hawker had prepared earlier. They all cried out in greeting, and resumed their discussion while Smith went to get the food kept aside for her.

"What's Sandra on about now?" she asked, nudging him amiably.

"Oh," he said, glancing over his shoulder at the group, "Jackie made an inadvisably positive comment about 'Uncle Joe'. She's not letting him off."

"Bloody right I'm not!" the culprit yelled. "Russkies say they need a strong authority figure to keep them in line. That's just evading responsibility. Ain't they got self-discipline?"

"I'll stay out of this," said Joyce as she sat down.

"I would," said Smith.

"Sandra has a point," Maggie put in. "At the start of the war *they* were the ones supplying Germany with oil and metal."

"Communism, Nazism... Dark skies all around," Donnel said, leaning back in his chair as he lit a cigarette.

"I don't trust any isms, me," said Sandra.

"No more isms," Proudon raised his glass.

"Hear hear." And all those with glasses raised them.

"It takes courage to oppose an ism," Donnel stated soberly. "Haven't all the law professors in Utrecht been arrested by the Germans?"

"No prizes for guessing where they've gone," said Sandra.

"I'm going to have to ask you two to shut up again," Hawker admonished. "You're allowing an ism *in* here. I suggest we leave the dishes aside and dance."

"I believe I owe you a waltz," Maggie said to Donnel.

They danced until the needles ran out, everybody taking turns with one another. Every arrangement provided comment, always complimentary; but it was when Hawker broke loose to 'June Teenth Jamboree', throwing his arms to the sky, chanting 'No more isms! No more isms!' and everybody stood aside to watch and clap along – *that*, everybody agreed, was the highlight of the evening.

"It was wonderful last night," said Joyce when Sandra came to collect her from the squadron office. "I daren't tell any of the other guys, but Ben is awfully good."

"I think they know. I noticed it didn't hold you back in favouring Trev."

"Hold on while I file these papers, then I'm done."

Sandra smiled at her friend's embarrassment. They had had a very similar conversation on the walk back to the WAAF quarters, but Joyce didn't tire of the subject.

She smiled again when Squadron Leader Francis came through from the back office. It was he who had met Donnel on arrival at Ravenscroft on the stairs. He and Sandra were too familiar with each other to insist on formalities, and he merely smiled in return.

"I wondered when Joyce's other half would get here," he said, as he ruffled through the papers on the desk. "Sorry to hold her back. Just one Yank in the mix and it's a bureaucratic nightmare."

"I was meaning to tell you, Sandra," said Joyce, looking up. "Jackie's flying tonight. One of the chutes you packed was for him."

Francis watched Sandra for a reaction, now he was aware of a connection.

"Oh."

"It's a Mandolin Op," Francis said, to be helpful. He always spoke candidly with her, often too candidly. She seemed to invoke trust.

"They're going for the railways," she said.

"Indeed."

"Jackie came with a lot of recommendations," Joyce added.

"Apparently the blighter can see in the dark or something," Francis said matter-of-factly. "Got two of my boys off sick and two on leave, so his name came up. I told him he won't always be strong and handsome, so we'd better use him while we've got him. His holiday is over."

"Which runway is it?" Sandra asked blankly.

"Two, if the wind stays where it is. 2130. I hope he knows to avoid the rock. I might not have told him about that." Roborough Rock at the south end of the airfield was notorious for near-misses, though no one had actually hit it yet.

"If he can see in the dark, I doubt that's a concern," smiled Joyce.

Francis looked unconvinced now by his own earlier declaration. "Donnel will be at supper in the mess. I'll make sure he's duly warned."

He found the paper he was looking for, and disappeared into the back office again. Joyce picked up on Sandra's glum expression.

"He's married," Sandra said firmly in response. "Or as good as."

"I know, but..."

"I don't do flings, Joyce. I don't have those utility knickers. Neither of us do."

"He doesn't wear a wedding band," Joyce commented after a pause. "I wonder what that means." Sandra didn't answer.

Donnel's absence left a gap in the hut that evening, but also a sense of excitement. Sandra was torn and said little. It was like growing up in the East End, awaiting the dreaded copper's knock.

"He has to bond with the other pilots," Joyce consoled not just Sandra but everyone. "He hasn't been spending much time with them."

They all went outside to observe the take-off. They stood as the sun set behind the trees and a cold wind rose gradually from the east. Hawker valiantly gave his jacket to Maggie, and she edged a bit closer to him, watching the skies. Great dark clouds were rolling over the horizon. Joyce hugged Sandra against the growing chill, and Smith put his arm around them both. A roar of engines could be heard in the distance. The glim lamps were on, lining the way in the subdued light. The metal beasts charged down the runway and lifted safely one after the other into the last rays glancing off the clouds.

Sub Rosa

From. McKay

To: Mathers

Mary, could you have a look at the enclosed bit of nonsense? It's from one of our regular authors Duncan --------. Till now he has proven a solid bet, providing interesting texts for our academic division. This is a radical departure. He claims it is a translation of an actual 13th century document, which he refuses to show me. Allegedly it was Latin before becoming medieval French. Personally I think it to be at best Chinese whispers, and much more likely the imagination of a desperate man recently returned from an extended vacation to the Bahamas. He has recently lost his position due to a scandal at the university, and may well be seeking revenue through the Da Vinci crowd. The erratic syntax makes me even more suspicious, as if in his desperation he couldn't decide whether to write in cod-Elizabethan or plain English. Still, he was once an expert in this era and there may be something here. I would appreciate your thoughts. Perhaps we can sell it as genuine to the public and piss ourselves laughing at how much money we made at the Christmas party.

Yours,

Keith

My lord, pray accept this humble account of our endeavour, as requested. You selected me as chronicler for my background, that I am familiar with the written word and as conscientious in my texts as I am in their illustrations. The lack of the latter is only one of the faults to which I must profess in this relating. This, due to the brevity of days before I next depart, is excusable. I am not sure I can claim the same for omission of details or inaccuracy in my portrayals of our deeds, and misdeeds. In these you yourself my lord must assume some responsibility, in selecting me as your unworthy narrator, and in that fault the All Father may forgive you in Light of the extraordinary risks that you undertook by enlisting us in this holy mission, and with such success. Thus all fault returns solely to my inadequate relating, and rests upon my shoulders alone. I also hereby state that, as agreed between us, no real names or titles shall be used, including my own. As an aspect of this adventure, I shall incorporate names of those familiar to all who relish lore and romance, as do we both. You may glean what you wish from the appellations that I select. Our adventure begins herewith less than one year before now in Twelve Hundred and Fifty-Five Anno Domini, at the western reaches of the land, in the main port and town before Land's End, known as Porthengrous. I and two other Knights had lodgings at our Temple in Madron nearby. We intended to examine the coasts south, west and north in the region to seek moorings far from the general eye. This was not to be. Geraint, he of the golden hair, returned from the north, proclaiming the seas unruly and the land wild, both inaccessible for our purposes though he did manage to acquire the sunstone Hafiz had asked for, and which could be found there. Bedivere returned from Land's End with the same news, whereas I differed not in my examination of the south. Porthengrous had established itself at the mouth of the bay with good reason. At this juncture I realised our anonymity at any odds highly questionable. Three Knights of the Order searching the shoreline for vantage would give rise to whispers whether desired or no. We wore our colours with deserved pride and as agreed would do so for the entirety of the mission. There is honour here, and we would have what we could of it. I returned to Porthengrous often to know the land and the people more, while the other two went east to summon the ship. Of Porthengrous, there is much to know. First that there are two abbeys, one for Franciscans overseeing the harbour, the other for Dominicans three score steps before, hidden as is their wont in a dark alley. Across the bay on the island of St Michael, were Benedictine monks, as far from these as possible. This division, being alien to us, I viewed with contempt, almost as much I did the Dominicans, and they no doubt me. The townspeople oft avoided my eyes and curtailed inquiry, though respect was always afforded me as to other servants of The Cross, though with the strange language they spake I cannot be sure. Another fact I wish to relate is that to the south of the town edge ran a stream whose waters were as clear and fresh as any I didst e'er take. To the south of this brook lay another town by the name of Porthenys, less than a stone's throw away, so named because of the small island offshore, on which a hermit resided. From whence came this division I know not. You and I, my lord, as so many of our brothers, have experienced unnatural division the world over, and the strife that comes about for no good. The two towns were on amiable terms I am pleased to say and visited the other's market on a regular basis, yet I cannot escape the sense that commerce is just sursanure, as can be faith and tolerance. Porthenys had what they called a natural harbour, but access was limited due to rocks and geography. At spring tide Porthengrous was suited to the most heavily laden ship, as ours would be with the horses, grain, water and foodstuffs. The Treasure would be the lightest thing we carried. I used my time wisely, making arrangements with merchants despite the difficulties with communication. The town occupants who surpassed all such barriers were the children who were mostly sanguine in nature and in awe of my apparel and sword. I knew the look of the boy who attended my horse, that he wished to join me on my quest, for we have seen that look in many. Alas twas not to be. Perhaps twas because of the children, or the idyllic waters, my spirits were affected so I found it in myself to tolerate the approaches of the various friars, who at least spake this country's tongue. Perhaps twas of my altered nature they deemed it acceptable to approach, and make inquiries of the Holy Land, how it fared under the saracen. I insisted on discretion in the name of the Church, and told them my name was Sir John. No other name would reach their ears. E'en as I spake with and became familiar with the friars by the sea, I could observe their benign souls and come to accept these were not the men I despised. Here, it appeared, so near the world's end, much remained innocent. Thus by the time Our Lady arrived, I had obtained many allies in the port, for the influence of the children and monks. Then less than a fortnight later cries did go about o'er the town and I didst glimpse the glorious cross on its sail of pure white innocence. My heart was rarely as joyful as on that day, I can tell you! As twas low tide Our Lady stayed off shore betwixt the island and harbour and put out a small boat which contained Artorius, Bedivere, Geraint and two others. The harbour thronged with townspeople. My lord, if you could see the joy in their faces, you would know what we fought for all these years, and the darkest nights will seem less dark. It took three days to ready the ship. In that time, questions were asked, such as why only six horses and twelve men with no black-robed sergeants. Although I related how our Order began with two knights on one horse, I pointed out that those who remained on the ship were not knights but sailors. However there rose the further question of why only half-a-dozen sailors on a vessel of such size, to which I had no reply other than that they were more than equal to the task. Our stay at Porthengrous was regrettably, and by necessity, very short. Noble lords in the area were few, but came quickly on hearing of our ship. Artorius dealt with them all as only a man of gentillesse could, so that they felt they had learnt much, when nothing was confided. It is time to talk of the women, of which Cornwall had many of note, for these were Celtic women with a wildness in their eyes and capacity to hold your heart in their hand whilst they assessed the weighings of your soul. In this way, they resembled closely those women who have been admitted secretly into the Order, and were worthy to comprehend the burden of our mission could we but tell. They appreciated the antics of Kay, he with the red hair and gentleness of a woman, whereas no crusader he met ever thought him anything but a Fool. I am sure of the nights he spent ashore, not once was he alone. He knew his bounds this time, you will be glad to hear, and no irate husband came our way. There were many unmarried women of low to high birth. It is one in particular of which I wish to speak. It was our final hour before departure, and the last to be loaded were the horses which we had been keen to enjoy the pleasures of fresh grass and open fields before the journey. As they were being led along the wharf I was by the gangway, ensuring they stepped safely on board. Many had gathered once more, and I saw on this fateful spring day, a group of nuns, I know not of which Order. As one of the sisters, tall and gracious, moved to see around another, long black hair fell down around her face, she gazed directly at me with wide blue eyes like the calmest sea, and I was Adam succumbing to the greatest temptation of divine innocence, falling in heaven. Ye and I spake often of my Lady before, her kindness and beauty, how it is for her I chose to go on this quest, and no other, for if I could prove myself worthy of God, I would be worthy of her. And you would oft laugh and remind me of my youth spent in the growing shadow of that great cathedral, playing with Elsie, my love of lesser years. She and I grew apart due to influences from without, and perhaps tis true I never loved again till having the fortune to meet my Lady. Perhaps twas true my love was contained betwixt that of a girl and that of a woman, and twas all I knew of love until the end of days in that harbour. The nun, if she were a nun, for with the long beautiful hair and candid stare, I was uncertain as to the truth of this, and this was a place of seeming. She altered me in an instant. At first, as I attended to the horses, I fantasised there was a shared monastery of men and women as in days of old, for if so, if she were a member, I would consider renewing my vows. Or perhaps she would consider becoming a Templar woman, thus joining another sisterhood. I thought of Elsie, and of my Lady, and how I had thought I had known where I stood in the order of things. How we limit the gifts of God through our own thoughts, and thus we chain our hearts! There was Great

Mystery here, in this place of moon-thought and charms. I confess, my lord, I would have stayed in that port, were it not for the vows I solemnly made to thee. I pray this will be the worst to relate of my feelings, for as you will understand, it is also the very best. We raised anchor and departed with much adieu despite the invisible tethers that now bound me to that place. I saw her walking away with the others in her flock, and I wondered in anguish whether I would live to see her again, to explore the mysteries of our souls together. The wind was in our favour, the waves grey and forceful, and the sun hidden behind cloud. Thus we departed to the sounds of cheers and cries of birds till they faded, leaving only the melancholy waves and the powerful wind as we headed out, it seemed, to garsecg, the Great Sea which enfolded all life and death and had no end. Still I thought of the maiden, and how if our task were known, how louder the cheers may have been, and how I may have won her heart through the deed I was to perform. I confess once more, that devotion to my Lady had been suddenly interrupted, and I from thenon never thought of her solely. You see how e'en I alone was altered irrevocably by our voyage, before it had e'en begun! Before nightfall, having observed nothing but fishing vessels who gave us wide berth, and having passed the westernmost isles, we continued into the open waters and deemed ourselves safe from human intervention. Ah! If only we had looked to ourselves, for in our own hearts lie the greatest monsters. I have read of a dragon in the English sky centuries past, but we have travelled to distant lands and seen none, thus I had fear of neither drake nor wyrm. We were past the islands before those of us disguised as sailors put on their tunics, including Hafiz and Lanval. Cornwall was familiar with men from afar, such as Moors and Phoenicians, it is said, with a path to the south of Porthenys named after such traders of tin and other metals, but to see one of these men in Christian garb, and that of a Holy Knight, would make them marvel and talk. From our pretence, nobody would know that we were all of the Order, and all trained in shipcraft, knowing well halyard, yard-rope and parrel. The Treasure itself left Our Lady not once, and always had two knights in vigil over it, as was agreed. It is time to talk of the noble ship itself,

94

and assure you she was everything of which ye spake, and more beside. We had seen cogs before, and e'en planned once to journey from Venice on a fleet of such, but Our Lady was a step beyond. Twenty-five feet wide and eighty in length, she could accommodate all we needed for the entirety of the journey, though water for ourselves and our steeds took a goodly part of the hold. She had a rudder to the stern, an excellent innovation, allowing much dexterity in movement, and both fore- and sterncastles in case of attack. There was also something called a capstan, a Spanish device for tightening the ropes. Such a vessel was worthy of all that you foresaw, including space enough for sleeping, though no more than six men would need such accommodation at any one time, due to the constant watch over the Treasure and more mundane duties. Artorius had been given his own quarters, but he did not wish it and desired them to be used solely for weapons and saddlery. He was, he said, our brother and would eat, sleep and die with us when the time came. Once we were in the open sea with no land or vessels whatsoe'er in sight, he spake with us gathered on the main deck, saying what we did we did not solely for the Church, nor our brothers and sisters, but for everyone. This we all knew. After that we set to our tasks, Artorius, Hafiz and I consulting the charts you had provided. I could understand but a few of the names and words, Hafiz of course all, but despite your assurances, the charts, and the aged cartographer to whomst we once did speak, there was fear in all of us. This ne'er did dissuade us from battle, nor did it now. There may not have been dragons where we were headed but there was a vast sea, uncharted except for these antique pages before us, and a journey that none in our lifetime had taken. The most we had, any of us, gone by sea was tween England and France. By the next day we would already have travelled further. I think I was not alone in feeling that our vows and the magnitude of our mission gave me courage, dwarfing my fears to insignificance. As night fell, the wind remained strong easterly and we kept our speed. As no stars were visible, Hafiz opened one of his boxes and showed us what he called a lopin, in our tongue a floating fish. Twas no fish but a magic spoon that when laid upon a special table of strange markings, wouldst always indicate north by its handle. Many of the knights marvelled at this, but the choleric Maufez spoke out against such a miracle, saying twas witchcraft, to which Artorius replied, it is a thing of beauty, harms no one, and aids us in our quest, therefore it is of God. There was no further argument from Maufez nor from anyone, for the course was to be righted, and collation to follow before prayers. Though none of us were novices subjected slavishly to the Rule, we each maintained what held meaning beyond form, and vespers were kept diligently for the entirety of the voyage. It was the one time we nearly all could gather, for morning and other prayers were subject to who was still asleep or awake, and there were numerous tasks to perform though sometimes Hafiz did choose to bow to Mecca and some of us would join him. After vespers I would attend to the journal. Alas, that it was lost in the events I will relate to the best of my ability! Twas sixty evenings' work and I feel the loss keenly, for the detail it contained, which this present account does not equal. To the best of my memory, I will continue. That first evening was typical of many to follow, with the creaking of the ship, the night sounds of wind and waves, and constant vigilance over the Treasure. This was located on the orlop deck, as there was space enough despite the proliferation of ropes, and this would make it central and visible to all those passing through. After prayers, I would attend to the journal sometimes simultaneously whilst on guard duty, and those not steering or maintaining the ship, would stroll about on the upper decks, clean their weapons, sit and discuss old campaigns or the philosophies of the ancients. Lanval oft produced his playing cards and invited others to join him. Bedivere proclaimed one evening that he had seen such cards used for foretelling events to come, to which Lanval replied all of the future and past are contained in the present, and can be read in all things. Some of the men wanted to know of their future. Artorius, who was there, said Lanval's abilities were not to be used for personal gain, that he was, like all of us, on this voyage for a greater purpose. Lanval afterward, during the games, would draw attention still to the pictures on the cards, inviting discussion and hence some meaning could be derived. I myself on frequent occasion drew a card depicting a man suspended upside-down. Lanval said that card was about surrender, about doing nothing, which I did not understand at the time. Many of the knights found the card of Death in their hands, at which Lanval would laugh, saying death was in all things, every moment of the day and night, for everything must always change. At which the knights also would laugh, for what feared any of us of death? Other calm evenings would be spent storytelling, in which Lanval was also proficient. Or Geraint, having such a powerful voice, would lead us in hymns and songs. Hafiz, when he could be prised from his charts and devices, had many tales and insights from his people. That first morning upon the open sea was truly a beneficent one. I believe we all forgot then the women and other loved ones we had left behind, and joy was upon us as we headed into the unknown, knowing twas of God. The waves were shining from the pure sky, and the wind gentle and easterly yet strong enough to propel us. Twas as if all the elements were united with us in our task, though on many days and nights twould not seem so. We would bring the horses up for exercise on the calmer days, as we did on that first. Usually twas my task as I didst so oft proclaim a love for these noble beasts in times past. Gawain was melancholic as Artorius forbade him before his favourite steed, saying we needed the meek power of geldings for such a voyage, and a stallion would prove ungovernable. I seconded him on the ruling, which Gawain never forgot e'en though in the spirit of fairness none of us could bring our own steeds. The journey continued hence. There were times of storm, and times of becalming, as in life, but without my journal I cannot say which days they were, and overall our progress was steady. Several times a day Hafiz would check the charts, consult his lopin or bring out his water-sapphire, hold it to the sky and deduce our direction from that. I will say it now that without him we would have been lost, our mission doomed. I do remember that it was three nights at sea before the night sky was sufficiently clear for Hafiz and I to check the stars, that we were where we were supposed to be. How comforting these fiery messengers of the heavens were to us, that we had a part to play in relation to the greater world. Every night conducive to viewing we would find ourselves at least slightly off course, which we would correct forthwith. Artorius had such faith in our prowess, he was at ease e'en with several enshrouded nights, saying that with Hafiz's sunstone and devices, the charts, my scholarship and our team of true knights, we could feel assured of good progress. E'en days of becalming he would trust as times for prayer and meditation, as well as fishing in the smaller sea for physical nourishment. Only by the third such day would he appear anxious, pacing the upper deck and peering in vain at the still waters. As I recall, only twice did such periods extend to four days, and ne'er more than that. I could tell of the various experiences we had with Our Lady and the elements, but without my journal I cannot vouch for the dates or sequence. Besides, apart from two incidents, which I shall relate, prior to reaching our destination there is little to note other than extremes of weather, all of which we found ourselves each time equal to the challenge. The first incident was our sighting of the Grey Islands. This occurred about three weeks after leaving Porthengrous. How far those last cheers and comfort seemed then! Although only three of us consulted the maps regularly, every man on board knew the significance of these islands, for they were on the charts and we had been advised to use them as reassurance. That is, if we sighted them when we expected to sight them, twould be validation of our course. You can imagine the joy when Geraint called out, and others joined him. We were not tempted by the land, for the sea was fierce at this point, we had provisions enough and these islands looked as forbidding as their name. What they gave, they gave in distance, and that was wonderful, in that it gave credence to our faith. At this moment we had no doubt of our goal no matter how fierce the elements. The other incident was perhaps a fortnight later when Artorius took me aside. Those nights and days I had been often at the helm. The contentment of such, being under the sail and skies, the wind on my face, was unparalleled. E'en now as I am safely back on land with people, and women and friends once more are my company, I yearn for those times alone with the sky, the ship turning at my hand. Tis power and grace combined. So twas with some surprise Artorius spoke to me of a serpent unforeseen. He hadst been in consultation with Lanval, he didst say, who had warned him of treachery. Was it Maufez, he didst ask, but Lanval could not tell other than that twas possible. Maufez had a surly look about him, Artorius didst convey to me, and was not a man of gentillesse. He may have errored by admitting him to the cadre, he knew not why he hadst done so. There are such people, he said, who seem as of everyone else and are well-liked but all the time plotting because of the evil in their hearts. According to our instructions, he didst remind me, only I would be permitted to gaze at the Treasure, and Maufez may be envious of that. Perhaps he e'en thought of taking the Treasure for himself. I am not afraid, said I, for if it camst to blows I believed myself a match, and e'en if not so, the others would come to my aid. Besides, all must follow Artorius, no matter the command. True, quoth he, but men such as Maufez are skilled at changing men's minds, enticing them to think what ordinarily they wouldst not, e'en the best of men. He left me with these melancholy thoughts, that stayed the course with me for many days afterward. I did think also of the Treasure and was grateful you had specified at least two men to stand guard at all times of the night and day. Thus e'en when I passed the orlop and Maufez was on duty, I felt assured. How vain that assurance seems now! Indeed, if I had looked more keenly when Gawain was with Maufez, perhaps I could have foreseen what was to come more precisely e'en than Lanval. For myself, when paired with Maufez, he didst scowl oft enough but was civil. We had fought at Acre so wouldst refer to those shared memories on occasion. Yet after our vigil I would feel unclean and uncertain about everything and would spend some time walking on deck no matter the hour or weather, in order to cleanse my thoughts. Any fears I had regarding the Treasure were allayed because of the two locks, of which of course Artorius had one key, I the other. No one could open the chest without much ado for all to see. Twas two months voyage, without further incident, when we didst arrive at our destination. We were now further south and west than any of us had been, and still no sign of the edge of the world. The sun would be higher at noon than ever twas in the Holy Land in the midst of summer, and the stars at night differently placed, though exactly how Hafiz and I had predicted. Because of the Grey Islands, the men had great confidence in us and were not surprised but delighted on first sighting of the Isles of Venus, of which there appeared to be many, scatterings of heaven in all directions. They were sublimely inviting, nesting in waters of sapphire and diamond, upon which dolphins would dance, and in which myriads of fish of rainbow colours would swim. However, the wind was as gentle as the waves, and we made slow progress. The men wished to go ashore, which Artorius forbade, saying we knew not what perils lay in wait and would take risks only on discovering the Island of Jewels, as ordained. We needed to explore the seas further to determine our whereabouts. Hafiz and I believed us to be south-east of the Isle of Jewels, and that we needed to verify this. This took several days of exploring because of the gentleness of the elements, then we came to what we thought was the southern shore of the Isle. E'en then we were not sure and asked Artorius to order a circumlocution of the island to be certain. As you are aware, the Isle is the central, small jewel in the Venus islands, protected by the larger Jewels surrounding. On one of the older maps it is named the Pearl, a name which is also apt, the other islands being the shell. What we needed for verification was to glimpse Paradise Island, an e'en smaller isle a few hundred paces to the north-east of the Isle of Jewels. The winds favoured a westerly direction, which we didst take in order to get the lay of the land. If twere truly the Isle of Jewels, it wouldst be best to know it well, was our thought. Night fell, and twas a beautiful night as we edged along the southern shore. Having been on duty, I wore my chainmail as I made my way outside. The moon was near full and flooded its portion of the sky with milky white, bathing the palms of the island with translucent grace, beneath the vast canopy of stars. Ah, but how truly this is a magic picture show, whose candles are the sun and moon! And how quickly it all can end! I was peering over the edge of the forecastle, wondering what beauty the silver waters held, when from nowhere the fiends Maufez and Gawain appeared by my side and hauled me over. I found myself in the waters which only moments before I had been admiring, now floundering for life as my armour sought to drag me down. My energies were divided betwixt crying out and fighting to survive. I heard laughing on the ship as it passed on. Whether this were Maufez and Gawain attempting to mask my voice, or Bedivere and Kay, who were at the helm, laughing at each other's antics I do not know. They would have been prevented from seeing my fall by the sail, and hearing my cries by the laughter. My efforts were soon focused on remaining afloat and it was with despair I viewed Our Lady diminishing under the moon. I was entangled in my armour and sodden tunic and doomed to certain death when to my surprise my foot knocked on something solid. Desperately I sought that life-saving hope once more, and both feet quickly reclaimed that impossible earth. Within moments I was standing, shoulders above the water, breath coming into my chest like savage daggers, my head reeling. My wits regained, I soon discovered I was on an outcrop of coral, and that I could make my way to an e'en higher point. Little had we known in the ship how close we sailed to danger, and how poignant that observation was now! Is it not so always in life? I tried but I could no longer discern Our Lady upon the benign-seeming waters. I was completely alone. As I pondered, I glimpsed a shark shoot past like lightning under the moon-waves. It was hunting and I waited for a while, knowing him to be back soon enough, which he was, returning the way he had come. I waited longer. With no sign of him nor any other predator, I decided to go on to the shore still with my armour on. Thus, if I were attacked, I would have some defense in addition to my sword, which I drew ready. The shore was but two hundred paces. I viewed it with anticipation. If this were the Isle of Jewels, which I believed it in my heart to be, I was looking at the sacred path betwixt the stations of Binah and Geburah. I knew the Divine Map in my soul, and that the path I was about to approach, merited caution being under the twin dominance of Saturn and Mars. There was danger ahead worse than I had faced when we were outnumbered thousands to one by the saracen. I placed my trust in the All High and ventured forth. By moving betwixt banks of coral, I never had to spend more than a minute beneath the waters, which grew shallower very quickly. Thus I soon lay prostrate on the shore, exhausted despite myself by recent events, lying on a brief shore of sand that lay amongst harsh unforgiving rocks. I remained there until noting the gentle enlightening of the shore and I realised dawn was approaching. I sat up to view that glorious orb as it rose majestically in the east. However dire the circumstances I experienced hope. I watched it rise awhile, my thoughts oddly quietened. A pelican broke cover and flew with its harsh cry in the same direction as Our Lady. When I did get to my feet, I was alive, and my gratitude knew no bounds whatsoe'er lay ahead. I stripped to wring out my tunic and boots and feel the sun's rays and balmy breeze upon my skin. I was naked but for the key about my neck. No doubt Maufez and Gawain had lusted after it but were restrained by it being under my tunic, and little time with which to dispose of me. After some minutes I was recovered and donned my garments once more. The cloth was still wet but the air warm enough to dry it soon. I climbed the rocks lining the shore easily enough and made my way through a grove of palms, their fruits as large as a man's head, high and beyond my reach. I was not hungry but my mouth already burned from the taste of sea-water, and I knew I had to find a stream if twere possible in this dry land, before the day was out. My strategy was to head directly towards Paradise Island in the domain of Netreth, for that was where Our Lady would be moored. This could be accomplished in a day, but I would need water. Other perils I would deal with in turn. How I had underestimated my trials to come, and the strangeness of this island! Already twas about midday when I had encountered no beasts of any kind other than sparrows and egrets. I have no idea where the hours went. Thirst was making its presence felt and my limbs were moving with an ache and more slowly than I had anticipated. I knew from memory that I was entering Daarth, the-station-that-does-not-exist. This seemed correct, going by the sparseness of trees, their twisted, grotesque nature, and the occasional crow that would alight upon their trunks, then fly away, for nothing could stay here. Twere essential I moved on as quickly as possible, yet as I did so, I glimpsed something that made my heart race. There in a wide clearing was what looked like a path. I approached it and wondered. It was straight as if managed by people, but the people of these islands were simple and without livestock and carts, so we had been informed. How was this track possible? Who could have made it? Was it truly the Divine Hand which we had been promised? I walked along it eastwards, marvelling, for I may well have been on the Sacred Path betwixt Kether and Tishareth, e'en if I were in Daarth. My spirit soared despite my body's sluggishness, then I saw what looked like a man lying ahead in my way, and I broke into a run. Of all I have to relate, this is the most marvellous, and the most terrible, its roots in the most dire treachery. Twas a man indeed, with armour shining in the sun. There was blood all around upon the sacred path. My terror increased as I knelt over him and turned him over, as he was face down. Twas Artorius. His face was a mask of anguish. His right arm was missing, and his chest a gaping maw of blood. I looked over to the edge of the track and could see the arm still clutching his sword. Then I didst notice hoofprints around, none of which I had seen before. Then to my further astonishment the scene unfolded before me. These were visions within visions. I didst see horsemen approach from the west, the leader of which was Artorius, the others behind those fiends Maufez and Gawain. In a moment it all did happen, the sudden trotting forward, Artorius in his last breaths sensing treachery, drawing his sword as he turned and Gawain severing his arm with one blow. Then the vision didst fade but I could imagine Artorius falling. E'en then he would have got to his feet, defenceless, blood spraying the air, as Maufez galloped forth, thrusting his weapon into Artorius's chest. The horror of such treachery caused a turmoil within, e'en as I turned back to discover the corpse of noble Artorius vanished. I had no doubt these were real events, perhaps due to proximity to Kether, to which I had been granted foresight and could thus prevent. My urge to return to the ship was now e'en stronger. Artorius was not yet slain, of this I was sure. They would

not have anchored to look for me nor any man other than
Artorius, this was understood. I laboured on from this
place of execution, heading in what I took to be north-east
though twas hard to discern with the sun so high in the sky.
What I would have given for Hafiz's floating fish! I
neglected to mention that when I had gone to the
forecastle, hours and lifetimes earlier, being off duty I had
left my helmet downstairs beneath the decks. Hence my
head had no cover and the heat was beating mercilessly
upon it. With the struggle to escape the influence of
Daarth and what I had experienced there, my thirst, fatigue,
growing hunger, and bewilderment, the relentless sun, tis
no wonder I did collapse. I knew not how far I had walked,
for how long, or e'en in what direction. Nor did I know
how long I lay there on that dry barren earth before
opening my eyes to see a figure standing over me. And
what a figure! I thought her another vision at first. She
was as tall as you or I, slender with skin darker than ours,
but lighter than Lanval's. Her hair was long and straight to
her shoulders, which were naked as was the rest of her but
for a small cloth about her waist and a coloured band
around her head. In her right hand she clutched a spear.
She moved deliberately to prevent the sun's fierce rays
from hitting me. I attempted to speak, to thank her, but
was unconscious again to a deeper shade. Vaguely I didst
wake I know not how much later. I was in a hut of some
sort, the sun now softened by way of gaps in the reed-
woven walls. The woman was pressing water to my lips
which I didst swallow best I could. There were others
present, their voices male and incomprehensible to me. I
slipped back into the darkness. When half-reawaking there
were discussions going on around my bed. I felt feverish,
and in that fever thought I could understand the words
impossibly. The men were insisting I be moved elsewhere,
whereas she was arguing, as she didst find me she didst get
to keep me. I wondered if I were to become a slave, and
would I mind such a mistress. Any such thoughts became
insignificant as I succumbed to darkness once again, and
remained distant each time I woke and surrendered to her
care. She would bring me smoked fish and various fruits to
eat, including those large ones I had seen before high up in

the trees, their flesh white and sweet, their scent like yellow gorse. Delicious fresh water would be brought in those same fruits hollowed out, their shells wooden and hirsute. I had no idea why I was so weak and feverish, whether twere the eight weeks at sea, the events at Daarth which remained most vivid to me, or sunstroke. After some time I struggled to the door, simply cloth suspended over a gap in the curved wall, to glimpse the sapphire, turquoise sea beyond the arid ground. Other huts were nearby and men, women and children of the tribe, all naked, and as part of the landscape as I was not. I collapsed and Teiko – for that was the name she told me – rushed to get me back to bed. In my half-sleep I was aware of more discussions around, and felt I could understand something once more, and that they thought I was likely to die. A decision was made, Teiko's earnest sing-song voice the last I heard till waking to the sound of drums pounding the night. I could see torches flaring chaotically through the reeds. The awning did draw aside and Teiko did enter. I could see in the star- and torch-light bracelets and necklaces glistening on her unguent body. She stood there outlined in the doorway, the stars behind her, and I realised I was gazing upon Venus herself. She came and sat astride me. She grasped my manhood tenderly then didst caress, though few such ministrations were necessary from her oiled hands. I felt a surge of life pass through me. She placed a covering of some sort over my manhood, then moved up and mounted me. Never was there such bliss! In that moment, as she did begin to gyre slowly, I was in no doubt that I was having congress with divinity, omniscience expressed in skin, touch and warmth. Men and women know carnal delights, and some the divine and, till that night on the Isle of Jewels, I like everyone else believed them separate. From that night I knew that not to be so, although how to recapture the essence of that knowledge eludes me now. That first time, to the accompaniment of drums, she didst ride me and draw the poison in my soul to herself, then with arms raised to the stars, she let it fly away with her cries. We didst love many times that night, no longer accompanied by drums which had fallen silent to be replaced by the murmuring of waves. She was a goddess, she eventually became a woman, and nothing can be more divine as resting next to one you love. For love it was though to be curtailed quite short. The next day I woke alone. Any immediate panic I felt was allayed as Teiko came in, bearing food and drink. We smiled and twas the smile of lovers. We sat and ate together, feeding each other morsels of delight. She would touch my body and scars curiously, for I was as naked as her, her fingers then inquiring after my strength, which was restored. I truly was in Paradise. E'en whilst thinking so, I didst look around, and could see how the tribespeople avoided us. Children would gaze at me wondrously then the mothers usher them away. There was an invisible shadow here, then as Teiko with soulful eyes didst give me a sweet drink, I realised the shadow was me. I never had opportunity to ask Teiko why she had drugged me so, nor did I need to. For when I woke alone on a barren hillside, I knew that as she had drawn and ejected the poison out of me, her people had to do the same. I was the poison. Thus were my thoughts. Next to me was my sword and scabbard, and some of the fruits that had proven nourishing to me. Six orange fruits with skin as luscious as peaches, I knew to be from Teiko, for she had lain them out in the shape of a star as was her wont, and placed her headband upon them. This I wound round my scabbard. I was dressed in my tunic and boots, the key returned to around my neck, but I was without my armour. They had saved my life so I did not resent this, whatever dangers new and old awaited me by the ship which I could see anchored below, betwixt this shore and that of Paradise Island. I ate some fruit to quench my thirst and mused as the sun descended to my left. Our Lady looked deceptively at peace. I would make my way as the sun set, then attempt to board it at dark, so I thought till I spied movement to the west. There were five riders coming along the shore towards the ship. At this number, my heart sank, for I knew with certainty that Artorius were slain in the manner which I had foreseen. I did head down the slope. My intentions now were to either slay one of the fiends by first ensuring they were separate from the others, or to reveal myself to one I trusted and enlist aid. Fortune proved the latter to be the means, for once I did creep down to the shore, and could observe the knights building a fire, one did separate and come towards me. As he drew nearer I knew him to be Geraint for his golden hair, and that I knew him to enjoy long solitary walks in nature. When he didst near I revealed myself. He was astonished. His hand flew to his hilt but remained motionless there. I didst entreat his silence whilst I told how I was pushed overboard in the night. His eyes were wide as he listened. Then he said, Maufez and Gawain told of how I had ambushed them when they searched for me with Artorius, that I had slain Artorius most cruelly and fled with his horse. Suspicious, I asked why Maufez had ridden with Artorius. Artorius did ask Gawain, I was told by Geraint, and Maufez didst offer to join their party. I realised Artorius did trust Gawain, and felt assured by his presence, and my heart sank further at this innocent fall into treachery's hands. Maufez had bloody wounds on his leg, given him by me, he claimst. He and Gawain did give great detail of the fight, and how I had enlisted the help of the savages of the island, that with surprise and brutality, I did outwit them all. They had escaped only just with their lives. To what purpose? I asked. Maufez knows not, was the reply, but he thought I worked for the Assassins and sought only sabotage. This is a lie, quoth I, for the Assassins work with us and for us, but whomst do you believe? Geraint regarded me carefully and said, Maufez hath the dead eyes of a shark when he talks, which thou doth not, and Gawain is his thrall. Also you and Artorius were always close in confidence. I do not believe you to be a traitor. At this we embraced and vowed to regain the mission, for the Treasure was now endangered, and Maufez was already giving argument to open the casket for all to benefit. The men are uneasy, Geraint said, and it will be straightforward to get them to act, for they would be overjoyed at my return. The landing party consisted of he, Maufez, Kay and two others. They were to stay on land with the horses, for embarkation was difficult without a pier. He would tell Kay to return to Our Lady under some pretence, really to persuade others to arrest Gawain. Then as night fell I could approach, by which time the odds would be in my favour. There is risk, he said, and you are much changed.

Indeed, quoth I, but we have known graver odds, and God is on our side, do what must be done, keep calm, and you will see both your wives again. He smiled at this and didst embrace me once more before returning to the camp. A short time hereon I could see the boat being rowed out to Our Lady, a solitary figure inside, as the sun did set a glorious red on our plans. This truly were Paradise. As the sun disappeared, I reflected that I had heard the saracens refer to this time as The-Light-Without-Source, a time of magic where a dog may be a wolf, a wolf a dog or some stranger creature. On that eve upon the Isle of Jewels all I experienced was a quietening, a deeper silence, and then a further half-hour into darkness, a certainty. I approached upwind for the horses knew me and would permit me to draw near. They greeted me in silence but for a quiet whinny from the youngest gelding as he jostled to be closer to me. I felt their breath upon my face, these trusted companions, then I drew closer to the fire. Esperance was standing alone, away from the others sitting by the flames, and he didst see me, then nodded, and my heart stilled somewhat. I did not draw my sword, for fear of the light from the flames upon my blade betraying my presence, and in a few paces I was upon them. Geraint had been alert to my arrival, and in a flash he had a knife to Maufez's throat whilst Lamorak leapt to his feet, drew his sword and pressed it to the villain's chest. Esperance ran forward and did the same. In that moment, I felt love for my brothers as ne'er before. I stand before you, I said to Maufez, with no armour and no sword drawn, yet I am stronger and more righteous than thou, who believest me dead, and knowest not this isle has a gentler, truer heart than thou. He did protest, his eyes rolling feverishly, but knew the game was up and no one to listen to his lies. I know that you and your vessel Gawain have slain Artorius, I spoke, without saying how I knew, and we will find his corpse, bury it with honours, then decide your punishment. He did protest that I was the murderer, not he, till Geraint knocked him on the head to be quiet. We bound his hands behind his back, and guarded him well while Geraint went to the waters and signalled with a torch to Our Lady. There were cries from the ship and a waving of torches, informing us all was well.

108

Bedivere brought the boat over, the pregnant moon rising as he did so and I asked Geraint how many days was I gone. He was puzzled and declared a good five days had passed. It had taken two days to get to the north of the island, when the wind was in favour. On the third they had anchored in the north-west and Artorius had ordered search parties of three to seek evidence of my fate. He, Maufez and Gawain had been the second such party. My thoughts were grim at this but I said nothing as we rushed forward to help Bedivere with the boat. He was overjoyed to see me, and said others onboard would be also, though not Gawain. He said after informing him of the situation, Kay had distracted Gawain with his foolishness, making it easy to perform the arrest. Lamorak said we should torture the villains to discover more, such as where Artorius lay, but I said no, we are not base crusaders nor saracens, and we will find out more through subtle means. I didst stay with Bedivere, Geraint and the horses, while the others took Maufez to be imprisoned in the ship with Gawain. These two had been my brothers-in-arms since the beginning of this quest, and I wished to hear more from them regarding the ship and the men. At first they desired to hear my story, and I told of my wandering and rescuing by the islanders, omitting only the intimacy with Teiko. They didst marvel at my telling of the events at Daarth, but accepted my veracity. They then told that they had seen the islanders, on land and on boats, but they seemed to regard our men as insubstantial as ghosts. Indeed, quoth I, the island exists outside of Time, and its inhabitants may have become accustomed to its strangeness. What of the men, I asked, how had they dealt with my disappearance, and the slaying of Artorius? To which they replied, it had been most difficult, they all knew something was not right but not what it was. That I could slay Artorius seemed impossible, but Maufez and Gawain had been valiant always in battle, and so were believed except by Hafiz who would not speak. And Lanval, I asked, did he not see anything? They didst look at each other strangely and saieth to me that Lanval had gone mad. This news was as disturbing as any of the reports but the night was balmy, I felt relaxed and content to be with my comrades, thus would allow concerns to be addressed on the morn. Tonight I would not weep my leader's death, e'en though the hours were long and still as I kept watch, alone with my thoughts. I had been asleep for days and had little need for sleep. Alone with my companions and the serene waters, I thought much of my quest. I had agreed through desire for my Lady, as you know, to find my certainty turned inside-out and around at Porthengrous, then transformed further here in the Isles of Venus. My allegiance to you was ne'er in doubt, what fuelled that allegiance was. I knew I would persevere e'en with these new doubts. And what of my Lady, you may ask, to which I can only reply, my Father's house hath many mansions, and in one of them perchance I am a happily wedded man, rather than one who dreamst so. All the adventures I have undertaken, the marvels I have seen, the dangers faced, and yet perhaps the greatest challenge is to live an ordinary life in peace with other people. I doubt neither monk nor warrior can comprehend that ecstasy. My musings ran so under a sky so magnificent I could believe I was in a nest of jewels, when I heard some movement close by the horses, one of whom cried out in greeting. I crept near without drawing my sword. Twas as if the headband of Teiko had sealed the scabbard! The animals were excited and, as I approached, I could see under the setting moon, there were now six. Artorius's steed had returned and stood quietly by the others. I kissed him affectionately and removed the tack. There was no need e'en to tether him, for he had proven his loyalty. At dawn when Bedivere and Geraint awoke, I didst tease them for sleeping so soundly, and they marvelled at the return of Llamrei. As the sun rose upon our little band of knights, so did our spirits. Kay brought the boat over. He was much pleased to see me and invited us over for breakfast, adding we had much to discuss. The horses would remain well in sight, so we agreed. You can imagine for yourself the reunion. Hafiz was the most silent, merely stating the calculations had been more difficult in my absence. I was keen to see Lanval, whom I found huddled below decks. He had not eaten for several days. He looked at me, wide eyes scarcely seeing, but I did entreat him to speak to me, his friend. He didst moan some more, clutching himself tight. I forced him to drink some water, at which he seemed to recognise me, saying, we are coming. Who is coming? I asked. We are, he said, many of us, an army in shackles, lovers restrained, beaten, children denied, the blood of a continent. He is spellbound, I said to the others, to which Lanval cried out no, no, tis you who art spellbound, then adding quietly in refutation, we all are. He then disappeared into himself once more. It is these islands, I said to the men, there is a magic here where we can see too much. We returned to the upper deck. Maufez and Gawain were bound in the hold, I did merely glance at them. I had nothing to say nor they to me. I also went to examine the Treasure casket and found it undisturbed. Outside, Lamorak did show me the key of Artorius, which he had found upon Gawain, who had confessed the whole story without torture, blaming Maufez for everything. I showed them that I still had the other key, and declared twas a sign that the mission was on track. At this they didst look at each other and at me. Geraint spoke, saying that though he was to be appointed commander being next in rank to Artorius, he and all the men wished for me to do so. I had the confidence of Artorius, they didst say, and didst understand the magicks of Hafiz. I protested that I was a scholar and had been a monk for more years than a knight, at which they all didst laugh and say I had fought more valiantly in those few years than many had in venerable lifetimes. This was no time for delay of humility, so I didst both happily and sombrely agree, and there was much rejoicing. First I noted that no one was guarding the Treasure, for all were here on deck, to which they immediately were shamed, till I didst proclaim this to be a good sign, for before we were divided and knew not, now we were truly united. Then I didst say, twas the time of lunar dissemination, which was ideal for completion of our task, as we were releasing divinity back to divinity. Soon after Hafiz and I did consult the maps and I could swear that he did smile secretly, pleased at my return. The Sacred Chart was our main concern. I did allude to my experience at Daarth, and he was most interested in the path of which I spake. He too had seen the semblance of a path 'tween Netreth and Chesed along the north coast. I trust twas a beneficent one, I said, to which he replied, more pleasant certainly than yours, at which we both laughed. We didst wonder at who had built these paths, this invisible landscape in the lap of Venus. Tis not for us to know, he said, only to marvel at the Sephirothic Plan, and to do our best by it. You have been here in Netreth for some days, I said, does this Station exhibit its qualities well? The truth was revealed to us, he said, and both you and Llanrei have returned without more blood being shed, and around here there is water and many foodstuffs to take as we need, this abundance and grace must surely be the blessings of Venus, and of Jupiter to the west. Indeed, quoth I, then must we ride south into the desert to determine the central path and our final destination. He pointed to the map and said, if we discover the Sun of Tiphoreth and ride east, Yesod will be the mid-point before Malkuth. This may take some days, I said, and we should begin presently. We rode for three days, Hafiz and I, accompanied always by two to three knights and returning to Our Lady each evening to consult further our charts, and make fresh calculations. We knew we had found Tiphoreth midway between north and south, east and west, by the abundance of a golden fruit and flower grown by the islanders, the Sun brought to Earth. I was grateful it proved unnecessary to revisit Daarth, though I suspected that would happen later. Malkuth at the easternmost point was not as you or I might imagine, but more Heaven and Earth combined rather than just the latter, with white tranquil shores, a glimpse of what mankind could aspire to if so inclined. There were dolphins there to welcome us and we five at the time sat upon our steeds and smiled broadly, for we knew that if paradise existed on this plane then we had discovered it. Then as one we were saddened as if by a sudden cloud, whether for the brevity of our stay, the weight of the world upon our shoulders, or the knowledge of man's dark heart. I know not which it was. We didst turn together and ride west, as calculated, till returning to what we suspected before as being the place of Yesod. There was a grove of pine trees native to this land, and a silence which calmed our racing thoughts. The peace that transcendeth all understanding came upon us,

112

as we knew we were at our journey's end, then we didst return to the ship. The following day before dawn I gave orders that all were to come, including our prisoners as they too were of the quest. Lanval also was now prepared, having eaten, and quietened, though still senseless in his random speech. He had not been much use to us since reaching the islands, and I was hoping he would regain more of his senses that morning. We used the two boats to row ourselves and the Treasure ashore. The casket was fixed to a cart drawn by Llanrei then our procession of eleven men and six horses marched forth. Hafiz was not using the lopin because he said the island was playing with the fish, and so the sun and our tracks became our main guides. Kay held our colours, which we also had been steadily flying from the mast, with no fear of discovery there at the world's end. By foot it took but an hour or two to reach Yesod. On the way we passed more islanders who looked at us from their fields, then resumed the tending of their crops. I was resolved in our task yet could not help maintaining vigil for Teiko despite knowing I didst not truly love her nor she me except in that she loved all. Those who had not seen Yesod appreciated greatly its tranquillity and all were quietened by it. I looked to Lanval who understood and nodded, that yes, this was the place. What else do you see? I asked, hoping he was returning to form. There is a church here, he said, for the wounded generations, much singing and joy, for this island will be a haven one day for them. Yes, he said, the Treasure will be safe, no one will know it is beneath. I put my hand on his shoulder in gratitude and he now did smile, and we began digging. Eventually twas time to bury the casket. I spake to the men and said we have done our duty, honoured our vows, we have sailed to where no one we know has ever sailed, we have found the promised sanctuary. This is the Cup from which our Lord didst drink, it is the receptacle of the Divine, and thus it is appropriate we ensure its safety until the Time of Judgement, here under the grace of Selene. I reminded them that only I was permitted to gaze at the Treasure, and with my back to the sun, though we knewest not why you had commanded thus, that Artorius would have honoured this decree. There was no dissent and e'en Maufez and Gawain remained silent. Lamorak did present me with the second key and they all stood back whilst I unlocked the casket. Kneeling down, I opened the lid. The men did tell me later they saw sun reflected from the Treasure within onto my startled face, which lit up gloriously, and my eyes opened in wonder. I was speechless. I then started to laugh. I closed and locked the casket then stood to face the others, tears streaming down my cheeks with joy. We are ready, I said, at which we buried the casket deep, the men looking at me incredulously as they worked. We prayed one last time o'er the Treasure now deep in the lap of Venus, looked over by Selene, then departed silently whilst duly covering our tracks. That night we feasted on board the ship, taking the prisoners some wine which they did accept sourly. I returned ashore with Kay to watch the horses, as I felt at home there and knew our days in Paradise to be numbered. At dawn the following morning I led a sortie to where I knew the body of Artorius lay, taking with me Bedivere, Geraint and Kay as I felt they would sympathise with my experiences there. Lanval would too but the island upset him too much and he agreed to stay on the ship. The corpse of Artorius was grisly for it had been many days in the sun and animals had devoured much of the flesh. It is not our leader, I said to the others needlessly, merely his vessel and he is finished with it, nevertheless we shall bury it at sea with full honours. Your instructions, sire, were clear that no trace of our presence was to be left. The men however looked darkly at the corpse, and after agreeing that there was something amiss about this bleak place, didst each mutter about wishing to kill Maufez and Gawain. They will be punished, I said, e'en if by living with themselves. We took the body back to the ship. If these were men who knew only violence they would have torn the prisoners apart, instead they merely forewent granting them supper that evening. The next few days we spent in preparation for our return, gathering what fruits and feed we could, some of the men e'en catching what they could for stockfish. There was no game on the island itself for us to hunt. Kay excelled at climbing the trees with head-fruit and tossing them down to us. These were the fruits of the milky flesh Teiko didst bring me, and every time hence I partook of it or the sweetwater within I remembered her. On the fifth day the winds were fair and we were ready to sail. Hafiz and I had returned briefly to Yesod to ensure that nothing was disturbed, and I assure you all was well at that sacred place of virgin earth, and I am sure still is. Thus we left the island, our hearts at peace, despite the occurrences there. I spake to the men before departing. You may be sorrowful at departing from this paradise, but heed this: others may be here one day yet to pass, ignorant of what lies below, seeking peace and happiness on these shores, yet having little of that within. Thus they will be missing the true grace of this realm. You may all be truly joyful for having succeeded in this most difficult of quests, and knowing thou dost have within what so few do. Let us return to our own lands, carrying eternity in our hearts. Methinks you should not read so many books when we do return, laughed Lamorak at my flowery speech. Thus we did leave the blessèd isles in good spirits and with a summer breeze that would take us home through many transformations. Towards the evening we were still within the outer shell of the islands. Having discussed this with the men, I gave orders to weigh anchor next to one of the many shores. Esperance, Bedivere, Lamorak and I escorted our prisoners in the boat, both of whom were expecting the worst, and deserved it, Maufez eyeing our weapons perhaps seeking a way of escape or determining how his life would end, I know not. We said nothing to them nor they to us. Maufez did glare with hatred, and Gawain look down as if already dead. Upon the white sand we gavst them merely a calfskin of water. There may be fruit and water upon this isle, said I, or there may not be. It is more of a chance than you gave Artorius. Then we didst return to the boat, leaving their hands bound which they would untie eventually. Comprehending our justice, Maufez did leap to his feet and run to the water's edge to call after us. He called me names, such as whoreson, to which I did reply, the beloved of our Lord and Saviour was a whore, so I take it as the greatest of compliments, at which he did curse more. As we grew more distant, he grew more erect, and his voice carried over the sparkling waves, his cursing more urgent and general. Our lands, he cried, would suffer greatly, with our crops seedless, water and trees poisoned, no man listening to another, mothers prostituting themselves, fathers lusting after daughters, our offspring either savage or weak, without purpose, temples and churches corrupt with Mammon, plagues infecting the populace... He said more but we could not hear. Are you not worried, Lamorak said to me, there is much of the sorceror about Maufez. Nay, saith I, a dog may crap on a grave with impunity, it means nothing to me. You, sire, may question our judgement, that we didst allow these murderers to live, but there had been enough blood spilt on this sacred mission. Besides, if you could see the vast maze that was the Isles of Venus, a fitting tribute to womanhood itself, your fears would be allayed, that there was no possibility of these vermin navigating the waters and returning to the Isle of Jewels. Our Lady was manifesting in numerous ways and her guile and beauty here were resplendent. Once we had passed the last of the islands the next day we didst perform the funeral rites of Artorius. As requested by Hafiz, we dressed without armour but in our white tunics for we leave life as we camst, without protection. The tunic of Artorius had been encrusted with blood, and his body had been wrapped many times in canvas because of the stench, the final wrap being a white sheet. We sailed not for three hours but spoke each in turn of our memories of our father, for that he was to each of us, as he was a friend to thee. We rejoiced in his life past and known, and his future unknown, then didst lay his body to rest in the eternal mirror of the sea. Hafiz led us in a prayer from his people. You may recall that evening in Limassol when he taught us in his language a song of devotion called The Shadow of Love. Twas that song, and its beauty touched us deeply and let our spirits soar, as it did that evening in Cyprus. He followed with a prayer whose words we comprehended not, but the sense we did all. After that we set sail again, now with a stronger wind. We were three men down. As two to three always guarded the Treasure, the loss was not felt practically. The voyage is not worthy of report. Besides, all my papers and personal effects had been destroyed by Maufez in a dramatic rage after reporting my alleged slaying of Artorius. Fortunately Hafiz's papers and charts were untouched and our return was as secure as possible. It is strange how one can retrace one's steps, essentially going back in Time, following that same course backwards, yet it is always forwards. A return has its own unique quality, in this case one of ease. Yes, there were storms but the seas threatened and did no harm and the journey was blissfully without incident though we were always busy. Again we passed the Grey Islands. This was not needed for navigation, indeed it added many days to the voyage. We felt the necessity more out of tradition, a different kind of reassurance from when we were going in the other direction. I think I can say with certainty we were all quietly cheered by the sight of those islands, so different in form from those we had left. Lanval was much improved by this stage and he did speak of legends of these islands where once had lived a powerful and magical race. They lived not there now. I asked him why he had not mentioned this previously, and how he knew these were those islands and not some others, to which he looked down and fell silent. It seemed he had not recovered fully from what befell him on the Isle of Jewels. Twas some weeks later we did glimpse cormorants sweeping low over the waters, and another sail, the first since leaving Cornwall months and an eternity before. We did not see the colours of the ship before it disappeared, but we knew in our hearts we were back in Christendom and rejoiced. Two days later we were e'en more heartened by the sight of the north coast of the Lordship of Ireland. There was little temptation to weigh anchor because of the uncertainties that lay within that country's shores, we knew not the situation of the Lodge. We glimpsed other sails, mostly merchants, as we continued on to Scotland. The seas were rougher than we had experienced for some time but we attended to our tasks, the ship held together well as always. After some perusement of the Scottish coastline we discovered the small isle you had stipulated off the coast of Mull. We weighed anchor on the far side, to be invisible to inhabitants of the main island. I spake with the men, reminding them our task was not yet done,

and here where we brought an end to what we had
accomplished, the need for vigilance was e'en greater.
Two knights went to light a beacon the next day to summon
the monks of Iona, as the plan dictated, but twas not
necessary as they had espied our approach and met us on
the island. We paid them as agreed, for which they were
most grateful and hence followed their promises to you
hereafter. We stayed one last night on Our Lady rejoicing,
with toasts to Artorius and to you. The next morn we stood
on the cold shore and fired flaming arrows onto the ship. It
broke our hearts to do so, for she was a fine vessel, the
finest anyone had ever seen, but her return to any port
with such a boat and just a handful of knights would invite
too many queries, and all evidence had to be lost to the
ocean. As she ablazed with all the charts on board I doubt I
was the only one to sense that this was also the funeral
pyre of Artorius, and almost the last tangible memories of
our mission. Satisfied with the imminent destruction, we
left her burning as we made our way across the little isle.
As guided by the Benedictines we found the waters
separating us from Mull to be only a foot deep at low tide.
On the other side we were given the extra horses and
instructions to reach Tobermory in the north-east. We
were also given assurance that stories would be told, and
the truth evaded, should any inquire about the burning ship.
I recognised these as men of honour and have no doubt
they kept all their vows and are keeping them to this day,
and will in the future. If they had known the true story,
that would have been something to keep silent about! As
we progressed over the sodden moor, so different from the
last island we had traversed, our closeness as brothers was
felt keenly, for we had accomplished much, and soon we
would be separated. We didst meet the representative of
the Order at Tobermory. He had been situated there for
two weeks and was most pleased to see us, having been
told of our arrival by an emissary from the monastery. He
had a ship standing by, newly readied and by nightfall we
departed for the mainland. To avoid undue attention, the
men decided to travel to Edinburgh in two separate groups,
while I would travel alone on my own final journey to thee.
In Edinburgh they would await their reward on word of my

safe arrival, though I swear we felt as one the reward to already be given. There was certainty we would meet again after that, and that certainty sweetened our departures though I am not so certain now. There is an air of freedom in Scotland, and we didst take that as succour into our lungs as our journeys commenced. Kay didst leap upon his horse backwards to our merriment. He was a Fool, in which there is great merit, for are we not all Fools, and I would miss him perhaps the most. My own journey was uneventful and I thank thee profusely for the warmth and welcome I have received, the riches thou hast bestowed upon me and not the mere riches in my hand. I understand, as thou knewest I would. Upon the blessèd and cursed Isle of Jewels, when I opened the casket to see but an empty box, its walls of bronze and copper, I was at first astounded, then I knew, and my astonishment turned to laughter and tears of joy. I know also that the World would not comprehend this, that they had been questing and fighting over Nothing. Your strategy, wise as it is, hath but one flaw. Thou hast relied too heavily on rumours to spread the story, the new myth of the Grail, for if there is one thing I know about our men it is that they will take this story to the grave and beyond. You wished for a legend, a suggestion of Hope, of Gentilesse, to inspire goodness and truth. Perhaps this will flourish in a different way, and you will understand why I must renounce the Order. For I know now that God is a woman, that all women are goddesses, and so I must go to seek one in particular, first to Cornwall then, failing that, perhaps to Spain. There is a likelihood she was on a pilgrimage to Santiago de Compostela, as there were many who went from Porthengrous. If, as Hafiz doth claim, we die only to return in another form, I pray that I always return to love women, to explore their mysteries, and provide what service I can. What you do, my lord, with this account is of course for you alone to decide. I ask only one thing. You granted me a boon, over and above the riches already showered upon me, and I ask but this. You have the plants, the succulents, the cacti, the yellow fruits, from our voyage and you have expressed a wish to incorporate their forms into a future temple, a church, as memento of what we have done. My humble request is that when you pass on the plans for that temple at the Holly Moor, this Roslin of which ye spake, stipulate as well two hundred and sixteen tiny caskets to be carved into the walls, representative both of our quest and each one of my Cathar brothers and sisters burnt by the Dominicans at Montsegur. Their sacrifice must be remembered e'en if cryptically, and the dark forces conspiring their death also. These same dark forces are everywhere, and they are also within us as this account doth prove. E'en thou hast questioned the recent spirit of the Order. We began with two knights upon one horse, and perhaps it ended as such on the Isle of Jewels in those fateful days. We travelled, as we all travel through life to death. Sometimes I wonder if we go anywhere at all, but are not just encircling the same space, the same time. Perhaps I am still at the Isles. Thus I endeth this tale of our hidden travels, the only true account of what did transpire. My lord, twas an honour beyond words.

I remain your devoted servant, Sir John Lancelot.

4

Loving

"Buster, Tilberg, come in! Buster! This is leader. Tilberg, are you receiving me? We are proceeding at vector three five zero. Over."

"I'm receiving you, leader, but I have no idea where I am. My compass is gone, my altimeter...and I can't feel my leg... It was the flak..."

It took seconds for Donnel to think this through. Tilberg was Johnny Scott, the youngest in the squadron. This was his second mission. With the rapidly worsening weather in the dark skies over France, Scott was essentially a child lost in the mist. Before the squadron leader even had a chance to respond, Donnel broke formation and banked to the right. The cloud was not so thick he hadn't been spotted.

"Merville, where the hell are you going?!"

"I'll get him, sir."

"How the blue blazes are you going to do that? Donnel! Oh damn that blasted Yank."

There was more chatter as the squadron leader attempted to keep the flight together. Donnel had sympathy but his instincts were firing on all cylinders and he continued to plunge downwards whilst heading south-east. The chatter became less and less coherent, drowned by static. Men he had flown with before believed him to be clairvoyant or just plain lucky. He knew it was neither of these things. His mind seemed proficient at absorbing various factors on a subliminal level, then acting on them decisively; two of those factors at this time being Tilberg's last known location and velocity. Nevertheless, in the face of such dark enveloping chaos, his instrument panel the only source of light and order, Donnel couldn't help but utter a childhood prayer, from a time when his world had been safe.

Adding credence to a belief in the supernatural, his senses became even more alert, from a foreboding, and a black shape revealed itself above, coming right at him.

He didn't know how they avoided collision.

Both pilots no doubt threw their sticks to one side. Neither got off a shot. Not only would he not fancy his chances at this high altitude, but he was out of ammunition anyway, having been too eager to strafe the railway yard. In this case the elements were his friend.

As he regained his direction and purpose, he began to wonder if the encounter had really happened. In this spinning world of turbulence, the mind could play tricks.

It helped to focus on his immediate task. He tried breaking through the static.

"Tilberg, this is Merville. Are you there?"

"Merville…Donnel?" The boy's voice was tremulous but clear.

"I'm coming for you, buddy."

"What do you mean?" He had almost given up.

Then Donnel's plane was the black shape hurling across Johnny Scott's vision.

"Shit, Donnel."

"Bet you're glad to see me." Donnel swung round in the dark and caught up with Scott.

"I am. Yes." He laughed, obviously relieved. The last lights glowing on his panel had felt like the remaining embers of his life, the cockpit a metal coffin suspended in a howling void.

"How's the gammy leg?"

"Bad. And I feel like I'm burning up, or freezing, I can't tell."

"Slow down then open the hood like I do. It'll keep you alert. We'll request a blood bucket to greet you before we land. Come on. Pancakes for breakfast."

It had been only a few minutes since Donnel had broken formation.

His debriefing took an hour. After the first twenty minutes, with general consensus that it had been a good show, they were dismissed.

"Not you, Jackie," said Group Captain Smythington. "Sit down."

Donnel, knowing what to expect, did so silently. Squadron Leader James Carmichael, as flight leader, had remained seated, as did an unnamed wing commander who sat next to Smythington's desk and so far had remained silent.

"I don't know whether to punch you on the nose or shake your hand," the group captain said to Donnel, leaning over his desk.

"Squadron Leader Carmichael expressed a similar sentiment after we landed, sir."

"You came in about five minutes after the rest of the flight, is that correct?"

"Yes, sir."

"If I may interrupt, sir," Carmichael spoke up, "now that I've calmed down and Scotty is back with us, I am more disposed to shake Jackie's hand rather than punch him."

"It's all right, Jim. We're not here to talk about that. Besides, I recall a certain impetuous Scottish pilot starting here six months ago..." Carmichael grinned sheepishly. "We're more interested in certain details. First, to get this out of the way, Jackie, you encountered a bogey on your personal rescue mission..."

"Yes, sir. What appeared to be a Focke-Wulf shot past before I found Scott."

"'Appeared'? How could you see anything?"

"Only the rough shape, sir. It was more the sound."

"Above the noise of your own kite, and the elements? I find that hard to believe."

"I don't always get it right, but I have a good ear," Donnel shrugged. He was reluctant to explain it wasn't so much the sound of specific engines, it was the unique *feeling* they each carried with that sound. Once he had thought he could even see colours emanate from a sound source.

Smythington paused. He had had to help investigate the mysterious crashes of Brewster Buffalos three years previously. Any suspicions that these were not accidental, but a mute protest from American pilots unconvinced by the worthiness of their planes, were quelled in the belief that the pilots were right. The 'accidents' had led to the arrival of the far superior Hurricanes, and the properly equipped Eagle squadrons. In a similar vein, he had known to stick by the Typhoons despite their erratic reputation. Once again, here, he was driven not so much by suspicion, as by gut instinct.

"Was it a 190?" he asked.

"Maybe. It seemed a bit different. I know how this sounds, sir, but the *tone* was different."

"Jerry's always coming up with new models," Carmichael put in.

"Good thing they're usually crap." Smythington leaned back. They were in a cul-de-sac and it wasn't really where he was interested in going anyhow. He leaned forward again, elbows on his desk, pencil between his hands. "I'm more interested in the weather conditions, and how you all managed. Obviously they were a lot worse than we anticipated. Jim?"

"They were, but only when we got to the target. There was enough visibility to drop our packages. We were gone before the fighters took off."

"You used the cloud for cover."

"We did but before we got there Scotty got hit by the flak."

"Donnel, you've got to give me something. How did you find him?"

"I estimated his position and vector from when we turned round. The rest was instinct, and luck."

"More than a little bit of luck, I would say." He turned to Carmichael. "You descended once over the drink, is that correct?"

"Yes, sir. Just before Plymouth."

"No trouble from our side?"

"None. Our parrots were squawking fine, and were heard."

"So I was informed. Except for Scott's."

"Mine was working fine," Donnel said.

"Lucky for him. What would you chaps say about adding to the IFF?"

Donnel and Carmichael exchanged looks.

"I'm not sure what you mean, sir," said Carmichael.

"Jackie and I spoke about this when we first met. Briefly."

Carmichael glanced again at the American, wondering if a lot more was going on with the sortie than he had surmised.

Smythington continued, weighing his words carefully. "What do you think about installing AI units in some of the planes?"

"'AI'?"

"Airborne Interception. Radar. If we're going to continue with these night sorties, it could prove quite an advantage. Wing Commander Allison here is the expert. We're likely to be introducing rockets by the end of the year, but we'd like to go one further, give us eyes in the dark."

Allison introduced himself and his role in equipping aircraft with the latest innovations. Since Donnel had first flown a Typhoon, the plane had undergone frequent alterations and improvements – the two were not always synonymous – so neither rockets, radar nor any other gizmo would surprise him. It was odd that despite all the changes, the cockpit was still too hot and they still wore oxygen masks in case of carbon monoxide poisoning. He was sceptical about cramming the small space with more equipment but voiced his concerns delicately. The four men chatted easily about technology, night flying and related issues, until the hour had passed and Carmichael and Donnel went to join the rest of the flight at The Rock in Yelverton.

It was one of those rare occasions when Donnel wasn't permitted, or expected, to buy a single drink. He felt embarrassed at all the remonstrations, and after two whiskeys refused any more only to have another thrust in his hand by Carmichael. News came from the hospital that Scott was doing fine, it was only a bit of shrapnel in his leg, and this lifted spirits all the more. So the evening went on till well after the small hours. The British, once their guard was down, could party with the rest of the world.

The women stood in the doorway looking at Donnel's recumbent form. Sunlight was streaming in behind them and through the window but he was in no state to notice.

"How sleep the brave," said Joyce.

"They're all like that," Sandra commented drily. "One bit of effort, then they're done. I bet he raided the larder too." She offered Joyce some gum, who refused it, and she stuck the stick in her own mouth.

They left him in peace and headed back towards the squadron offices. Sandra, as happened frequently of late, was on clerical duties with her friend that day.

The weather had calmed since the night, leaving only a quiet gloom over the airfield, relieved by sporadic bursts of engines here and there.

"Oh let's just make sure we pass by the Bellman," Sandra said. "Who knows who we might see."

"Very funny."

"Bet you never thought you'd fall for an erk. You were always more 'officer material'."

"He *is* an officer."

"I meant a fly boy."

"He is that too. Besides, do you really wish me to bring up the subject of pilots?"

They were interrupted by the arrival of Maggie parking ahead of them half-on, half-off the grass. She had surprised them by coming up abruptly from behind.

"What are you chaps doing Saturday afternoon?" she smiled through the open window, blowing a strand of hair off her eye.

"I might be on duty," said Joyce.

"No, you're not. Neither of you. I checked."

"Well, nothing then."

"Shall we go to the matinée at Egloston? It's about five miles away."

"I know," said Sandra dubiously. "What's on?"

"Does it matter?"

"It does if it's about steely-jawed American yokels and dumb-arse Gestapo agents."

"Let's hope for a comedy, shall we?" Maggie said. "Truth be told, I'm really scouting for a dance venue. Because of what you said really, Sandra. There are plenty of small ones every week but there's a need for a larger, more inclusive one, and the hall at Egloston might be adequate. I thought we could all go for a recon. Is Jackie on an op then, do you know? *That*, I couldn't find out."

"Nah. They want him on the Thursday sortie, then the squadron will be full again. He won't be needed."

"How about the rest of the gang?"

"I think Trev can get the time off," Joyce answered. "I don't know about Ben."

"No one knows about Ben." Sandra chewed her gum, looking down happily at Maggie. "Ben doesn't know about Ben. I bet you do though."

Maggie was uncertain how to take this. Sandra noted the other woman's fragility, and suddenly regretted her own tendency to be belligerent. She didn't know how to retract and remained silent.

"David is away right now," said Joyce, "He won't be back till next week."

"Just us six then," said Maggie, shifting into gear. "I'll be in touch! Maybe see you tonight."

"Bye, Maggie," Sandra called out warmly, but the car was already speeding away. "That woman knows a lot more than she lets on. Like how come she's got that posh bag for her kit, while we're still carrying grubby gas-satchels. And why does she use first names... I know we often do around 'ere, but she's even called Spiffy 'Derek'."

"It will be nice, going out together," Joyce said, ignoring her as they continued their walk. Smith was obviously in the hangar and out of sight, but they waved anyway. "I'm glad David Proudon

126

won't be with us. I have nothing against him," she added quickly, "I think he's marvellous, and I know the guys call him the fourth musketeer..."

"In actuality he's a seventh wheel." Then it was Sandra's turn to add quickly, "Not that Jackie and me..." She didn't finish.

"There is something between you. Maybe you should just accept that, Sandra."

"Maybe *he* should accept that," she came back fast.

"You'd make a super couple. I could come and visit you in California. Trevor and I could," she said boldly with a smile.

The conversation could have gone on along the same lines indefinitely but Sandra was pensive, and wished to impart something before they reached the offices. So close to the hub, personnel came and went, some greeting them, but she was oblivious. When an officer came past Joyce had to nudge her to get her to salute, which she did somnambulistically.

"My family...well, you know about my family. I've gone on enough about 'em. Well, you know how nuts they'd drive me... Sometimes I would just need to get the hell out. I have an uncle – my dad's brother – who lived a few streets away, and I would go and see him when he started living there. I often thought he was the most interesting person in my family. He was a conchie in the last war though he did join the Ambulance Corps. Now he's too old but still managed to get into the Fast Response Team for our area.

"Anyway, as this war started and we were gettin' used to rations, gas helmets and the like, I went round to see 'im before I enlisted. 'E 'ad so many stories to tell, 'e'd been all round the world, an' his living room was filled with books. I thought he knew everythin' about everythin'. But this last time I saw 'im 'e was prattlin' on about Eastern philosophy. Normally I'd be listenin' but he was burnin' sulphur candles t'get rid of the bugs which I could see crawlin' under the wallpaper. The place was dirty – not particularly, just sort of *male* – books on the carpet, crumbs on the settee... That, and the smell of sulphur, the bugs...an' I thought, this is one of the smartest people I know, I would even call him a hero. He went on all sortsa adventures, bucking all sortsa trends. Gramps never forgave him for that, said he shoulda been a teacher or somethin' insteada just helping out at the local. I think Gramps helped him with the rent. But what struck me that day was that he was alone. He could talk about the 'divinity of solitude' all he liked, 'eck, I would even call him a loving person, but his being alone had a sadness to it 'owever wise e' was. Somethin' was missin', and that was love – messy, infuriating, wonderful, 'uman love. Buddha wasn't married far as I know."

They were at the squadron offices, and Sandra had clearly finished. They hesitated before going in. It was Joyce's turn to be cheeky.

"It seems the answer must be exactly half-way between your family's house and your uncle's."

"That's where our local perv lives so I 'ope not."

Squadron Leader Francis looked up, despite himself his spirits lifting at the sound of their laughter as they entered. It had been a dull hour.

Defying the laws of physics, they all six had managed to get in the Hillman outside the base, then out again at Egloston chaotically, Sandra laughing as she hit the ground. Donnel helped her to her feet, picking up her pillbox hat and dusting it off. It was made of green felt, and with a veil that would dangle over her eyes. He felt very conservative next to her, in his borrowed black suit.

"Next time you sit on *my* knee."

"Where's the fun in that?" she retorted, brushing off the dry dirt whilst holding onto him for support. Catching sight of Hawker standing, grinning ear-to-ear, hands in his pockets, trilby tilted over his face, she couldn't stem the flow: "Oh Ben, so smart in your brown suit, laughing at us poor mortals who had to squish in the back."

"You're looking pretty fine yourself, Sandra," Ben said appreciatively.

"He's right," Donnel remarked, brushing some debris off her green velveteen jacket. "You could be Ronnie Lake."

"Oo's 'e?"

"*Veronica* Lake. A very glamorous movie star. 'Sullivan's Travels'?"

"She plays a hobo in that," Hawker pointed out helpfully, at which Sandra belted Donnel on the shoulder.

"Ow! Only for a bit," he protested. "She looks beautiful for most of the picture. Really beautiful," he added, looking intently at her. She narrowed her eyes playfully at him. "Again, ow," he said, rubbing his shoulder. "I can't believe I survived the Luftwaffe so far to face this."

"You said the last mission was a piece of cake," she said.

"It was, but... Heck, I was only trying to give you a compliment. You do look...smart."

"I look 'smart' in my uniform."

"Yes, but..."

"For heaven's sake," Maggie broke in, walking around the car. "You look wonderful, Sandra, as do we all."

"I've gotta admit," said Sandra, walking up to her, "I was admiring your jacket in the car."

Maggie, like Hawker, was wearing a trilby but hers was a warm terracotta, matching her elegant peplum jacket and gored skirt. Sandra, in her floral dress that was one of two re-stitched years ago by her mother, felt Maggie to be on another level of elegance from the rest of the group. Even her white handbag offset her clothes perfectly.

"It's three years old," Maggie said amiably. "Still very simple, note. only three buttons, no cuffs or pockets..." She did a little curtsey. "*Il faut 'skimp' pour être chic.*" Hawker, the only one who understood, laughed. "Let's see what's on, shall we?"

"Hello, Jackie," said a petite brunette WAAF with wide eyes as she passed, smiling knowingly.

"Hello, Jackie," chorused her blonde friend perkily.

"You've become very popular these last days," Sandra said as they crossed the busy cobbled street. Military personnel, most in uniform, were mixing with civilians, and Americans were chatting to awestruck boys and girls, plying them with sweets.

"Not with you though," he said candidly.

She was about to respond when she looked round suddenly. "Where's...?" She fell silent. Behind the car, Smith and Joyce had thrown caution to the wind, oblivious to everything but their kiss. "I'm so glad. It was like sitting next to Vesuvius in the back of the car. I didn't know when it was going to erupt."

"They do know they're still in uniform?" Donnel remarked. The lovers, being on duty till the last minute, hadn't had time to change. Smith gripped his hat by his side, while he held Joyce's to her head with his other hand to prevent it falling off, her wispy golden curls astray.

"You try telling them," Maggie said. "Come on, guys."

"It's always the quiet ones."

129

Maggie was pulling Hawker gently by the sleeve, and the other two followed slowly, Sandra the only one unaware of the hostile glances the group was getting from white Americans. Maggie pulled Hawker closer to emphasise he was with her. "They're all...what do you call it?...rednecks," she said to him. On the short drive he had talked a bit about his aborted secondary education. She was already aware of his intellectual upbringing by a black mother and mixed race father. Academia had done him little good in the world, but he worshipped his parents, and respected their ambitions both for him and themselves. The chasm between aspirations and actuality in his life was consequently home to a perpetual storm of inner conflict.

"Ah shoot," Donnel exclaimed. "'The Philadelphia Story'? How far *are* you Brits behind the times?"

There was a portly man with glasses and a threadbare suit outside the hall entrance, smoking a cigarette whilst viewing the small crowd and nodding benignly at those entering. Squinting in the bright sun, he eyed Donnel with interest.

"I do apologise, sir," he said, flicking ash into the street. "As we are not a proper cinema we cannot obtain the latest releases. "As a matter of fact, we have just stopped limiting ourselves to Ministry of Information films."

"It looks promising," Maggie said keenly, squeezing Hawker's hand. "Are you Mr Stephens?"

"I am, and you must be Sergeant Drummond," he said holding out his hand.

"Maggie, please. How do you do. This is Ben, Jackie... Sandra, what are you doing?!"

She was pressing her face at different angles to the glass of a display cabinet. Within it was the poster for 'I Married a Witch', starring Veronica Lake. "I want to see if I really look like her. If I merge my reflection..."

"It's a *picture*, Sandra, not a photograph."

"I'm...Jeremy," Mr Stephens said, shaking hands with the two men. He was uncomfortable with the first name basis Maggie had established, but was going with it. "Maggie said you chaps would be over today. Something about a dance night...?" Donnel and Hawker were clearly baffled, it being news to them. "I take it you're both American."

"We are," said Donnel.

"Nice to have you with us."

130

"Shouldn't we be going in, Jeremy? Isn't it about to start?"

"That is unlikely. Harry our projectionist had a few too many last night and he's not light on his feet at the best of times."

"Hey, look!" Maggie called out. She now had her face pressed to a poster. "If Sandra's Ronnie Lake, I'm Rosalind Russell!"

Donnel grinned at Mr Stephens as if to say, "What can you do?"

"Why do you show only American movies?" Hawker queried.

"Because Mrs Stephens chooses them," said Mr Stephens.

The women, returning, overheard.

"Hey, any chance of getting…what is it called, Jackie?" Sandra asked, hanging onto Donnel's arm and looking up at him wide-eyed. "'Gullivan's…'"

"'Sullivan's Travels.'"

"I'm afraid not, young lady. They won't let us have it on these shores. We've asked."

"Whyever not?" she cried.

"The powers-that-be don't inform the likes of us as to their reasoning."

The film discussion ended promptly with Mr Stephens escorting them in, and picking up four tickets from the table that acted as a kiosk. "Your money's no good today," he proclaimed. "I hope you enjoy the film. Let me know what you think about the hall, Maggie."

"I will. Thank you, Jeremy."

The room was smoky, lively and nearly full. Most of the wooden chairs with their elegantly arched backs were occupied, and arranged in neat rows, empty food cans scattered here and there acting as ashtrays.

At the front on the right side of the central aisle were two rows of Italian prisoners with the tell-tale circles blatantly large on their brown uniforms. They seemed to have the afternoon off from farm work. There were two soldiers guarding them, which might have been unnecessary as they seemed exhausted and content to be there, smoking and talking quietly amongst themselves. Few of them could have been over twenty years of age, just boys really. Maggie felt a surge of pity for these children caught in an arena of bewildering conflict, now in a foreign country watching a film in a strange language.

The rows opposite the Italians were mostly occupied by elderly ladies, focused on talking and knitting rather than smoking. Behind them were a few black GIs and civilians, while on the right side of the aisle where Maggie and the others headed to a line of empty seats, was a more varied assortment of civilians and military personnel, both in and out of uniform. All of them were white, Maggie noted as she sat down, ensuring those behind were locals who would be unfazed by Hawker's presence. Egloston's proximity to both the black GI camp at Gunnislake and the white one at Bere Alston must have led to some pugnacious evenings, especially at weekends. The snowdrops would be busy. Here in the dark, she mused as the lights dimmed and she shut out any sense of hostile attention, at least all would be at peace. Her musings continued along these lines even as the Pathé news began, its opening volley shaking as Harry the Projectionist blundered into his machine, eliciting roars of approval from the audience. There were more cheers as the invasion of Sicily was featured even, bizarrely, from some of the Italians. More sobering news about the advance of the Japanese was tempered by that of the Soviets hammering the Germans in south-west Russia. Maggie's mind began to drift with her eyes as she attempted to scrutinise the audience in the dim flickering light available.

When the newsreel finished, and the lights came on accompanied by a surge of chatter, she glanced towards the courting couples at the back, and smiled.

"Look," she nudged Hawker, thus alerting the other two next to him.

There in the back row could be seen, through the smoke-veiled audience, Smith and Joyce staring straight ahead, her head resting on his shoulder.

Harry seemed to be waking up, for the lights went down and the feature began promptly. Everyone's attention returned to the screen.

Maggie rarely went to the cinema so knew nothing about the film, but found herself enjoying it eventually. For the first twenty minutes she was concerned for the Italians, that there wasn't enough slapstick. By half-way through she was so wrapped up in the tale, that when Tracy and her father were confronting each other, she became aware for the first time that her fingers were entwined with Hawker's. As the farcical elements in the film increased alongside the Italians' jocularity, particularly at Tracy's obvious and innocent confusion about her infidelity, Maggie was relaxed enough for her head to be leaning on her lover's shoulder.

The film ended to great applause and dozens of couples straightened up just before the lights came on. Not, though, Donnel and Sandra who had been sitting stiff as boards the entire time. Of the two, Sandra was perhaps the most relaxed and even she was rigid with terror and uncertainty. Donnel, conflicted as always with his own moral code and innate licentiousness, had no idea where he was going, what he was doing. Neither of them noticed much of the film whilst staring dead-ahead at the flickering images.

As they were all exiting, Maggie nodded in the direction of the Italians who had been ordered to remain seated until everyone else was out. A couple of them were blowing kisses at any girl within range with cries of 'Ciao bella!' and 'Belissima! Amore!' Some of the Allied men were visibly getting angry, and a guard told the prisoners to calm down, whilst smilingly accepting a cigarette from one of them.

"The film seems to have hit them in the right places," she commented.

Sandra forced a smile. "I think they were simply eager to have a good time."

"Well, it's a commendable philosophy."

"What shall we do now?" queried Smith innocently, as the six of them gathered in the bright sunlight.

"First of all," said Maggie, letting go of Hawker's hand, "what do you think about the place as a dance venue?"

At the unanimous approval she went to have a word with Mr Stephens.

The remainder talked vaguely about the film. There was a shyness between them all, as if on the verge of a great new adventure, with unknown protocol.

"This is a summer to spend in gardens, drinking under the stars," Donnel spoke up. "Normally we are in a muddy field, so let's make the most of our freedom and go to a pub."

"Jolly good idea," said Smith.

"Marvellous," echoed Joyce, holding onto his arm firmly.

On rejoining them, Maggie needed little persuasion and mentioned the pub they had noticed on the way in. As it was less than half-a-mile, they decided to walk. The three couples became even more discrete as they ambled up the lane, Smith and Joyce leading the way, Maggie and Hawker in the middle. Donnel attempted to prevent this with banter, particularly aimed at Hawker, but in vain. The silence from his friends was too encompassing and permitted no random, frivolous chatter.

Falling behind, the reluctant couple started to accept the situation. The birds were singing fiercely, it was a light blue sky and the hedgerows plump with wildflowers. Donnel took her hand playfully and she smiled, relieved.

"The road's a bit ripped up from your countrymen's tanks," she pointed out.

"Yes. Sorry about that."

"I don't hold you personally responsible."

"I thought most things were my fault," he teased.

She didn't know how to respond and looked around vaguely, her hat and veil shielding her hazel eyes from the sun. At a time when most women were limited as to their make-up options, she was comparatively spartan, using a pink shade of lipstick delicately applied, and just a trace of blush. It gave an honesty to her features, like a beautiful rock unadorned in an otherwise homogenous landscape. He felt himself falling into unknown territory once again.

"Foxgloves," he said appreciatively. There was a large group of them protruding from the hedge.

"Do you have them in America?" she asked.

"Of course. But what I really love is what you call willowherb."

"I know it. I've seen it growing on bombsites. So we call it bombweed."

"Yes, it flourishes on wasteland. It brings colour where there is little. I've seen it all over airfields in the States. The Indians used to use it in cooking."

"You know about a lot of things, doncha."

"Probably not the important things," he admitted.

"Oh look." She pulled him closer to the hedge where late-blossoming red campion burst forth.

He felt her body press close to his. He named the flower automatically but his consciousness was with her proximity to him.

"It's more pink than red," she commented.

"Here." He let go of her hand and plucked some. "Please allow me." He placed them in her hat-band. "Beautiful," he said ambiguously, standing back.

Nervous, she took off the hat to have a look. "Very fancy," she said, grinning shyly, and placing it back on.

"It really does suit you," he said, taking her hand again.

They walked comfortably in silence.

"The road's totally quiet," he observed needlessly.

"Apart from country sounds. Hey, do you notice how fast Trev is walking?" He and Joyce were almost at the pub, now in view fifty yards ahead.

"You're right. He doesn't even have his stick. It's as if he's putting on a show for Joyce."

"Or he just doesn't notice the pain when he's with her."

"That's very romantic."

"I don't think so. I think it's biology."

"Is that not the same thing?"

"That's debatable," she said enigmatically.

"'The Ship and Compass!'" Maggie called out at seeing the pub's sign of a gold compass and a ship on a stormy sea. She had no idea why she did so, the sound of her voice erupting strangely into the landscape, and she drew back quietly once more to Hawker's body where she felt she belonged. There was a warmth and understanding from this man unequalled by anything she had previously encountered. For all their mutual erudition and eloquence, silence proved the stronger bond.

Sandra and Donnel caught up with the others who waited for them on the terrace. Only one table was occupied by a family of seven, including a baby in the process of being fed by the mother, who had lifted her breast out of her bespeckled dress.

There was a tangible sense of discomfort amongst the group, with the exception of Maggie.

"It's quite common in the country," she laughed *sotto voce*. "Besides, we have a *real* problem here," she said to Donnel with her light smile, drawing his attention to a notice pinned next to the entrance:

'*Only coloured Americans permitted on these premises.*'

Donnel was astounded, the others more amused.

"Put it down to quirky English humour," suggested Smith.

"Maybe you can just keep quiet," said Joyce.

"What are the chances of that?" quipped Sandra, squeezing Donnel's arm.

"The GIs must have caused some trouble," said Donnel.

"The white ones."

"I'll go and put in a good word for you, old chum," Hawker said, slapping Donnel on the shoulder before going inside.

The others followed, except for Maggie and Donnel.

"Are you all right?" she asked.

His mind was on something else.

"Your pistol," he whispered urgently. "You didn't leave it...?"

"In the car? What do you take me for?"

"Oh. Good."

"It's in my handbag."

He had no time to respond before Sandra returned.

"Come on," she said, pulling him by the arm. "The landlord's been persuaded to give you a chance. Don't blow it."

He didn't blow it. In fact, even when the car's axle broke two miles from the base late that evening, he offered to walk Sandra home as she had to attend church parade early the next day. Smith wasn't capable of any more walking so Joyce opted to stay with him no matter how late. However, an American jeep came by soon after and the two crammed in with the GIs to go and get assistance.

Hawker wasn't going anywhere without Maggie if he could help it. The two of them watched the lights of the jeep fade under a rising moon. They leaned against the bonnet and she nestled into him, her thoughts racing further ahead.

"Jackie's fiancée," she said. "What is she like?"

"I haven't met her. But, from what I know... You've heard about body language? Well, let us say, she speaks many tongues..."

Half-a-mile ahead, Donnel and Sandra were lit up by then overtaken by the jeep, its occupants cheering and waving.

"That *was* Smithy, wasn't it?" he asked.

"And Joyce, yes."

"So we're not the rescue mission."

"I think that's what they were yelling."

Tentatively he put his arm around her waist. She didn't resist. There was an odd comfortableness in the space they occupied, between easy intimacy and distant formality. They each felt heightened in the awareness of what was within and surrounding them: the fields blanketed by the moon's silver, the whitewashed sky with a few stars visible, the calling of an owl, the sound of their hard shoes beating the road and their quiet breathing of the cool scent-laden air.

They could avoid Crapstone and the busy community area, with its officers' mess and sports facilities, by taking the lane north of the village. It made their walk to the WAAF site shorter, only not too much. It was an uphill walk. The whole way they found they had no need to talk, but did so occasionally, about the moon, the

136

stars, England, America, all words fading swiftly and gracefully to blissful deaths.

When reaching the first barrack hut, they stopped. Other groups and couples were coming and going. They seemed far away.

"My digs are further along," she explained. "I'd invite you for coffee, but the neighbours will talk."

"That's okay…"

"We don't know how to make coffee anyway."

"True…"

Her eyes were laughing at him in the silver light. He leaned towards her, wanting to disappear in the kiss.

It lasted a long time, their lips exploring each other lightly, delicately, incapable of rest and content with the play of parting and coming together. He felt aroused, yet the arousal belonged to something greater, to the trees standing watch, the shadowy people around, the sky overhead and the earth under their feet.

She had no choice but to surrender, knowing in that moment there was no one else, there never was and never would be.

Opposite him on the train was a gaunt elderly woman reading a book, next to her a few seats away, a portly middle-aged man reading a paper. Two seats along from Duncan, to his right, was a Muslim girl staring straight ahead. At Camden he exited the Morden train, and dashed along the connecting tunnel in hope of getting an earlier Charing Cross train on the other platform.

Getting there, he saw a train about to leave. Without knowing if it were the right one, he jumped aboard and sat down. The doors hissed shut and the train shifted into the tunnel. He was occupying the same seat as before.

As he looked around that section of the carriage he noticed opposite him a gaunt woman reading a book, next to her a portly gentleman reading a paper. Fear mounting, he looked to his right at the Muslim girl staring straight ahead into something incomprehensible.

They were all the same people.

He woke. It was a dream, but once it hadn't been. It had actually happened, except it hadn't been the same people, they had only looked similar. It had given him a start at the time.

He remembered that era of his life with a clarity denied him at the time. He had been sinking into a subtle despondence. He and

137

Rose were staying with her family at Barnet, Jasmine about to flee the nest but surrendering to one final family winter break, and Rowan on his gap year in Thailand. Duncan was on a mission to the Imperial War Museum. Rose had refused to join him; out of lack of interest in him rather than the exhibits, he now knew. Jasmine, after being up half the night web surfing and chatting to her boyfriend in Ontario, hadn't surfaced by the time he left the house. This was pre-Evelyn, but the writing was clearly on the wall, even if he weren't able to read it.

He stayed out late deliberately, and after a forgettable pub meal sat on the train, rigid and tired. His eyes were half-closed. It was the journey into town that had provided the eerie echo of personnel. This time he knew an array of young revellers were seated around him. The girl to his left, her face and hair covered in glitter, was trying to amuse her friends with strange expressions, pursing her lips close to his face and moving her hands over him mock-erotically. Slowly he smiled, turned to face her, his eyes suddenly wide, playful, challenging.

She yelped then laughed. Planting a real kiss on his cheek, she said, "I love you." Waving a child's wand, she got out with the others at the next stop, laughing.

The girl may have been high on something, he didn't care. She had provided a moment of warm respite in what was becoming an increasingly bleak, cold and airless world.

He rubbed the cheek she had kissed, sitting up in bed now, remembering. He was joining Kay and the others for a walk that morning.

A few minutes later he stood in his pyjama bottoms, opposite the mirror above the bathroom sink, shaving carefully. He thought about the film they had watched the previous night. It had been one of those he had inadvertently bought when hiding in Tavistock Market, about an Englishman trying to make it in America. The others laughed throughout. He had felt sad, the romance at the core of the story so remote now from his world.

As he changed, he had left the annexe door open as recommended by Kay, in order to let some air in.

She was coming to summon him for breakfast when she glimpsed him in front of the mirror on the outside of the bathroom door, preparing himself. He had two different socks on, a Cambridge tie askew, the bottom button of his crease-ridden shirt undone, and the shirt itself only half-tucked in. He scowled at himself in the mirror, rearranged his belt so that more of his stomach protruded, then smiled.

She stormed back to the house, into the sitting room, pausing only to kick off her shoes. She plonked herself down in front of her husband, furious.

"He's doing it deliberately!"

"Doing what deliberately?" George asked, peering over yesterday's paper. The subject of the exclamation was not the question.

"Dressing provocatively. I saw him in the annexe."

Folding his paper, George put it aside. "As I keep saying, the garden is the eyes and ears of the house."

"That's not the point. I saw him rearranging his belt, and I know, I just *know*, he'd moments before been pulling his shirt out of his trousers. It's a co-ordinated symphony of disasters. And the doughnuts. What happened to all the doughnuts? Why? Why would he do this?"

"It's armour, to repel women. Or perhaps 'camouflage' is more accurate."

"What?!"

"Think about it. They've been nothing but trouble to him for the last few years."

"He *likes* women."

"Voilà la problème. He needs some space to re-evaluate his life, which he gets by removing himself out of the equation. I doubt it's entirely deliberate, more development on a theme. Quite brilliant, really – you've got to give him credit. Any pretty girl who tries to manipulate him with a coy look and a smile is wasting her time, because he knows he doesn't have a chance."

She looked at him, sullenly pleased at how he still managed to surprise her. "When did you get so...?"

"Perspicacious? Since I looked it up in the dictionary."

At sounds of activity upstairs, Naomi's screams of outrage and Heinrich's laughter, they both glanced at the ceiling, smiling fondly.

"That's the cue to make the coffee," George said.

"I'll do it," said Kay, getting up quickly as he started to rise.

She was greeted by the apparition of Duncan stepping through the door, in his wildly coloured socks, both flaps of his shirt now loose, his fly half-open and a grin on his face.

"Hmph!" She pushed past him to the kitchen.

George merely chortled at his bewildered and bewildering brother, and picked up the newspaper once more.

They went to a small reservoir to the west. "We can have a short walk, then go to Egloston for lunch and see that movie. I can go to the wool shop as well," Kay had said as they got ready.

Duncan, not knowing what movie, yet aware he had ostensibly been part of the conversation concerning it the night before, was silent the whole way in the car. They took Heinrich and Naomi's car because it was her father's Mercedes and had more room. All the same, Duncan crouched in the corner at the back as if squashed, staring out of the window at the drizzly landscape. He had refused the passenger seat through obstinacy, reading the subtext that he was by far the widest person there. The sulk was not solely because of that, it was also due to the feeling that he had done something wrong again. The feeling never really left, it had been with him his entire life; which was ironic as the one thing he had always attempted to do was the right one. At times such as this the feeling was merely reasserting itself.

His musings continued as they got out at the car park and began walking. There was a cold, erratic wind and traces of rain. He fell behind quite quickly despite being the only one in proper moor gear, with his wax coat and hat. "I'm the limpy pig," he told himself, picking his way along the rocky trail.

The small reservoir did little to improve his mood. It was basically an over-hyped tank of water with a few token trees planted around, many of which were leafless, dead or dying. Someone had got their analysis wrong or didn't care as long as they got paid.

The others went around a hillock and were out of sight not far ahead. He took advantage of his solitude to urinate behind a rock. He kept twisting, attempting different directions, in order to control where the flow went in the wind. A red setter ran past towards the car park, glancing briefly at him. He smiled, distracted, when the dog's owner strode around the corner in her pristine Barbour coat and shiny green wellingtons. Duncan, in the presence of this bastion of the middle-class middle-aged demographic, ceased whirling and spraying to quickly tidy up.

After an initial shocked intake of breath, she yelled, thrusting her walking stick in his direction.

"You blundering oaf! Where do you think you are?!"

"Um, in the countryside?" he offered.

Her eyes bulged beneath the silk scarf wrapped around her head. "You should use public conveniences!"

"They haven't built them yet. I can't wait that long."

"What if a child had come by, you disgusting pervert?!"

No doubt if she had been of lesser breeding she would have spat at him. As it were, she merely shook her head lamentingly one last time and strode after her bitch. Duncan remained still, pondering whether the animals in her life were treated to similar reprimands. He looked around for sheep as obvious fellow reprobates but seemed to be in the one area of Britain where there weren't any.

He caught up with the rest who had been wondering where he'd got to. They said nothing, simply disappearing with smiles into a copse of conifers. He followed them. The trees seemed to be doing better comparatively than those outside the wood, but even so had lost many of their needles, forming a yellow-golden carpet fading in the grey light. There was a silence, not a comfortable one, more like that of a morgue with no birds singing.

They emerged from the wood. As they completed the circuit, Duncan became more perturbed. Did they not see? Did they not feel? How could anyone accept this shoddy facsimile of Nature?

"Don't worry, Duncan," Heinrich commented as they reached the car, misinterpreting his sour demeanour, "you're the best-dressed for the occasion, even if it did not rain much."

"Only mosquito piss," said George cheerfully.

How could they just go along with what was happening? he asked himself.

The answer, he knew, was that they were happy. They weren't striving, and were at peace with the world, what it had given them. He really should grant them a break, it was he who was at odds with everything, everyone, himself. However smart he was, he had to admit these four really did love each other. It was expressed on a daily basis, with the mundane minutiae of love, the gentlest of considerations. He had never experienced that, he and Rose being too clever to so demean themselves.

Most people he knew in a partnership, wanted out; most of those he knew were out, wanted in. Being in one required work and a certain knack. He didn't appear to have it. The real challenge now was to be alone, where other treasures awaited.

They were passing a pub which – oddly when they were so far inland – had a ship on its sign, when he suddenly became aware he was in the passenger seat. He had obviously been enwrapped by his personal cloud when getting into the car. He glanced to his left at Heinrich who wore his customary grin as he negotiated the winding road. In the back seat all were silent, each occupied by their own thoughts.

When they arrived at Egloston Theatre car park, the half-hearted rain had now ceased and the sun was beginning to show.

Feeling he'd been an ass for too long, Duncan was eager to make amends. Once out of the car he pointed out to Kay a young couple indulging in some tonsil-hockey.

"They're happy," he said, with cheerful deliberation.

"At that age it's all that matters," she said, looking at him curiously.

"I never had a first kiss," he said.

"What...?" The display of ingenuousness shocked her more than the revelation itself.

"At university I went straight into inebriated sex. I often wonder if I missed out an important stage in life."

"Perhaps. Romantic love is never easy, nor is it for everyone. Though we pretend it is. Ironically, spiritual love is accessible to all, and is always sweet. Yet few people want it."

His immediate reaction was to protest at her moralising. Only her uncanny echoing of his own thoughts restrained him.

They were preparing to go into the theatre café when three boys on skateboards, whizzing past, hurtled to a halt as one, their boards leaping into their hands abruptly and elegantly. Duncan was accustomed to being tormented by boys on skateboards – he saw his duty now as lying somewhere between being their butt and being their nemesis – but it wasn't him they were interested in. It was the car.

"Is this yours?" the smallest one, with long mousey hair and a nose-piercing, asked Heinrich who had just locked up.

"Yes, it is," he answered warmly.

"*Ja, it is*," mocked another boy.

"Heil Hitler! Heil Hitler!" they chorused with accompanying salutes, before leaping onto their boards and rattling away into the distance.

"The little monsters," Naomi said forcefully, watching them go.

"Let me reiterate that," said George. "The little effing monsters." He produced his pipe and proceeded to light up, as he was known to do only very occasionally when disturbed.

Naomi put her arm through her husband's, drawing him close, his good nature crestfallen.

"We've experienced this before," she said. "It's as if Britain is trapped by its own history. It never grew up."

"America is worse," said Heinrich, coming back swiftly. "I find it hard to respect a country that believes Burroughs and Salinger to be worthy literature. The Great American Novel remains forever elusive. You English feel sorry for your cousins but are too polite to say anything."

Naomi smiled, hugging him, when Kay cried out, "Oh my golly gosh! Look who it is."

Weaving towards them amongst the cars, a wide smile on her face, was a Bohemian-looking woman in her late thirties. She had long straight blonde hair, and an inner grace which shone from weather-beaten features, rendering her transcendently beautiful.

"Charlotte is part of our singing group in Totnes," Kay explained after hugging her, and introductions were made. "She *was* in our am dram here before she moved. She's famous for asking the director, 'How many ways exactly *can* one say "A handbag?"' This is very far from the moor for you, Charlotte. You'll have withdrawal symptoms. What are you doing back here?" she asked delightedly.

"I'm going to be cat-sitting for a friend. She's leaving in an hour."

"Come to dinner tonight," Kay urged. "Even better, join us now…"

"I can't," Charlotte replied, eyes glittering as they softly assessed the group. "I was on a mission to get some pickles for lunch, when I saw you. I'm happy to come for dinner though. We can have a sing-song."

"Oh Duncan won't like that," George said, puffing on his pipe.

"Won't he?" She looked at the man himself, curious after never having heard anything about him. He looked quite the odd-ball, refreshing in a way.

"He claims he's tone-deaf," Kay said, then in a stage-whisper, "even though we tell him there's no such thing."

Duncan's awareness of the attractive new arrival drifted as he started thinking about his condition. This particular one, from a legion of lesser entities, had shut him out of so many shared experiences: church choir, birthday songs, camp fire singalongs, and now New Age woolly mysticism. People were very eager to inform him there was no such affliction, it was all imaginary; while he was left with the reality of symphonies becoming cacophonies within minutes, social ostracism, and an inability to hear subtle distinctions in tones in various languages including English.

He was still lost in related thoughts during lunch, and only came out of his reverie, roused and irritated by the roaring of the coffee machine, to make a fuss about tipping. Nobody had even considered it, but he queried whether, as one ordered at the counter then waited for the waitress, whether a half-tip would be acceptable. "Do I need to get out the paper bag?" asked Kay. They managed to distract him, by drawing his attention to the film poster on the wall.

The film – and Duncan now remembered his part in the decision to see it – was about a premature attempt to bring the Age of Enlightenment to Denmark in the 18th century, though from the advertising it looked like a love story. In his rediscovered enthusiasm he went straight into the auditorium after lunch to get comfortable.

Having consumed a pint of Dartmoor ale even before eating, he needed to relieve himself once again.

Placing his box of popcorn and carton of Diet Pepsi on the floor by his seat, he looked around. Screwing up his eyes, he could discern a glowing sign with an umbrella over a door at the front. He went to check, and sure enough it was a toilet. Two toilets to be precise. He crammed himself into one of the cubicles, lifted the seat and did his business.

It was only when washing his hands in liquid lavender soap and admiring the coral pink décor with gold highlights, and a young woman in high heels walked in, did he realise his error.

Bustling past her indignation and out the door, he saw the theatre was still mostly empty. Naomi and Heinrich were in their seats however, and they burst out laughing at his emergence.

"The open umbrella is for girls, the closed one for boys," stated Heinrich helpfully, pointing to the bathroom on the other side.

"I hate art," growled Duncan, taking off his heavy coat after extracting his glasses, then throwing it with his hat into the aisle as he sat down.

"The girls' one is pink, the boys' one blue," Naomi said, touching his arm affectionately.

"Stuff and nonsense. It used to be the other way around."

Any argument on the history of colour bias had to be postponed as Kay and George arrived. A few minor dramas were in evidence off screen rather than on, once the film had started. First, a man with a bald head and startlingly white strands of remaining hair – at least, from Duncan's perspective – sat in front of him, and he decided to move due to the reflections on the said head and hair. He found them luminous to the point of distraction, standing out like beacons in the darkened room. He then moved only to experience the subtle dialogue being swamped by the rustling of a crisp packet of apparently infinite depths from some unknown location. He moved again and was happily settled in when a neighbour started exchanging texts on their SmartPhone. The light invaded Duncan's vision to such an extent he realised he was in a worse situation than with the bald head. There were now no other easily accessible seats available, and so he returned to his original seat. The head diminished in importance as he became enthralled by the story on the screen.

They all enjoyed the film, or at least were edified by it. Even Duncan limited himself to but two objections: that Queen Caroline Mathilde's beauty was reputedly more inner than outer, and the optimistic ending was probably more symbolic than factual. They discussed on the theatre steps how society tended to punish those ahead of their time, Heinrich commenting that in the current day it was left to the media to do the deed.

The couples dispersed to do some shopping. Left to himself, Duncan sat on the theatre steps, observing the scene, musing that he could not be considered ahead of his time, but behind it. The sun was out, the air becoming rapidly warmer at the tail-end of the afternoon, and his coat was draped over his knees. He felt the wax material with his hands and, returning to a familiar theme, he watched people coming and going, in their various attire specific to this place and time. It was funny, how he'd always been so disparaging about fashion. He'd argued that it was superficial and ephemeral; yet in its constant change, its shifting balance between pragmatism and celebration, perhaps it was one of the more accurate reflections of eternity.

Satisfied with his return to these musings, he decided to wander for the twenty minutes allotted to him. Two minutes later he espied a newsagents and went in. His eyes scanned the shelves randomly, and were drawn inexorably to the top shelf. He was alone apart from the Asian shopkeeper behind the counter, not that it would have made any difference if he hadn't been. He picked up one of the magazines, flicked through it, scowled, put it back and took out another. After several such attempts, the shopkeeper intervened.

"Can I help you, sir?"

"Oh no…" Duncan said politely, going up to the counter with a magazine, and flicking through the pages, showing the man in order to make his point clear. "This is like a catalogue from which you can never buy anything, don't you think? I've seen teenagers watching music videos which do exactly the same thing, but they don't call it pornography."

"What is it exactly you are looking for, sir?" asked the man, uncomfortable with the fickle flesh flickering past his eyes.

"Beauty," said Duncan, closing the magazine and leaning across the counter in great earnestness. "There is nothing more beautiful than a woman's body: it moves right, it looks right, it *is* right. What I'm looking for is a celebration of that fact, an artistic flourish. In life, rather than art, all women are beautiful if only they knew it, and all are attractive to someone. I'm not talking about art as such, perhaps a sensual art…an art of passion, something to take you further…"

The man came around the counter, grabbed the magazine and returned it to its rightful position on the shelf.

"What sort do you like?" asked Duncan, following him eagerly.

"What sort…?" The unfortunate shopkeeper couldn't finish his sentence. The Duncan Effect was working triple time on him.

"Yes. You can be as PC about it as you like. Men will always like looking at women's bodies, even if they have to hide the looking. That is the conclusion I have come to. However, there is a deficit of aesthetics in these particular tomes. Surely there must be some available of superior quality? Look…" Duncan reached out and pulled another one down, opening the centre pages wide as a visual aid. "What is the significance of this? I'm not a gynaecologist. I'm not a nutritionist either, but this lady definitely looks malnourished. Do you think she takes care of herself? Do you think she may be in trouble?"

"You get out now!" yelled the man, pointing to the door, then pushing Duncan helpfully. "Get out! I've had enough of you people!"

"'You people'?" asked Duncan, confused. "What people?"

But then he was pushed so forcefully out the door, he fell backwards onto the pavement, his hat flying into the road. George and Kay, naturally, just happened to be approaching and – along with numerous other people – witnessed the door being thrown open again, and the shopkeeper emerging, his arms full of the offensive literature. He stood in the doorway, tossing the magazines one by one on top of the recumbent Duncan before yelling abuse and returning inside.

"I think we'll definitely win that whisky," said George.

Kay went to help Duncan to his feet, but was taken aback by what was decorating him.

"Planning some light reading?" George chuckled.

"Are… Did you want to buy these?" asked Kay tentatively.

"No, no I didn't," said a puzzled Duncan, on his feet and scratching his head. "I believe that was the problem."

Kay focused on the task at hand. She gathered the magazines into a neat pile. Opening the shop door, she glanced timidly at the owner safely behind the counter once more, and placed the pile just inside.

The incident was so mercifully brief, it had drawn the attention of only those in the immediate vicinity.

There was a stilted silence on the way back, Heinrich stifling his laughter after hearing the story. Duncan was oblivious as he sat in the back with George and Kay, admiring the abundance of wildflowers in the hedgerows.

"First of all I can't believe you were in Porthengrous all that time, and you didn't call. Secondly, I can't believe you thought I'd take Mum's side? Whenever did I take Mum's side. That was Rowan's job, and he's a prig. Okay, maybe you were the guilty party, literally speaking, but she didn't make it easy for you. She's an horrendous flirt, Dad. But this Evelyn woman… I'm sure she only loved you for your mind."

The speaker was Jasmine. She had finally called the house at an opportune moment, and managed to get hold of her father. Duncan listened to his daughter rail on with the greatest of pleasure. When she had finished, and he agreed with all that she had said, he promised to return to Cornwall after a week and make up for his earlier shortcoming.

He remained quiet at the beginning of dinner. The others noticed his happiness and didn't intrude, pleased. He was waking up after a long sleep, and took note of his surroundings gently. He felt he was emerging from a culture that valued opinions more than it did people; it made love to and woke with them and had little else to offer. As every wise man knows he is a fool, every intellectual should acknowledge their ignorance.

He gradually became more aware of what was transpiring in the room, and that the conversation was about disastrous earlier relationships. As appropriate with one's spouse present, the subject was kept light.

"Meditation in my youth was a disaster," said George. "I used to have my mind buzzing with thoughts about women. Now they're about recipes."

"Alison was very beautiful," commented Kay, regarding her only real predecessor.

"Ahh yes, but as a beautiful woman she had an entire history, a back catalogue. She didn't come alone…"

"That's such an oafish thing to say."

"Her beauty was just the tip. The rest of the iceberg had all sorts of rubbish attached to it."

"You're mixing your metaphors again."

"I've always liked cocktails, you know that."

"It's impressive how relaxed you guys are talking about ex-lovers," put in Naomi. "I'd say Heinrich and I are very secure with each other but that's still an uncomfortable area. I got mad with him once for talking about his first kiss."

"She wanted to kill me, and not in a good way," her lover agreed.

"*I'm* impressed he actually got you mad," smiled Kay. "Do you both feel – unreasonably – that your early years were a waste, because you weren't with each other? I say 'unreasonably' because you're young now. George and I were in our late twenties when we met."

"That…that could be it," Naomi smiled radiantly across the table at her husband.

"It's so refreshing to listen to you all," Charlotte, next to Heinrich, said. "It's clear you're all totally in love."

"Weren't you, with Jim?" asked Kay. Charlotte had split up a year earlier from her boyfriend of ten years.

"We were in a *relationship*," she answered. "Yes, we were loving towards each other, before the end time. But we were never *in* love. We fancied each other when we met, had plenty in common and a good time, and it worked. People are quite cynical, or at least sceptical, about romance these days. There's a pragmatism I admire in many 'relationships', but it didn't work for us…in the long term; and I can't help feeling these 'relationships', as with online dating, are like arranged marriages. They lack the dramatic shifts in life that romance offers."

"I agree," said Duncan opposite her. "My marriage ended badly, as you may know. It would be easy to be cynical about our falling in love, but it's only recently that I'm looking back, and thinking it *changed everything*. So what if it were a rollercoaster? There *were* good times; and we're moving on."

"And you have two wonderful children, *and* a grandson, let me remind you," said Kay.

"Whom I still have to meet, yes."

Charlotte looked across at him, becoming more intrigued by the minute. She could imagine others perceiving him as a chubby clown; an image, to some extent at least, she suspected to be self-cultivated. This made him even more intriguing. What was he hiding, protecting? She appreciated his large size, even more knowing there were hidden depths. His thin moustache, his attentiveness to women, those roving brown eyes with their soft intelligence were reminiscent of a 1940s charmer such as Clark Gable. Yet he was lost, he was like a wounded bull who didn't know his role in life anymore.

She drew him out over cheese and biscuits.

"Kay tells me you've been playing solitaire alone in your cabin. Oh. Is that tautological?" she teased.

"'Solitaire alone'?" he responded with a smile. "Not if you were specifying me being alone in the shed, which I am." He was enjoying her presence opposite him whilst being aware of the illusion of hair over the eye, a song he should no longer hear. This type of Bohemian waif that George and Kay were always bringing home had never appealed to him in the past; but Charlotte had a rounded maternity to her, a fullness that was very attractive. Perhaps he was changing despite himself.

"I play as well," she said. "Especially since my break-up. With the television I mean, not with Jim! I'm tired of that nonsense." Which nonsense she meant was not clear.

"Yes, it certainly relaxes me. I actually lost my cards, then Kay showed me the game on the computer."

"Oh I've had enough of screens. I still do it old school."

"Normally I would agree, but the ability to undo what you have done I find extraordinary. It is as if you can actually go back in time. It's taught me a lot. For instance, I don't understand how, but intuition can be spot on. When I don't listen to it, I go back and find I should have gone with my gut-feeling."

"Mmm. Intuition is a fickle mistress. She can mislead you." Charlotte wrinkled her nose whilst blowing another wisp of stray blonde hair from her eye.

"That is true. Which is also interesting. Why isn't...she...more reliable? If it's a natural human function, then surely more dependable behaviour is to be expected?"

"Maybe it makes life more interesting not to always get it right."

"Ahh yes..." He was intrigued but fixed on a theme. "It's fascinating how, with an apparently unsolvable problem late on in the game, I can go back, begin again, and everything works out – and I have no idea how I did it. Though some problems always remain unsolvable. How do you manage it, when stuck?" He couldn't remember how he himself had ever managed.

"Oh," she said, spreading butter onto a cracker, "I play best out of three. If that fails, best out of five, and so on."

He was astounded by this revelation.

As the discussion moved on between them, Kay watched fondly as they interacted. At the other end of the table, Heinrich was entertaining George and Naomi with an historical anecdote.

"Then when they finally downed a Spitfire, all the Luftwaffe engineers descended on it. 'Vat is the secret to zis plane zat is knocking all ours out of ze sky?!'" He exaggerated the mock-German accent well. "They opened up the hood, and went, 'Vat?! Zis does not make sense!' Then they realised, the edge the Brits had was that they designed intuitively, not logically..."

Their laughter, Duncan's and Charlotte's conversation, were like music to Kay, heaven here on Earth. Yet she couldn't help sensing that someone was missing. Who was it? Charlotte's presence balanced the table, filled a need, but it wasn't her. It didn't make sense. She couldn't think of anyone she was missing, yet the void was obvious. She thought about her children, grown up and with their own lives; and she thought about Time, how somebody really important can be in your life as if they always were – yet they weren't. Or perhaps they were. She couldn't imagine a life without George, or any of those present really – but she had once been without them. What was it she wasn't seeing?

Duncan did his morning walk that night once dinner was over and Charlotte had left. The moon was waxing and rising above the old airfield, the air chilly and still. He always thought the moon indifferent and remote, now he felt and understood its romantic associations. He even remembered a moment with Rose, dancing to Roxy Music at the Students' Union.

'I hope I'm great, but not too much
Out of reach is out of touch.'

So, even his past was altering, the monsters of history being shoved aside by more positive aspirations.

He was once quite a smooth dancer. Did he have any moves left? He attempted a few steps by himself there and then before resuming his walk.

Roxy gave way to Naomi's kind voice talking about the mauersegler, the colourful, artificial birds sent to drift over the Berlin Wall during the Cold War, messengers of hope. Then, her voice gave way to Charlotte's whose – irrespective of the words – was full of warmth, delight and compassion. People really were wonderful if you gave them a chance.

The trouble, he decided, as he stomped across the silvery ruminant-clipped lawn, was him. He was like a potato, only half-baked, glassy and frustratingly trapped between fullness and raw indigestibility.

He found his rock, startling a pair of horses who whinnied softly and went to find somewhere else to sleep. He sat down, patting the stone's rough surface.

"Jealousy," he said. "Nobody really looks at what jealousy is. I do. I've had to. Rose flirting with those men, then Evelyn leaving me for someone her age. I had to wonder about jealousy, because I was experiencing it, yet when I was a young man I believed in love. Do they exist together? No, because jealousy exists like a horrible siren going off, warning you that you're not being humble, that you need to learn something. And for a start, possession is not what you're learning. And me? What did I have to learn? I learnt that I didn't love my wife, and that Evelyn wasn't the way out either. I have learnt that I don't know what love is."

Having said his piece, he fell silent. A few minutes later he clambered to his feet and headed back across the shadowy airfield, which was seemingly devoid of any other people.

5

Chasing

"Although I still adhere to the popular notion, those who don't know their history are condemned to repeat it, it is what even the experts don't know I find somewhat disturbing. All those dark unknown deals echoing through time. It is the job of the historian to examine the evidence, but what if there isn't any evidence? Even I have to acknowledge the distant past may have little in common, to the point of zero recognition perhaps, with the present. People assume that as survival issues remain always to the fore, the same applies to deeper motivations."

"Is this to do with your new book you mentioned?" Kay asked whilst brushing his sports jacket down vigorously.

They were in front of his full-length mirror, he motionless as she sorted him out. Surprisingly, he had managed to iron his shirt by himself, as he had done – so he informed her nonchalantly – throughout his marriage. As far as other domestic virtues were concerned, Rose and he had engaged a regular cleaner – taking care of bathrooms was not in his repertoire. Kay had been the one to impart such wisdom so late in life, which was something of a victory in itself.

"Sort of," he grimaced, then launched forward: "The greatest thing about history is you can never know for sure. History is always mystery. What we *don't know* has always been the attraction. That is the paradox of it. Even now there is a suspiciousness towards history, as politicians seek to control the judgement of unknown descendants. Also the film industry, as it replaces guns with flashlights, and removes cigarettes from actors' lips. It is like that fiction of a spy network in Europe during the war, created in order to draw attention away from Bletchley – I sometimes wonder if all we're doing is studying such fictions." He paused his subdued tirade, conscious of himself. "I have to be careful that I'm not so down on my own profession," he sighed. "I become like those magicians who go out of their way to convince the world there is no such thing as magic."

Kay smiled at his good mood and was about to comment – accompanied with a warning not to indulge in diatribes on his date – when she stopped, aware that putting light on such an immediate event could force it to retreat back into the shadows behind a camouflage of colour. Instead, "I think you're ready," she said, as they stood facing each other. "How are you feeling?"

"Good. This should be fun." He didn't quite know what he was doing, but knew it was the type of thing single people did; and everyone said he should get back on some horse or other.

"It's super that you say that, Duncan. I think the English tend to be too serious with dating on the whole. We forget to have fun."

"Romantic expectations."

"I imagine so, though Isabelle wasn't particularly romantic. Just serious. The boys...I don't know...they were all over the place, being boys I suppose. Only Jason's settled down now."

"Rowan I would judge as a realist, Jasmine a pragmatic romantic."

"It's marvellous you're seeing her soon," she said as they headed back to the house together.

"Yes, though I do have my doubts about parents getting too involved with their adult children. Even now I feel I don't entirely have my own life, that my parents live through me in a discordant manner. Family's opinions are rarely to do with reality, only their reality."

His expression was becoming so sour by the time they reached the kitchen, she poked him in the ribs.

"None of that. *Fun*, remember?"

He smiled. "Thank you, Kay." He put on George's fedora that he was borrowing, and left. She watched him go from the door, haunted by the feeling that whoever Duncan should be with, he had yet to meet.

George emerged from the living room to watch his brother closing the front gate, and disappearing up the lane.

"So that's Duncan off on his adventure. Do you think it will work out?"

"They got on very well at dinner. Though, as we both know, personality will only get you so far. She does have an accepting, understanding nature, which bodes well for him."

"We are talking about the man who managed to enrage Buddhists."

"Tch. Only the once." She now found herself straightening out *his* shirt. "Are you off to the orchard meeting now?"

"In twenty minutes. Time for a quick coffee."

"I might still be at the doctor's when you get back."

He went quiet, grabbing her shoulders gently and looking her in the eye.

"It'll be fine. Don't worry."

She wasn't assured, but she smiled in order to assure *him*.

Before leaving the house in Egloston, Charlotte drew two cards in preparation. First was the Eight of Swords. A woman blindfolded, having to make her perilous way in a field, surrounded by swords. Something unseen. A situation where intellect wouldn't cut it, intuition the only ally. Her second card was The Moon. More of the same. Also, 'things' coming up for her. She had always loved both of these cards for the risk, the adventure. She didn't need any more information. She would get to the rendezvous early to check the lay of the land, that much she *could* do. One last scrutiny in the mirror – and boy, did she look good – she grabbed her keys and left.

Despite being overtaken by a sudden cloud as he tramped across the heath, mocked by Rose's sarcastic taunt from long ago ("That's what I like about you, your sense of adventure.") Duncan went on to what was, by and large, a successful date. Her taunt, which had popped out of nowhere both at the time and presently, seemed to have kept its teeth permanently embedded in a particularly vulnerable nerve. Where was his sense of adventure? Was he really alive, or happy? Reputedly singing, dancing and drama made people the most happy, and he didn't currently do any of those things. Could people not live without unhappiness? They always seemed to have to create new problems, new dramas – and not the fun kind, unlike one of Kay's amateur productions. He should take up dancing again, he thought, as he continued across the airfield, but he didn't have a dance partner. He didn't have a partner.

The thoughts started to dispel as he reached the pub. He had enjoyed Charlotte's company when she came for dinner, and there was hope there. He got the sense she saw beyond the obvious, which was fortunate for him.

At the bar for about ten minutes, he was delighted to see her approach, smiling, and sit on the adjacent stool.

"Hello," she said cheerfully. "Oops sorry," as she wavered, finding her balance and having to rest her hand on his shoulder to steady herself.

"That's okay," he said, enjoying her touch. "I'm having a tin and gonic. Would you like one?"

"That's very nice of you," she said, amused. "Yes, I would, thank you."

They chatted about Yelverton, the weather, various other generalities, and it all flowed along smoothly. He shifted the subject back onto the oddness of solitaire on the computer, how he would go back to the start, and recommence without over-thinking and everything would then work out. She was genuinely interested; and he wasn't thinking about the cards really, the correct placings of kings and queens, only about how her long blonde hair seemed more lustrous, her eyes more liquid and absorbing than he remembered, her soft Devonshire accent even more captivating. He was falling for her quickly. She really was a special person. He was so lucky.

It was only when he mentioned her housesitting at Egloston they hit a snag.

"Who do you think I am exactly?" she asked, leaning back, away from him.

Charlotte drove back to Egloston, holding back the tears.

After reaching Yelverton, then realising it wouldn't do to seem too eager, she had gone for an amble on the old airfield. It was another perfect day, the sky all-blue with just a slight breeze, sparrows and swifts darting around. A time made for happiness.

She had braided her hair, a look which made her glamorous, she had often been told. She had replaced her usual tie-dye ensemble with a thin beige jacket and skirt, elegant black shoes, and a little green woollen hat to top it all off. She was also wearing large light brown sunglasses. Duncan was more from the straight world than she was used to, but she could get used to that. It might mean a new life. Hence she dressed what she thought of as appropriately.

Having put so much effort into transforming her appearance, she was confident and delighted when she saw Duncan approach.

His head was down. He seemed full of contemplations.

She stopped to wait for him. He too had made something of an effort. His sports jacket seemed new, and he was wearing a rather fetching fedora, the 1940s charm in evidence once again.

She was about to speak, when he glanced up at her, scowled and looked back at the ground.

Stunned, she stood frozen as he walked into the distance.

Not sure what to do, she waited a while unmoving then slowly, reluctantly followed the old runway back to Yelverton and her car. She walked into The Rock tentatively just in time to witness Duncan precisely where he said he'd be – he'd been very adamant on that – and in deep tête-à-tête with a blonde several years younger than herself. She looked more his type, with the thin cashmere sweater, the expensive hair and green manicured nails. Very Middle England. There was an easy and undeniable intimacy between them.

Charlotte turned, controlling surging emotions with deep breaths, going back to her car.

She had journeyed only a mile or two before having to pull over in a gateway, switch off the engine and start crying.

Once the sense of humiliation had diminished with the tears, she was left with the residual awareness of something greater having been at stake; otherwise her reaction was woefully disproportionate. Was it because she had deep feelings for Duncan? No, she hadn't. She liked him, she had a certain fondness for him, that was all. So why the deluge? She realised why, immediately after asking the question.

It was because she had always had a partner, and she was getting older. Gaps between men had been few and brief. Now after a ten-year relationship, at this time in her life, she was panicking.

Sod it, she thought, gripping the steering-wheel determinedly. This had been passed down to her, as to most people: there's something amiss if you're not married. She had faced similar judgements by not having children. That's what it came down to in the end, particularly for a woman. It was not a new revelation, she had always been aware of this unconscious lineage; but now for the first time she was going to act on that awareness. In the past she had moved swiftly to new relationships, now she had to move swiftly to something else.

What though? What was she going to do? Who was she exactly, she herself, alone, rather than one-half of the relationship animal? What did *she* like?

She liked horses, she thought as she turned the ignition; always did, always would. She'd left that part of herself behind as a teenager. Maybe it was time to reclaim it, even get enough cash together to start gathering a small herd.

The signs had already been there, she mused down the road to Egloston. Since the break-up, to get away from it all she had been seeking solace regularly on the moor with the ponies. Lying flat on the spongy ground she could hear them milling around, hoofbeats as individual as fingerprints. Now and then one or two would approach to investigate, make sure she was all right, and nuzzle her recumbent form, tickling her face with their hairy, delicate lips and warm breath. Perhaps she wouldn't be as alone as she thought.

On her return Kay found George in his office stabbing the keyboard of his computer angrily. He was obviously composing one of *those* letters.

He stood up on her arrival. "What did the doctor say?"

"Nothing new… How did the orchard meeting go?" she asked, nodding meaningfully at the computer.

"The idiots want to accept an offer of twenty free saplings. I told them they're not free as they wish to put deer-proof fencing around, each one at ten quid a pop, despite us not having any deer around here. The real problem is bullfinches. But they won't listen, though I'm the only one with experience."

"So you're writing a letter to them."

"No, that would be pointless. I guess if you sign on for community projects you have to occasionally accept asinine decisions in the name of democracy. This…is because I only just opened the letter from the car park company."

"The people you paid despite them being in the wrong?"

"Only because I didn't want to go through the appeals process. They must get a lot of people that way. So I paid whilst voicing my objections, *vociferously*, then they lost my cheque. I sent them another one once they told me. Now they're fining me extra for late payment. This whole state of things is because councils wish to evade responsibility by letting cowboys take over."

His rant was punctuated finally by the sounds of the front door slamming, and a pygmy rhinoceros charging through to the garden.

"I'll speak to him in a minute," said Kay softly, "find out what happened."

He caught the shadow under her expression.

"Kay...the doctor?"

"It was one of the new ones. He didn't really listen, his head was too full of all his expensive knowledge. He told me the heart monitor from six weeks earlier showed clearly that I wasn't experiencing palpitations when I said I was. Blood results were normal etcetera etcetera. I explained about the constrictions around my chest, and he suggested that I was merely getting older. George, I just can't accept the gatekeeper to life and death is a pimply-faced know-it-all! There's something wrong, I know there is!"

As she collapsed into his arms, he held her tight as always, allowing the flux of her emotions to reign as long as required. He was a practical man. His level-headed attitude applied to virtually everything he encountered. It was that attitude which made him concede to moving to Crapstone all those years ago, despite his subtle dislike of the airfield. They needed a larger house they could afford, so they would go for this one. Kay had echoed his taciturn feelings at the time, admitting "So many people must have died here"; yet also his pragmatism: "This is England. People have died everywhere, no avoiding that."

Thus, his pragmatism extended even to questions of mortality, and his rock-like demeanour permitted her feelings to roil around him, no matter the cause, as always.

Kay had composed herself sufficiently by the time she got to Duncan. Even so, he was more perceptive to others' feelings than generally acknowledged, and she was relieved that he was immersed in a sea of books – pretty much literally, squatting on his bed; volumes he'd already had, volumes he'd found in charity shops, volumes ordered over the phone, surrounding him, one bookmarked by being draped over the head-rest. He looked up as she cleared a corner, aware she may be upsetting his filing system, and sat down, facing him.

Reluctantly, he told her what had happened.

"So," she said once he had finished, "do you think Charlotte must have come in and seen you all over this other woman?"

He actually blushed.

"And this woman, Robin," she smiled, "are you going to see her again?"

"She was waiting for her boyfriend," he mumbled, feigning indifference by picking up another book.

Kay took a deep breath. "What about salvaging things with Charlotte? Simply explain about the face blindness, that you were relying on her identifying you first..." She trailed off, wondering how a woman, particularly at an insecure stage in her life, would react to the fact that her looks were indistinguishable from others'.

"Actually, I was hoping you'd have her contact details. I can at least try to explain."

"You don't?"

"Our meeting was so determined, and clear...she was rushing home after dinner to feed the cat...we didn't exchange numbers. Though I guess she has your number, she doesn't have a mobile phone. Another thing we had in common."

"That's the problem. She doesn't like new technology, and even refuses to check her email more than once a month. I'll leave a message on her landline but she's housesitting for much of the summer, and I'd be very surprised if she checks messages. She's notoriously retro – I think that's what the kids call it – and difficult to get hold of, even when domesticated." Duncan already looked resigned. She decided on another tack. "Have you had lunch?"

"A liquid one. I'm not hungry."

She found that hard to believe. Another man out of touch with his feelings. He was obviously in a sulk. She stood up.

"Come on, Duncan. We're about to eat. George is making tuna salad. You know how you get with your hypoglycaemia."

She held out her hand, he took it and she helped him to his feet.

"We're going to Tavistock this afternoon. Do you want to come? It's bigger than Egloston so who knows, Charlotte may be doing some shopping there."

"It's something to do," he said as they headed to the house. "When are Heinrich and Naomi back?"

"Tonight, I think. Their friends in Bristol only have a small apartment, so they couldn't stay long. Do you miss them?"

"Heinrich makes me laugh."

"Well, let's hope we all regain our chuckles this evening. George could certainly do with a respite. He doesn't like bureaucracy, and there's some more awaiting us at Tavy."

160

Duncan had no faith that he would bump into Charlotte, nor was he sure he wanted to, but he ambled around the town anyway. Hope was no more logical than love. Personally he felt the date had been a noble experiment, no more than that. To his mind, experiments didn't fail – they just didn't always give the results desired.

The weather had turned whilst they were having lunch, and he had regressed to his wax coat and hat, thinking the little drops of rain justified it.

George and Kay had to go to the bank, then on to some community survey at a primary school where Duncan would meet them. He had nothing to do for half-an-hour so bought a bag of chips, and while he was at it, several bars of chocolate which he stuffed into his pockets. Following directions, he crossed the bridge on the Plymouth road and carried on to the school, munching on his vinegar-saturated potatoes for sustenance. He wandered into the car park, peering under the brim of his hat through the drizzle to espy a sports ground encircled by three-metre high fencing. There were young children playing what could have been rounders, baseball, cricket or an amalgamation of them all with some rugby thrown in for good measure. No adults were in sight.

Three girls about nine-years old were standing by the fence. One of them called out to him.

"Hey, mister!"

"Yes?" he said disinterestedly, wandering closer. Girls tended to be less cruel to him than boys, so he felt relaxed around them.

"They look good," said the girl, her shoulder-length blonde hair pressed miserably to her face by the damp.

"Geez us one…please?" pleaded her lanky friend with short dark hair.

"Okay." Moved by their bedraggled, forlorn faces, he started passing chips through the wire fence. "Why are you here? Is it not the holidays?"

"We have to do *math camp*," said the third, who could have been a pre-Raphaelite princess with her long beautiful auburn hair, "because our *Attainment Targets* were too low." She had a penchant for comedy, it seemed, as her mimicking of adult phraseology was on the mark.

"This doesn't look like maths."

Other children were abandoning their anarchic game and starting to head towards the welcome distraction.

"We got thrown out of class."

"All of you?"

"Yeah."

"To 'let off steam'," said the dark-haired girl.

"You don't know what it's like!" cried the blonde, her mouth full of potato. "Can you get us out? Or give us some food? Anything!"

Duncan was so moved by their pleas as they clung to the fence in their wet, muddy clothes, faces streaked with rain and sweat, he began eagerly to empty his pockets and hand over the contents.

"Share them out fairly," he insisted.

"Mister, you're so cool," said the blonde girl as she shared the first Wagon Wheel with her friends.

George and Kay had driven in to the car park, and got out to be greeted by the sight of Duncan passing sweets from the depths of his long coat, to a crowd of excited children.

"It's your turn," Kay sighed.

"I'll go and extricate him before the police arrive," George said. "You carry on without me."

Resigned, Kay went into the building. There was no relevant signage. However, she used her instincts to navigate the empty school's labyrinthine corridors, and eventually found the office she sought by the sounds of activity. There were about ten people present, all busy with paperwork, one of whom she instantly recognised.

"Brian!"

A slight man in his sixties, smartly dressed in a tweed jacket and tie, stood up and shook her hand enthusiastically.

"Good to see you, Kay."

She nodded at the wad of documents clenched in his left hand. "I trust you're helping them see the big picture."

"One would like to think so. I attempted this online but their web page kept crashing."

"So you came in all the way from Egloston."

"You'd think they'd set the survey up there, but oh no, it has to be several miles away and only for a few hours on a few days, in another town."

"Hours which only suit the retired, unemployed and night shift workers."

"Funny that."

Brian was an expert in sustainable communities, and unlike most of those who brandished the term he actually knew what it meant. The survey was concerning development plans at Egloston and its environs. If anybody's opinions carried more weight, it should possibly have been his.

"We also had problems online," said Kay, picking up a questionnaire and sitting down on a plastic chair next to him. "Ahh. Here's George."

The men shook hands, then sat flanking Kay.

"Where's Duncan?" she asked suspiciously.

"He says he needs to go to Morrisons to do some shopping. I suspect he wants to replenish the mobile tuck shop in his pockets."

"Where were the teachers?"

"From what the children told me, there were some injuries and both supervising adults went inside."

"Both?"

"They were the injuries. I got the impression they couldn't quite handle St Trinians and their male counterparts. So, Brian, let me guess – you didn't manage this online either."

"Correct. Although I am not sure it was entirely their fault. My broadband is getting slower and slower."

"Do you leave it switched on?"

"No, I don't trust those things when they're left alone, don't know what they're up to. Also I switch it off in order to save electricity, minimal as it may be."

"If it's off for long periods, the modem goes into a sulk, feeling unwanted. It starts to underperform."

"I see. You try to do one thing right, and something else goes wrong."

"That's how it works, old bean."

The next twenty to thirty minutes worked in such a way that by the time they met up with Duncan in the car park, all three were rendered quite despondent by the inefficiency and informed pointlessness of public consultations.

"They set the cardboard committees up, then do what they want anyway," moped Kay.

"Not if we can help it," said Brian. "This is the Age of the Internet. We'll gather the forces and fight them in the digital trenches. If I *can* gather the forces, that is. People tend to be so enamoured with their new toys these days, they're forgetting about people."

"You need to sell it to them," said George helpfully as they stood around the car. "People will accept anything as long as it comes with melted cheese on top and sandwiched between sugar-enriched buns."

"I was hoping for a more grass-roots…"

"Hold that thought, Brian," George said as his phone rang out from his jacket with its traditional ring tone. He smiled as he saw the name of the caller, and nodded at Kay. "Where are you chaps? Really…? Well, we're in Tavy but headed off for a drink with a friend… You remember that pub on the road to Egloston? That's the one… We'll see you there then." He snapped his phone shut. "Heinrich and Naomi, back early," he said to Kay and Duncan, then to Brian: "They'll be joining us, if that's all right."

"Of course. Whoever they are."

"Now can we get in the car before we get totally soaked," protested Kay as the threads of rain started becoming ropes. Duncan, feeling invincible in his long coat and under his wide hat, was grinning.

George apologised, and promptly unlocked. They were giving a lift to Brian as he had come in by bus, the idea of going to the pub being serendipitous in its arrangement.

They got to the Ship and Compass to find the Mercedes there before them in the car park. They disembarked and went inside to the lounge where Heinrich and Naomi sat with a pint of local ale and a gin and tonic respectively. "I am fitting in!" Heinrich exclaimed, lifting his glass. "Warm beer! No one will know I am German, *ja*?!"

Brian was introduced and everyone started offering everyone else drinks, except for Duncan who was experiencing one of his increasingly regular inner attacks regarding his financial situation. This had been triggered in the cramped car by the heated discussion on local budgeting. He stood now to one side first perusing a brochure for Bretton Moor Theme Park, then a National Trust leaflet which stated he could 'Explore More for Free', while his tongue played havoc with a loose molar in his jaw. He had cancelled the remaining dental appointments when the dentist had become disconcertingly eager to remove two more teeth. One was enough. Was he to become a gap-toothed old man already? Could he afford to be so? He sighed, reflecting that he would really miss sex, or at least the chance to have it.

His worries were allayed by a reassuring grip on his shoulder, and George asking him what he would like to drink. Conversation around the table steered perilously close to becoming exclusive, focusing on the activities of children and new arrivals of grandchildren. Brian, whether deliberately or no, launched things in a different direction by talking about his youngest.

"She was working in Admin for that new university Becks in Cambridge. Fortunately she quit, despite having no prospects. She said it was like working for the Nazis. They're intent on using the city's name to their own ends, building in every direction they can, irrespective of local and environmental concerns, and they treat their staff like slaves. She was bullied and coerced on all levels. The atmosphere was awful. Women generally only fitted in by agreeing with the men. It's ridiculous, unsustainable at best. Ironically, the unwitting students, delighted to be educated at 'Cambridge', have no idea that every thirty of them are supporting one pen-pushing nitwit. Not to say a sociopathic pen-pushing nitwit."

"Interesting," said Duncan, sipping his second gin and tonic of the day. "You – or your daughter rather, compares them to Nazis, but I suggest Romans might be a more fitting analogy. The Nazis never managed to invade. The Romans on the other hand occupied all the key areas. They also were not interested in spiritual conflict, only material. The gods were acceptable under any name as far as they were concerned. It was material expansion they sought whatever the cost."

"Construction workers as the new legionaries," smiled Naomi. "I can see that."

"Yes," said Duncan, who was about to expound on Nietzsche's theory of the horizontal movement of diseased cultures, as opposed to the vertical and healthy, when in his enthusiasm he knocked his crisps onto the dark wooden floor. A lustrous hound, which till then had been sitting obediently by another table, bolted across the room, dragging its lead behind, and pounced. At first it seemed completely disinterested in any scattered crisps, solely obsessed with throwing the bag around and tearing it to shreds. Then three seconds later it started devouring the contents of the gutted bag.

"Washington! Washington!" yelled the owner, a huge man in all directions, as was his moustache. He came to the rescue.

"I'm so sorry," he said as the dog came to heel, and was taken back to its rightful table to be nurtured and restrained by the man's wife and teenage children.

"They're cheese-and-onion, aren't they?" he said, returning, and dutifully cleaning up the mess. "It's the smell, and only crisps."

"And Quavers!" yelled his wife. "And Cheesy Puffs!"

"Same diff. He doesn't do it with anything else. We wanted a Lithuanian – Uliana there is Lithuanian – but they're impossible to come by, so a Latvian had to do. Harry!" he called out to the barman. "Washington's done it again!"

"One cheese-and-onion coming up," said the barman.

As the loose ends of the comedy show were tied up, the floor swept – crisps remunerated, apologies made, their necessity denied, and everybody back in their rightful places – Brian returned to the main topic with remarkable alacrity.

"I take your point, Duncan. The wars nowadays are economic rather than ideological, no matter their mantle. This makes it even more difficult, for *who* is the enemy? I'm pretty sure we have one, or more than one. Even in the Second War that was true, but now our foes are nebulous. They don't wear uniforms."

"Look for a lack of humour," said Heinrich, raising his finger in a pedagogic manner. "That is a dead giveaway."

The general mirth assured everyone that he, at least, was clearly not the enemy.

"In fact," he continued, raising his finger again, "my main objection to the Chinese taking over the world, as they seem intent on doing…"

"Oh they are not alone," George interrupted.

"Indeed, my good man, but it is their lack of a single good joke that concerns me, and I am a German!"

Kay, who had been quietly enjoying proceedings since their arrival, from the initial discussion, to Duncan's and the dog's vaudeville, to its current direction, looked upon Heinrich with ever-deepening affection. Despite his last remark, it struck her now that he easily transcended any notion of nationality. He and Naomi more than anyone she knew embodied the sense of being true global citizens. They may have considered themselves first European, then German, but she saw them as much more. In comparison, she and George remained quintessentially English, Brian too as he rallied the troops for one campaign after another. Duncan she wasn't sure about. She watched him discreetly as he watched Washington who was also watching him from across the room, both wondering who was going to make the first move. Duncan's fingers would creep across the table to the unopened bag of crisps, then like a spider sensing a subtle muscular tension in its foe, would retreat. Kay wasn't too sure what he was anymore, only that she loved him too.

Brian meanwhile was having his own reflective spree as he observed Heinrich get to his feet and march rigidly on the spot, chanting, "Ve vill not laugh! Ve vill not laugh!"

"You two were just in Bristol, I understand," he said once Heinrich had calmed and sat down.

"We were," said Naomi.

"You wanted to see a movie," Kay said. "Were there any good ones on?"

"Not really," sighed Heinrich. "Tom Cruise was saving the world again."

"Not *again*..."

"What do you do in Bodensee, may I ask?" Brian asked.

The question was not an idle one. Early years as the head of Human Resources of a large accounting firm in Slough had been mind-numbingly dull. It was only when Brian realised that the true role of his job, was to determine what people *really* wanted to do, that he had started to enjoy himself – having discovered what he really wanted to do. He had to rein in his perspicaciousness when numerous long-standing employees realised they did not want to be accountants. Even so, he found ways to circumvent his employers' polite despotic rule by 'casually' meeting other workers in a nearby pub. His subtlety was such that he managed to stay on for many years, eventually retiring with a full package. Both he and his wife loved Devon, so it was the obvious move for them. Neither remained idle. She was part of Kay's macramé circle plus several other groups endorsed by the WI; while he gained an MSc in environmental science, before becoming rapidly involved in local politics, despite objections that he was not really a local. He either completely charmed or ignored the objectors, and simply got on with what was needed, having insight into the Big Picture.

"They're not moving back to Munich, that's for sure," George said.

"Right," Heinrich agreed. "It's a good city, full of interesting people, but we're – how do you say it – country bumpkins at heart."

"Though I didn't know that till recently," put in Naomi.

"Anyway, to answer your question, we don't know."

"Well, we…" She looked softly at him with her wide eyes.

"We have a plan. Being of the eclectic persuasion, it's hard to focus our disparate interests, but we're considering setting up a local arts centre. It'll be hard to make it pay, even with funding."

"We're going to combine resources with the running of Heinrich's parents' guesthouse. We do all get on fortunately. Patience will be requisite as I don't have a clue what I'm doing."

"Well, it does sound like a plan," said Brian. "What kind of a centre? Why there, apart from nearness to family?"

"Although it is a radical departure from Naomi's studies, it will tap into her interest in local folklore," Heinrich explained. "We can build on that. Then I can find a way to subvert the populace with the blues."

"A Billie Holiday fan, I take it."

"Absolutely!" Heinrich's eyes became even more animated. "And that can lead to political subversion. That's my master plan. Hee hee." He rubbed his hands theatrically. "I will do a lecture on my theory that the FBI prosecuted her simply because they were bored once Prohibition ended." His pedagogic finger was raised once more, till Naomi hit him on the shoulder, and he lowered it dutifully. "To be discussed."

"There's a poem," said Naomi, "by Yehuda Amichai about a man who photographed the view outside his room rather than photographing the woman he'd just made love to. We would like the centre to bring a deeper enhancement to visitors' appreciation of the landscape, rather than just adding to the superficiality."

The point could have been obscure – even Brian, who was quite taken by her, felt out of his depth – but Duncan understood perfectly.

"When I was walking up the hill from Porthengrous one day," he said, purposely ignoring Washington, "there was a beautiful rainbow arcing over St Michael's Mount and the bay. A sports car stopped and a young woman got out from the passenger's side, with one of those tablet thingies. She held it up. I could see the spectacular view beyond her, then that same view crammed into the tiny, inadequate frame of the device. She took the picture, got back in the car and left."

There was a brief silence, then Heinrich muttered, "The pictures aren't even that good quality on those things."

Naomi's face was glowing as she looked at Duncan who was back to looking at the dog warily. She felt understood, seen, by him. She didn't always need to be seen by Heinrich, he was along for the ride unconditionally and permanently, but she enjoyed it when it happened.

When it came time for them to go, and email addresses exchanged, and promises made to keep in touch, Duncan stuffed the unopened crisps into his coat pocket, and went for the door, making sure there was always someone between him and Washington.

It was turning into a marvellous evening with rosy-tipped pillars of clouds marching in from the east, and the warm breeze carrying blossom-scents, subtle and multitudinous.

"Here," said Brian, waylaying Kay, as he produced a notebook out of his jacket pocket. He scribbled something down, tore off the leaf and gave it to her.

"What is this?" she squinted. "A German company, isn't it?"

"Yes, it's the specifics of a phone they make. I couldn't help thinking when you described the pains in your chest, it might be something to do with your cordless phone."

"Oh that's why you were asking. George said the signal isn't very strong."

"Not enough to cook popcorn, no, but it's *constant*, that's the thing. I don't know much about biophysics, so I can't explain it, but the symptoms you describe remind me of what a friend also had. He replaced his phone with an old-fashioned one and the symptoms went. If you feel you need a cordless model, this one doesn't transmit between calls and is low energy generally. The company has a strong ethical policy."

"Thank you so much, Brian," she said, her eyes welling up.

"A pleasure. I'll be in touch."

"Are you sure you want to walk, Brian?" George called out from the car.

"On an evening like this? Who wouldn't?!" He waved dismissively as he headed off down the lane to Egloston.

"Come on, Kay! Naomi's making pancakes for dinner!"

She couldn't move for the moment, clutching the piece of paper Brian had given her to her chest, overcome with love and a sense of gratitude for the life she was living, the people who surrounded her.

Then Heinrich and Naomi whisked past in the Mercedes, George pulled up to her in their car, she got in, and they followed the others back home.

That night after an excellent dinner, Duncan went out to walk on the airfield. The sky was now overcast, which didn't affect him as his gaze was inward. For all the bonhomie evident in recent days he was feeling increasingly isolated. He wasn't part of their group, or any group. Any transcendence granted by a collective seemed destined to remain elusive to him.

Even in the poor ambient light he managed to find his rock and sit down next to it. For some unknown reason, perhaps because of the illusory nature of dates that was becoming more evident to him, he started to think about the Lusitania. "Seventh of May 1915," he said to the rock, "Nobody can say for sure why it was sunk. It is possible it was a conspiracy to egg the Americans on to fight. I don't know why I'm thinking of this." Then he fell silent at the pointlessness of it all. When he started thinking chaotically, and just as pointlessly, about the Bahamas, he got up, fed up, and went home.

Despite Hawker's idiosyncratic behaviour – cultivated, natural or both – he attended to certain duties every day conscientiously, one of which was delivering mail to the huts. He knew the importance of contact with folks back home and would do all he could to facilitate. Other areas along the lines of communication could be more capricious however, with deliveries ending up being at any time of day or night.

Thus Sunday morning after the cinema outing found Donnel alone in the hut, stretched out on his bunk. Light was streaming in through the dusty window, bathing him in gold as he smoked a cigarette and perused his mail. He had restrained himself sufficiently to first read the one from his parents, before going on to that from Tallulah. Another photograph was enclosed, if anything more saucy and daring than those that had gone before.

So she had gone for another session. The meaning was clear: 'Look what you're missing, buster.' She was completely naked, reclining on a Persian rug, looking over her shoulder at the camera, one dark lock playing peek-a-boo over her right eye. He wondered about the photographer. He wondered how many hands had

170

touched the picture in the name of censorship. At least it had got to him, in more ways than one. If he hadn't been called up, he would be enjoying her company now. They had slept together on a number of occasions, and it was often all he thought about at nights. During the day she was like a ghost, intangibly present, popping up unexpectedly from time to time, often in spasms of jealousy brought on by imagined trysts. He really wondered if she were being faithful, but then, was he?

The letter implied nothing to the contrary. It was impassioned, talking of the Californian heat, of sunbathing, the latest movies, and consequently about her aspirations – so far unrealised – her body, how much she missed him, and when was he coming back? All this accomplished with just a hint of salaciousness, nothing as overt as the photograph, yet saying so much more, his yearning increased.

He put the letters aside and stared at the sky through the window, drawing heavily on the cigarette, flicking ash onto the floor. He thought of Sandra. She'd be at Church Parade with the other WAAFs. There was a chapel somewhere nearby, he'd been informed, with services he could attend. A lot of his countrymen did, but Catholicism had become more cultural than spiritual to him, and Tallulah had long since shaken him out of any loyalty to such perfunctory duties in life. It was a new world evolving, with a hell of a shaky start.

He thought of Sandra. He could still feel the sensation of her kiss. She was here, Tallulah was there. Yet paradoxically the opposite was true as well: there was a distance to Sandra that didn't exist in Tallulah who seemed to have a hold on him from afar, a hold sustained for months with every letter, every photograph. Surely they were as good as married.

Elsewhere, a maelstrom of another sort was building in Maggie who was not at Church Parade. She had been summoned to a meeting with the station commander at Ravenscroft. Spiffy she had no concerns about, he was a decent man and a good leader who knew when to leave something alone. What gave her cause for some trepidation was that she had been informed Wing Commander Gleeson would be present. Like any WAAF, she was used to hardened cynical women delighting in their new-found power when in charge. This man, however, as her self-appointed nemesis, this walking fossil, was as dangerous as he was absurd.

171

People died because of fools such as he, and would do so again in this case if she didn't keep her wits about her.

There was a relaxed feeling all around this Sunday morning as she got out of her car and mounted the steps at Ravenscroft, but it couldn't reach her inner anxiety. She was aware of too many things.

She was made to wait for fifteen minutes outside the office. She had already tied her hair back and checked her uniform so there wasn't much she could do other than collect her thoughts, head off the maelstrom at the pass as it were. The summons hadn't even given her time to make a phone call. She really was on her own, and would have to wing it, to use another metaphor – one that had come up more than once since agreeing to the mission.

The phone on the desk buzzed. The sergeant picked it up, listened briefly, then put it down again.

He nodded at her amiably. "You can go in, Maggie."

She raised herself nervously, and rapped on the heavy wooden door before entering. Closing it behind her, she marched to the centre of the room and saluted the two men smartly.

"At ease, Sergeant," Smythington said languidly. He seemed bored, irritated but also amused by his companion seated next to him, which gave Maggie hope. She felt the threat of the maelstrom rapidly dissipating. "Please, be seated," he gestured to one of the chairs in front of the desk. "We have something to discuss."

She sat down, feeling a sense of relief come over now that she had read the room. This was despite the grimacing walrus sprawled next to the group captain, his legs wide open as he clutched the walking stick between them,

"You know Wing Commander Gleeson?" Smythington asked.

"I do, sir."

"He has brought to light a number of irregularities regarding your behaviour at Clearbrooke. He has taken it upon himself to contact your previous CO at Bletchley."

Gleeson, missing any subtext, was looking even more pompous and pleased with himself. The inference Maggie made was that this unsolicited correspondence was the source of Smythington's irritation.

"'Irregularities', sir?" Most subordinates knew not to talk in such a situation, but it was in part Maggie's temerity that had got her into this position and she wasn't about to relinquish it.

"Your fraternising with the Yanks, and all manner of reprobates," Gleeson thundered, holding onto his stick with sudden, barely-contained rage. "Don't deny it, Sergeant. You were seen even yesterday…"

She remained perfectly composed. "It is my job to fraternise, sir."

Smythington saw the need to head off a different maelstrom at the pass, and interceded.

"Be that as it may, Sergeant, I did receive a letter by special envoy from your Commander Denniston."

He unfolded it now. She tried not to look at Gleeson who had no idea what forces he was antagonising. Smythington should have berated him for ignoring the chain of command, but any reprimands would have been tempered due to respect for his age. Thus, the chastisement was probably very subtle, and Gleeson didn't do subtle. Whatever the contents of the letter, a couple of things would happen soon. Maggie could see them unfold. First, Gleeson would get a visit from MI5 who would simply tell him to stay quiet. This would be followed by a posting to somewhere he could do little harm, somewhere like Cornwall. The old boys' network was, ironically, doing him more harm than good because he should have been put out of his misery a long time ago through forced retirement. A remote post like the further reaches of Cornwall would only condemn him to a slow drawn-out lonely death whilst subjecting others to his views, which would live on long after him.

Smythington glanced over the letter obviously not for the first time.

"Commander Denniston reminds me in no uncertain terms – and he has been given authority in this case, as I was informed moments before your arrival – that you be allowed to do what you wish to do. However, he is also concerned with any ripples your behaviour may be causing, and advises that I remind you to be cautious."

How like Alistair, she thought, holding back a smile. He could have contacted her through the channels they had established, but his reverence for protocol and for others ensured he took the more circuitous route of writing a letter. Smythington outranked him, but that wasn't a factor in this case, whereas etiquette was.

"He asks that I give you this." With the letter was a sealed envelope that he handed over to Maggie, both having to rise out of their seats to make the exchange and meet half-way. "You are to open and read it in the presence of Wing Commander Gleeson and myself."

The men remained silent as she sat and opened the envelope. An Avro Anson swept past, causing the windows to vibrate with the soft, synchronous beat of its two propellers as it descended to Runway Three. Only Smythington seemed momentarily distracted by it.

"You are smiling, Sergeant," he commented, coming back to the room.

"It's in code, sir," she said, looking up.

"What does it say?" demanded Gleeson.

She couldn't stop her delicate smile as she produced a pencil and proceeded to work it out, which took less than a minute. Denniston had obviously got one of the cryptographers to write the note. It was a basic cryptogram. Her name at the top was the key. The playfulness of the code had been carefully selected to highlight the frivolity of the situation.

It simply stated, 'TELL THE OLD FOOL.'

She understood more than the words. Gleeson would be dealt with in the manner she had surmised. Before that, it was essential to defuse the situation, to play it down, by speaking the truth.

"It says you are to be informed what it is I am doing here," she said, folding the missive, placing it back in the envelope and into her jacket pocket. From the same pocket she produced another piece of paper. This one was entirely different. The men were fascinated as she stretched the paper out to its full length, about a yard, and half-an-inch in thickness. There were capital letters and numbers written along it at random intervals.

"This is a copy of an original coded message that was intercepted here at Clearbrooke…"

"'Intercepted'? By whom, may I ask?" Smythington interrupted.

"An American naval intelligence officer. He found this blowing about on Runway Two near the Bellman."

"He must have been unusually vigilant. I mean…a piece of paper?"

"I believe you are correct, sir. There have been problems in the past with American security. Two years ago the Germans intercepted and managed to interpret vital info between Cairo and Washington. Because of such occurrences, American Intelligence is more than eager to make up for its past mistakes. If anyone other than that officer had seen the paper, they would hardly have bothered to pick it up let alone recognise it for what it was. We have since found more, and suspect there are other discarded attempts around that have not been noticed."

"And what is it?"

"Among other things, this one is a description of squadrons and aircraft operating from here."

"All that on a thin piece of paper? And why so thin?"

"To answer your first question, sir, it's very succinct. To answer your second – " She stood up and faced Gleeson, holding out her hand. "If I may borrow your cane, sir?"

The wing commander glanced at Smythington as if for reassurance, before handing it over to her.

As she stood in front of them, there was no doubt as to who currently commanded the room.

"This is an old medieval coding system known as a skytale. It can only be read by wrapping around the correct hilt of a sword – in our case, a walking stick. We know this from the particles of oak and polish found on the original paper. It could possibly have been something like a table leg but we consider that unlikely because of the amount of dirt also in the paper, and that discarded skytales have since been found at adjacent airfields. The spy is moving around unnoticed, and won't be doing so with a table leg."

She carefully wove the paper around the stick and held it up horizontally.

"As you can see, the letters start to line up more intelligibly. Not completely, because it's the wrong stick."

"So I am in the clear," Gleeson guffawed.

"You were never out of the clear, sir. I admit I couldn't help glancing at the cane when you spoke to me before. It's a bad habit, which I am now trying to control, and for which I apologise. No, I have been tasked specifically to track down an American."

"How do you know they're American?" asked Smythington, who had become more animated since she'd taken the floor.

"He refers to the attempt to camouflage Runway Two with black rubber, spelling the word 'color' without the 'u'. Here." She moved the skytale around till the word appeared clearly. "The other skytales reveal an identical syntax. We are sure he's an American, one who moves around the local airbases with ease, and who has been here for at least a year."

"That's not a lot to go on."

"It is all we have, sir."

Maggie returned the stick to Gleeson then sat down again demurely.

There was silence as the men contemplated what action to take next, then Smythington turned to Gleeson.

"I think that tells us all we need to know – all we *should* know. Do you agree, Wing Commander?"

Gleeson's cheeks blew red as he puffed, considering.

"Yes, sir," he admitted begrudgingly.

"Do you have any more questions for Sergeant Drummond?"

"No, I do not."

"If you could leave us now, Wing Commander, I need to speak privately with her."

Gleeson got to his feet stiffly, put on his hat, and saluted Smythington. Maggie also rose but he was out of the room before she had a chance to salute, though not without one last rebuke.

"Worst bloody spy I've ever met," he grumbled. The door shut with a thud.

Shyly, Maggie sat down again.

"Now, Maggie," Smythington chuckled, settling back in his chair. "He may have a point. You have stood out remarkably. For instance, an unofficial shooting match…?"

"That was simply a group of old chums getting together, sir."

"Is discretion not a prerequisite for espionage?"

"I'm not really a spy, sir."

"Then how did you get the job, may I ask?"

"People knew and trusted me…"

"I see. The old girls' network, is it?"

"Something like that, sir. I'm also very good with puzzles."

"Being affable, charming and a good shot I'm sure are also factors. Well, reading between the lines – " He tapped the letter on his desk. " – Commander Denniston may be regretting having sent you here. Don't take it personally. I get the feeling Bletchley – whatever the hell they do there – does not readily let go of personnel. Indeed, one of the reasons you're here may be that they wish to keep things in the family.

"We're fighting an invisible enemy, and you're in the front line. Me, I prefer my foes in uniform where I can see them. I will of course continue to offer you carte blanche as originally requested; *and* my support, though I doubt you'll require it other than in exceptional circumstances like today. The sooner you complete your mission, the sooner we get you back to Bletchley, and the happier we'll all be. Tell me, if you are able, how close are you?"

Maggie felt a sudden cloud descend over her, one she had been pretending wasn't there for quite some time.

"I'm not, sir. I've been given a list of possible suspects by MI5 but it doesn't seem to be any of them."

"Why are they not more directly involved? Unless they are. I would have thought this was their cup of tea."

"They're favouring a light touch, I believe. I'm not even sure they're taking it that seriously. That the spy is using a skytale, a code a child could break, suggests we're dealing with amateurs."

"Children can cause a lot of damage if unsupervised."

"As far as we can tell, none of the information has been used by the enemy. I'm here to ensure it never gets to that point."

His eyes drifted towards the sunlit window as the sound of a distant engine reached their ears. He looked sad in the rounding off of their interview, as if he were facing a change in his life for which he wasn't quite ready. She had no doubt he would push to get back on the front line and in the air before long.

As she left the office, Maggie felt the relief of direct contact with someone on her side, someone to whom she could talk. The rest of her team seemed vague and far away. As she descended the staircase, the relief was pushed aside by increased pressure from the relentless concerns, and she had to force herself to breathe in order not to pass out.

One thing she hadn't told Spiffy was that the discarded skytales all carried dates. They were discarded because it could be tricky writing cohesively on them, mistakes easily made. But one thing they all had in common was the date, probably of the hand-over, when the spy met with his contact.

The date for this month was the coming Thursday, and expectations were on her, and within her, to find out who it was before then.

Donnel himself had a meeting with the group captain that very Thursday morning. While Maggie was desperately following tenuous leads as distant as the GI camps the other side of Egloston, Donnel was relieved to find a distraction from his more personal unease. He hadn't flown all week, occupying his time with hanging out with Hawker, exploring the countryside or chatting with anyone available, whether ground crew, pilots or civilians. Sandra and he spent most evenings together in the hut, always followed by a walk home and a lingering kiss before the inevitable parting. Once he had tried going further, merely exploratory hands under her blouse but she arrested his fingers two buttons down.

"Steady, tiger," her hot voice sweet with gin upon his neck.

"But…"

She pushed him to arm's length, staring at him in the darkness. "You're still engaged, right?"

"I don't know…" he muttered, looking down at the road.

The meeting at Ravenscroft was comparatively less awkward. Nor was it quite as relaxed as previous meetings with Spiffy, due to the presence of a third person.

Donnel's surprise at seeing the USAAF major wasn't so great that he didn't manage to salute properly.

"Take a seat, Jackie," Smythington smiled. "This is Major Jacobs." There was a lightness between the superior officers, as if they had just shared a joke.

Jacobs's tightly-cropped bright white hair sat upon a large rectangular face that belied his obvious affability and intelligence.

"You're a sight for sore eyes, sir," Donnel couldn't help commenting.

"The Captain's been feeling somewhat neglected," said Smythington.

"All that is about to change, Jackie… May I call you 'Jackie'?" The major had a mild mid-western twang.

"Of course, sir. Everyone does."

"I'm here, in part, to inform you that your isolation is over. I understand you've been living in a hut with one of the locals."

"Flight Lieutenant Smith. Yes, sir, that is correct." He pronounced the rank in the English manner, whilst barely containing his smile. He'd forgotten Smith was the only other official inhabitant. Hawker pretty much lived there at present, Proudon often chose not to go back to the mess, and even Joyce and Sandra had on occasion commandeered bunks for themselves. ("It might even be like this when you're married, mate!" Sandra had yelled across to Smith in the dark from a top bunk, Joyce smiling quietly to herself in the one beneath.) In the past week, Maggie and Hawker's had proven the most gently unassuming of the relationships, and she never stayed too late.

178

"The segregation orders were from above," continued the major. "In part, this was an Air Force/Navy thing. We still don't trust each other entirely, which we're going to have to in order to win this war. Interestin', ain't it, how we and the Brits are learnin' to work together whereas *we* ain't quite figured it out yet! Anyhoo, the long and the short of it, is our Navy needs the hut for accommodation, and you and Smith will be moved elsewhere."

"When, sir?"

"In the next few days. I understand there's a shindig of some sort this weekend."

"Saturday, sir. In Egloston." Maggie had moved fast with the arrangements.

"Let that be your swansong. On Monday you'll be posted elsewhere."

"Can I ask where, sir?"

"That depends." The major's smile was as dazzling as his hair. "How does Fort Lauderdale suit you?"

"That's…"

"Navy. You'll be there on detachment. They'd like to borrow you."

"Why, sir?"

"My opposite in Naval Intelligence has requested you. They're having trouble with navigation over the Bahamas. The equipment doesn't always work. Not sure why. There are Nazi subs there so it's a significant issue. I showed him the reports I received – including the one from the group captain here – regarding your night-time exploits, and he thinks you're what they need."

"Can't you just tell him I eat a lot of carrots?"

"I won't beat about the bush, Jackie. This is a new era of co-operation, and in this case you're the sweetener. I realise you may have formed attachments here, but we'll also make sure you get a few days with your girl in Cali."

"Thank you, sir." Donnel was stirred up, even more uncertain than in the past few days. This was an order masquerading as a request. "Is this why I've been shunted around, Major?"

"Is that how ya regard your vacation?" Oddly, Jacobs didn't smile when making jokes though did for much of the rest of the time. "No, that is related to your actions before we entered the war." He glanced at Smythington, saw that he understood, and continued. "This doesn't leave the room. You were contacted by Colonel Sweeny, weren't you." It wasn't a question so Donnel remained silent, trapped. "You almost made it to Canada but caught sight of the Feds on the train. They did later get hold of papers with your name on them."

As he went silent, smiling broadly, Donnel was aware that they knew everything, and there was nothing to hold back. "I was contacted the same time as the others at Mines Airfield in LA," he admitted. "Tobin and Mamedoff were on a different train. I had to settle things with my family first, so got a later one." Talking about this made Donnel pensive. If the adventure hadn't been curtailed, he wouldn't have met Tallulah in the following weeks.

"My town is full of Germans, and was opposed to us entering the war," the major continued. "As far as I am concerned, you and your pals were doing the right thing. You saw what was coming, and wanted to help, you wanted to fly. The pen-pushers didn't quite see it that way though. Even those who made it here to fight alongside the Brits and the hundreds of other foreign nationals against the Luftwaffe were viewed ambiguously. This is a World War. You knew it then while the politicians were still catching up. In that respect, Captain, you've been an embarrassment and no one knew what to do with you. Now we don't have the luxury of caring about such things."

Seeing that he had finished, Donnel pointed out, "I've been shunted around since arriving in the UK, while others who tried to join up are firmly established in Eagle Squadrons." He was trying not to sound petty or resentful, but the acrimony was evident.

"What can I say, Jackie. You've been caught in a bureaucratic backwater, and things are never quite logical in those places."

"If I go to Florida, will that clear my name?"

"With bells on."

He went for a walk with Sandra around the peri-track that afternoon. He was sullen and thoughtful yet not indisposed to enjoying her company in the sunshine allowed to burst sporadically by the tumbling clouds, as the odd gusts conspired to tug her brown hair loose from out of the kerbigrip. The airfield was tranquil, filled only by birdsong, the distant testing of a Whirlwind engine with its deep-throated rumble and calls between ground crew. By now she was used to his quiet moods, and knew not to take them personally, and that he appreciated her rambling nature.

"Around 'ere they believed Nazi parachutists were amongst 'em, and kept tellin' stories about hairy-handed nuns. Can you believe it?! The funny thing is, back in the Smoke we could take anything Jerry was throwing at us. It was our own government which would cause problems by being too honest with the bad stuff – we couldn't take *that* – so they would relent, and give us more balanced news. The rose-tinted stuff didn't work either. They showed an ability to listen, then respond, which I think is pretty impressive..."

He loved how she could see a far larger picture than most, yet deliver its interpretation in such effervescent manner.

Despite all his concerns, he found himself smiling, letting go.

That evening Maggie joined them all in the hut long after dinner. Hawker and Smith were enjoying making cocktails, coming up with more and more elaborate concoctions, using any supplies – no matter how bizarre – Hawker kept providing miraculously. The ice, the one thing everyone knew the source of, he got from a contact in Ravenscroft.

"This is like engineering," Smith espoused, cigarette dangling, as he checked the vermillion colour of a liquid in a jam jar. "I *love* engineering. Everything makes sense. Various combinations you wouldn't normally conceive of, reveal how wonderfully they work together. Have you seen the Merlin engine? I tell you, it's a thing of beauty."

Maggie took in the scene: Joyce in a deck-chair, fondly watching the boys perform, Donnel and Sandra sitting upright together on the edge of a bunk like a newly-engaged couple, too shy to be demonstrative, all eagerly anticipating the new drinks. Hawker briefly left his duties to give her a kiss.

"Are you all right, Maggie?" asked Joyce. "What are you up to?"

Maggie dropped down in the deck-chair next to her. She looked exhausted.

"Giving up," she said, lighting a cigarette.

Hawker looked over at her whilst applying the final touches to his and Smith's potion. He could see something was wrong but had been aware from the day they met, there were layers in her work of which she didn't talk. He would have to think about the best form of approach. In the meantime, he would ply her with various drinks, just enough to relax – she was always cautious about the amount she drank.

181

The evening went on and the window darkened, so that the main source of light came from a glim light which had been broken and abandoned, then retrieved and fixed by Hawker and Smith. It gave a warm glow from the far wall where it was placed, and deep shadows to the room.

Donnel hadn't told anyone about the changes to come, and delighted in the distraction provided by a mock sword-fight with Smith, while Hawker attended to the gramophone. The women looked on and chatted, the drinks in their hands now viridian with crimson streaks, though barely discernible as such in the strange light. Maggie, remaining forlorn, never inflicted her moods on others if she could help it, and was conversing affably when the sword-fight caught her attention. Donnel was using a long straight piece of wood which hadn't been broken up yet for the stove, and Smith his walking stick.

"I'll teach you upstarts a thing or two!" he cried out. Then, with an adroit side-parry, he mock-pierced Donnel's chest.

"That's me dead," said Donnel, resigned. "Again."

"Bravo to me!" Smith exclaimed, holding up the stick triumphantly. "See, I don't even need this thing to walk with anymore. I disapprove of the word 'hero' but…"

Maggie leapt out of her chair and pounced, snatching the stick away from him.

"Steady on, old girl."

She ran her fingers up and down the stick, examining it closely, almost feverishly. The rest of the room froze, watching her.

"Where did you get this?" she demanded – coolly, despite her fervour.

"From David," Smith, bewildered, answered. "After I chipped my old one poking it in an engine…"

"*He's* given up," she said aloud without meaning to, throwing her cigarette on the floor then, whilst rushing to retrieve her jacket from the back of her chair: "When was he in the States?"

"As a teenager, I think," Joyce said, looking on with concern. "Then he came back to join the Air Force. Didn't you know…?"

Everyone became more baffled when, deciding action now took precedence over subterfuge, she produced the long slip of paper and wound it around the stick. Satisfied, sober, she gave the cane back to Smith.

"I have to go now," she said firmly, putting her jacket and hat on, and the paper back in the jacket. "Does anyone know where Squadron Leader Proudon might be?"

"Try the Officer's Mess," said Hawker, feeling awkward, like an onlooker, when he wanted to help, be involved.

"Ravenscroft?"

"No. In Crapstone. He was going to meet some friends."

"Look after the stick," she said. "I'll be back for it."

She had become almost oblivious to what was around her, thinking solely about the errors which had led to everyone missing Proudon. She assumed his parents were English, as was his accent. She was furious that he wasn't on the list MI5 had given her, and more furious with herself, that he – along with that blasted stick – was right under her nose the whole time.

She left without another word.

The atmosphere in the hut was at first tense and rife with speculation. Not so with Hawker, who smilingly embarked on another chemical experiment.

"Are you all right, Ben?" Joyce came up and put her arm around his shoulders.

"Ahhm fine," he declared cheerily. "My girl will be fine too. She knows what she's doing."

Donnel wasn't convinced. He sensed a disturbance around, something he could play a part in fixing. Under the pretence of taking a leak, he went outside and crossed the peri-track. Leaping over the fence, he made his way to the community area at Crapstone.

Without a cap or jacket, he was under-dressed and he kept to the shadows whenever a vehicle came by with its shaded headlights.

He hadn't yet got to the site entrance before a particular jeep caught his attention. On seeing it approach, he slipped into a gateway, catching a glimpse of its driver as it swept by.

It was Proudon, visible under the delicate light of the waning moon, looking resolute, staring straight in front with unnaturally wide eyes.

Donnel went on to the site, and was working out a plausible way to get past the lax security, when another car shot out and towards him. There was enough light now from the buildings' lights to see clearly that it was a Hillman Minx.

He stepped out in front of it, holding up his hands.

It screeched to a halt.

"Jackie? What are you doing?" yelled Maggie, leaning out the window. Her hair hadn't been tied back since leaving the hut, and her face looked ghostly white under the moon.

"I know where he's gone."

"Where?"

"I'll have to show you."

Before she could say anything, he was around the side and leaping into the passenger's seat.

"Keep going," he said, slamming the door, and pointing straight ahead. "He's not far."

"What do you know about this?" she demanded as she pushed into first and they took off.

"Only that you work for Intelligence in some capacity, you've realised David Proudon is the guy you've been looking for, and – going by your urgency – he has a rendezvous tonight."

"Where?"

"I'll show you. Keep going. Head towards Plymouth."

"I kept missing him, then he was gone. You saw him then?"

"A few minutes ago. I thought he looked a bit…deranged."

Neither of them spoke as they passed the turn-off to the hut then, skirting the airfield, shot past Ravenscroft and onto the Plymouth Road. Donnel mused that till this point it was the reverse of the journey he had taken with Corporal King, that misty day of his arrival, a lifetime ago.

"How far?" Maggie asked nervously.

"Not far at all," Donnel answered, leaning forward. He didn't question the veracity of his hunch. He was certain. He felt it in his gut. The only problem was the lack of signposts. He'd be more secure in the air, with a compass. "There," he said. "Turn left."

She did so. "Where are we?"

"If I'm right, this is the official entrance of a decoy airfield. Proudon will have chosen the unofficial one, but it will be easier to sneak up this way."

"I didn't even know it was here."

"I only know about it from Trevor. Clearbrooke's never been under attack, so it hasn't been used. You can't even see it from the train which passes right across."

"They don't work," she said sourly. "Once the Luftwaffe knew of their existence, they used them as guides to the real airfields."

"The perfect location for a secret rendezvous, don't you think? There. That must be the OR."

An unassuming building crouched a few yards back from the road, amongst some trees.

"Most of it must be underground," she observed as they pulled in, and drew to a halt. She killed the engine and the lights. "The way they're supposed to draw fire, I should hope so. They'll have heard us arrive though. From what Trev told me, the side-entrance to the dummy buildings and planes is south-west from here. We can walk."

"No," she said firmly. She reached into her door's hidden compartment, and pulled out the gun. "I need you to deal with whoever is here officially. Just hold them off for a bit."

They got out the car, closing the doors quietly. He looked at the adjacent building in the darkness.

"Nobody's coming," he said. "They've probably got the wireless on."

"Stay here," she commanded, and left, holding the pistol at arm's length.

He watched her fade into the darkness, looked at the motionless building in front, decided he was bored, and went after her.

In the faint moonlight, dimmed by a rippling veil of grey cloud, Maggie could see the shapes of planes nearby. Her eyes were good enough so that she could also see some of them were merely bits of scaffolding covered with canvas and on trolleys of some sort. Other planes looked more convincing.

The buildings were a similar mix of substance and fabrication, yet even the real ones often lacked doorways or windows. Everything here seemed devoid of logic, of purpose.

She moved carefully from one building to the next, inching along the walls, weapon at the ready, listening for any sound that didn't belong. So far all she had heard were scurryings in the undergrowth, presumably rats, a call from a bird she couldn't identify and an aircraft's engines in the distance. Everything was still, not even a breeze.

Then she heard a sound that didn't quite fit. She couldn't make out what it was.

It was coming from a building at the end, a few yards along.

Fully alert, heart beating wildly in her chest, she began to feel foolish. Who knew what she would find, how many people, how well-armed?

185

Too far gone to go back, repressing her fears, she got to the doorway – a real one, though without a door.

Someone was inside, making the sound.

Before allowing herself to hesitate, she stepped inside, holding the gun straight in front with both hands.

The sound was louder, and from the next room.

She stepped very carefully across the rubbish-strewn floor, aided by the dim moonlight shining through the broken rafters.

She went boldly into the room, pointing the gun – simultaneously flicking off the safety – at the huddled shape in the corner.

The sounds were of a low keening with occasional sobs and incoherent ramblings.

"Squadron Leader Proudon?"

He looked up at her voice. His moon-white face was that of another person, one of the dead. He didn't see her as he looked in her direction. His moaning continued.

"Squadron Leader Proudon, you are under arrest."

"He doesn't hear you," said Donnel behind.

Unsurprised by his presence, and somewhat relieved, she lowered her weapon.

"He's not coming, your contact," she said to the broken man. "He hasn't been coming for a long time, has he?"

Proudon didn't answer but resumed muttering to himself, and staring at his cap which lay amongst all the other discarded bits of rubbish at his feet.

Then he went silent.

"Sir?" she said anxiously. "David?"

"There's no one there," said Donnel.

6

Dancing

The following morning Donnel was once again in the station commander's office, facing the same two individuals as before.

"That's quite a brouhaha you got involved in last night, Jackie," said Major Jacobs.

"Yes, sir, it was."

He was exhausted. Maggie had a pair of handcuffs secreted in a pocket, and insisted on using them on Proudon, then taking him back to a secure location in Plymouth. This was followed by phone calls, waking up officials in the middle of the night, lots of waiting and several interviews. This one, taking place immediately they returned to Clearbrooke, was hopefully the tail-end.

"He was one of Kennedy's," the major confided. "We can't prove it but when the ambassador was in London he implemented a spy network that was feeble and short-lived."

"So Proudon wasn't a German spy then."

"Far from it. As you know, Joe Kennedy opposed us getting involved in the war and we suspect was one of a group establishing a way to keep an eye on the Brits. They were part of a larger network extending to the military and government. Charles Lindbergh belonged to the clan,"

"Lindbergh, huh?"

"Yup. He looked into using sea-planes against the Brits at Hudson Bay." Jacobs looked over to Smythington, grinning both at the misguidedness of the past, and with a sense of daring, that he was actually saying all this in front of the previous supposed enemy. "You wrote a letter to him as a kid," he said, turning back to Donnel.

"Yes, sir," Donnel admitted, beyond surprise now. "He was one of the reasons I learned to fly. This network must have been pretty big."

"It sure was. Fuelled by paranoia, or prudence, depending how you view it. They suspected Britain of being resentful of America's rise in power. However justified or not, clowns like Lindbergh, Kennedy and Proudon seem to have been the order of the day. This whole thing here was half-assed and an embarrassment. Proudon must have been the only operative still left."

They were interrupted by the phone ringing. Smythington picked it up. "I'll come out and have a word with him," he said to the receptionist, then put the phone down. "Excuse me, chaps, I just have to deal with an unrelated matter outside. This is all a bit too Barking Creek for me anyhow."

As he left, Jacobs chuckled at the exhausted Donnel. "Quite a brouhaha," he repeated. "But you see how your connection with Lindbergh further muddied your waters."

"Not really, sir. I was just a kid."

"Yeah, I really don't know why they call us Intelligence sometimes. You know how we interrogate someone? We threaten, we intimidate, we beat the bejeezus out of them, pardon my French. You know how the Brits do it? The smart ones anyway. They trick the person without laying a hand on 'em. It's an art form, a joy to watch. You and I, we're guests here, and we have a few lessons to learn. I suggest we make the most of it."

Donnel was about to reply that the education was probably reciprocal but felt churlish, and remained quiet. The major was suddenly pensive and resumed talking, whilst smiling broadly.

"But don't be fooled neither," he said. "There's another side to the Brits, one that makes the Gestapo look like Boy Scouts, despite the tea and biscuits."

He was interrupted when Smythington came back. The three men resumed chatting, for that was all it was, part of the epilogue necessary to tie up some loose ends. The remaining part was with two men from MI8 in another room downstairs, that proved remarkably straightforward once it was established everyone was on the same page.

He found Maggie waiting for him in the foyer when he was leaving. She stood up on seeing him. They couldn't speak at first, and merely looked at each other. She was also exhausted but properly attired for once, her hair tied back and her hat in place. He was in the same clothes as when he had left the hut twelve hours earlier.

"He must have had a lot of problems back home," Donnel whispered, aware of individuals milling around, curious.

"I don't think anyone cares about that right now," she whispered back then, taking him by the arm, led him outside to the sunless, still morning.

"He was our friend," he insisted, louder once they were alone.

"Not a very close one," she said realistically. "He mostly just slept a lot."

"We should have noticed something was wrong."

"I'm sure he'll get the help he needs," she said in a calmer tone. "We can visit him after the war."

"I'm headed back to the States," he confided, as much to change the subject as anything.

She was surprised. "When?"

"Next week. The officer who told me suggested your little party tomorrow be my swansong."

"Have you told Sandra?"

"I haven't told anyone except you. There's more. Trevor will be moved to the mess, and the hut used for more American sailors. It's the end of beetroot cocktails for you guys, and back to boiled cod and horse-meat."

"Ben?"

"I guess he'll go back to sleeping in the trees. Or with you."

"We'll all have to exchange addresses," she said, ignoring him. "I'm also going next week."

"Where?"

"We have to decide what to tell the others," she insisted, still ignoring him.

"Easy. We tell them there was a ruckus involving David we can't discuss. They'll accept that. Then we distract them with all the other news. Besides, we've got a party to plan."

She sighed. Could life ever really be that simple?

Sandra accepted the imposed clampdown regarding the previous night's drama. Remaining silent throughout, at the time, she had anyway felt herself a mere witness to events whose outcome was already written, involving things that didn't concern her. Jackie could tell her after the war, she decided.

It was their habit now to walk together along the peri-track around lunchtime. He had managed to get some sleep, and thought he'd be prepared to tell her about his imminent departure. He now found he wasn't prepared, nor did the secrecy around the previous

189

evening serve as a distraction, as he'd hoped. Fortunately, she was on a roll.

"Sometimes the siren would go and there'd be no planes, sometimes there'd be planes and no sirens. The worst shelters were damp and full of litter, smoking, couples shagging, kids spewing mucous, and wardens scaring the crap out of us all. The good ones had community-minded wardens who got us singing so much we couldn't sleep. Then there were the people who would hog space, using bedding to stake their claims." She fell silent, then resumed in a sadder, less furious tone. "You would often see the homeless wandering without shelter. And you would get rich motorists with empty cars refusing to give lifts. Then people started blaming the Jews. I was glad my family left to go hop-picking in Kent. They've gone back, they liked it so much."

She glanced up at him shyly, and he put his arm around her for as long as he could without them being seen. He loved listening to her voice, mellifluous with its abrupt shifts of tone. For such a rebel, she looked surprisingly neat in her sky-blue uniform, shirt-sleeves rolled up in the subdued warmth. Her clothes and her face seemed the brightest things around.

They forewent lunch in order to circumvent the entire airfield, not even stopping at the hut. He left her at the squadron offices, and they parted, both in high spirits; that in Donnel's case relegated the guilt for his lack of candour to a remote, dark place which he could comfortably – mostly – forget.

Sandra found Joyce waiting for her in the office with Squadron Leader Francis. They were both standing by the desk, looking somewhat jovial and, paradoxically, uncertain.

"What's happening?" Sandra asked, closing the door behind her.

"How would you and Joyce like to accompany me to Malta, as part of my admin team?" asked Francis.

The two women were so full of the news, and its uncertain implications, they spilled it out to the others as soon as they arrived in the hut that evening, in what was to be their last gathering. While they were doing so, restlessly pacing back and forth, gesticulating wildly as if in some thespian roles – a show meant predominantly for the men in their lives – Maggie shot a telling glance at Donnel, and he confessed, with occasional glances of shame at Sandra.

"The truth is," he said, to allay his conscience, "we're all headed to different places."

"I'm not," said Smith.

"I probably am," Hawker muttered. "I just don't know where yet. Maybe I'll stay in England. After all, they did name an aeroplane after me."

"At least you're going somewhere beautiful," Maggie said to Sandra in particular, who looked in need of consolation.

"Yeah, great," Sandra responded, quickly lighting a cigarette. "I 'ope the screams don't distract me when I'm lyin' on the flippin' beach."

Donnel made to comfort her but she shrugged his arm away. She was being unreasonable, he thought, pouring himself another drink and sitting down. After all, she too was leaving.

Maggie found Hawker the next morning in Yelverton Post Office. He was posting dead pheasants by tying address labels to their legs.

"For my pals in Suffolk," he explained.

"Does that work?"

"They always get there. How did you find me?"

"I also have connections," she smiled as they emerged into the sunlit air. "Jackie told me."

"Are they all right?"

"I think so. He walked her home as usual. Anyway, can I be your CO this afternoon? Who *is* your CO? All this time, and I still haven't been able to work that out."

"That will be *my* secret," he grinned. He looked particularly dapper in his uniform this day, she thought, his buttons neatly polished and hat on straight. "What do you need?"

"I need you to rally some help for the dance tonight. These things run themselves by and large, so it won't be a lot. Certainly to help clear up afterwards. Sandra, Joyce and I are busy preparing something this afternoon for an hour but we'll be there by four. We could do with a hand then. There's another dance at Tavistock, which I'm hoping will take away some of the pressure." What she hadn't told anyone was that her initial rush to make the dance happen was motivated mostly by the need to cast a wider net out into American waters. She had known about the dance in Tavistock and calculated that that was where most of the British fish would swim.

This knowledge was not what made her quiet, peering at him under her peak.

"You're sure you've got my details written down?   Both addresses. It might be months before we get to see each other."

"Don't worry, Maggie. I'll always find you." He smiled in that way he had so that she couldn't quite tell how serious he was being. "When does the fun begin tonight?"

Officially the fun began at seven.   Unofficially people began to arrive long before that, many of whom were commandeered by Maggie to help set up.

It was generally acknowledged that children were allowed in for the early part of the evening.   Maggie suspected that that rumour had been spun by homesick Americans, who came before six with local families they had befriended.   Donnel was well up to the occasion and cheerily administered candy to a group of little girls who thought he was a film star.   He and others started teaching the children to jitterbug.   The band, having secretly partaken of some Devon cider, was slightly tipsy and welcomed the early start.

Donnel was engaged in teaching the right moves to a happy plump nine-year old when a voice sung like crystal in his ears.

"Can I cut in?"

He stood up straight to see Sandra dressed in a white rayon dress that flowed like silk down her ripe body, with filigree lace upon her neck and shoulders.   On her head was a teal net holding waves of her lustrous hair in place, and on her feet white high-heeled shoes.   The effect of the clothing was to frame, to enhance her lightly tanned skin, her luminous brown eyes and forthright smile.

"Sandra...I..."   They had parted after a brief, awkward fumbling the night before.   Now, everything he wanted to say, or felt he should say, was swallowed by her presence.

"You're a very pretty lady," said the girl. "Even your shoes are white!"

"A friend lent them to me," Sandra said, looking down. "I'm Sandra.   What is your name?"

She was drawn in rapidly by the attentions of the excited children, and she and Donnel reigned in a colourful court of games and spontaneity, aided by the occasional delivery of more candy from Hawker.

The couple still hadn't danced together by the time the children were called home, and Maggie pulled Sandra through the now-crowded dance hall, towards the stage where they were meeting with Joyce.

"Our women are looking *fine!*" Hawker proclaimed as he and Smith came and stood next to Donnel.

Maggie, of course, was as elegant as ever in an understated aquamarine dress and a black Bolero jacket; but Joyce easily matched her in a black strap-less gown with a lace neckline and sleeves, that complemented Sandra's ensemble.

"I think they've been working together on this," Donnel commented, well aware he and Hawker were wearing the same suits as the Saturday before.

"That's not the only thing they've been working together on," Smith responded as the women headed on to the stage. "Hey, do you notice we're sort of the odd ones out, Jackie?"

Donnel, looking around to see what he meant, realised for the first time the dance floor was dominated by black American servicemen. Officially, thanks no doubt to Maggie's inveiglements, it was not actually a military dance and many, but not all, of them were in civvies.

"Yeah, how did that happen? Most of the Brits here are women."

"It's Gunnislake's turn for a night out in Egloston," said Hawker drily, as the band finished its number. "The camps take turns to avoid trouble."

"And Clearbrooke? I see only a few of our colleagues here," Donnel said, slightly uncomfortable.

"They all went to the dance at Tavy 'cos it's rumoured they're serving booze there."

"Are they?"

"No."

The three men started chuckling at the whole comedy of things, when the lively music started.

It was Joyce taking the lead.

"It all began in a cabana in Havana..."

Her voice sang out clearly, soaring above the band and the hall's multitudinous chatterings. People were divided, whether to respond to the song's infectious beat and dance, or to stay still and watch the show.

By the time Sandra and Maggie joined into the chorus, most had opted for dancing – it was hard not to. Among the exceptions were the three men who couldn't take their eyes off the stage.

"Yah yah he would serenade on his guitar…"

"Joyce is really really good," Donnel said aside to Smith.

"They're all really good," was the reply as the girls sang the chorus in turns, playing off each other's turns.

"Yi yi, yi yi…I remember when we kissed goodbye…"

It was true, they were an impressive force combined. Certainly, Joyce came alive on the stage in a way that outshone her friends; but they were all so harmonised in colour and sound, they each shone the brighter.

"…far away from a cabana in Havana."

They ended together on a glorious finish with the band, and to rapturous applause from the crowd.

The band leader stepped forward.

"Thank you to The Clearbrooke Girls. And now for all you go-getters out there…"

The girls exited the stage as the band launched into 'Take the A-Train.'

Donnel was aware of nothing but Sandra as she came before him, shining, and he put out his hand.

"Would you care to dance?" he said.

Smith was Orderly Officer the day after the dance. His duties included, among other things, saluting the flag at reveille, and inspecting lunch at the airmen's mess. With all that, plus another Walrus to scrub down, and he and Joyce spending the night away at a B'n'B – she borrowed a wedding ring for the endeavour – it was late afternoon and he was exhausted before he managed to track down Donnel, who was smoking whilst admiring a Whirlwind being worked on in one of the dispersal bays.

On seeing Smith approach, his limp painfully in evidence after so much rushing about, Donnel offered him a cigarette. Smith ignored him.

"I was at the squadron office this morning," he declared, gazing at Donnel forcefully, brushing away sweat from under his eyes. "What happened with you and Sandra?"

"What do you mean?" Donnel responded defensively.

"Her eyes are red from crying, there's an atmosphere thick as porridge around her. Joyce doesn't know. Sandra won't talk to her about it."

"Nothing happened."

Donnel was telling the truth. Even his fumbling had been half-hearted as they'd kissed goodnight, Sandra dissuading him easily with a light brush of her hand.

"Well, she's really upset about something, and when she is, so is Joyce." Smith looked at him with suspicion. He approved of plain speech, and had a sense it was something unspoken causing the rift, which made him uncomfortable.

"What is your intention towards her?" he demanded.

"'Intention'?" Donnel too was feeling increasingly uneasy, not least because of the look in Smith's eye.

"Have you committed one way or the other?"

"I'm still engaged to Tallulah."

"Then you've made that clear to Sandra?"

"No, and it's none of your damned business."

"You can't keep her dangling, man! What the dickens are you up to?"

"Nothing with her, that's for sure."

"What do you mean by that?"

"Her knees are locked together."

Both men were riled up, but it was Smith who finally relinquished control and did what he had never done and never would again. He punched Donnel on the jaw dead on, so that Donnel – taken by surprise – fell backwards onto the ground.

Those working on the plane, already alerted by the raised voices, stopped what they were doing, part-amused, part-apprehensive at the sight of two officers dropping any veneer no matter how briefly.

Smith limped away.

Donnel sat up, nursing his jaw, watching him go.

The last partaking of tea together was conducted with all the frills, much to Heinrich and Naomi's delight. "I hope we qualify for the same treatment when we go," Heinrich said, lifting a pinkie as he sipped his Lady Grey. They were not to leave for another three days. This was Duncan's farewell, and with the home-made scones, cream and jam, it was the full works. The only thing missing was George who, after placing the scones in the oven, had dashed off to Yelverton for a last-minute meeting with Dave Allen.

"So, Duncan," Naomi said, probing gently, "do you think you might settle down in Cornwall?"

Duncan flushed. "No, I, well... Settling down didn't really work well for me..."

"Are you talking about your marriage?" Kay scoffed. "Duncan, you had twenty years or so together, a successful career, and two wonderful children. Don't be so dismissive."

"I rather enjoyed my adventures abroad," he said, piling the cream and jam on a scone in a gravity-defying way.

Kay was doubtful. He had never seemed so lost.

"Without our so-called burdens we fly all over the place, at nature's whim. Perhaps at one level you always knew this."

"Yes," Duncan mused, "one can change train carriages to escape inconsiderate passengers, only to find oneself with another set of inconsiderate passengers." He might have lost his audience were it not for the sight of half a scone with three storeys of butter, cream and jam disappearing into his mouth. As a teacher, he had always understood the benefit of visual aids.

"I believe that is what the Americans call 'leftfield'," observed Heinrich.

Duncan was avoiding further discussion by eating. The New Age therapists would talk about how being alone was playing it safe. He didn't find it safe at all. As a single man he was always under suspicion, or supposition, and others' moods and opinions would hit him like savage gusts of wind to and fro. People were very eager to shout their views to the radio, however informed, whereas now he was seeking quietude. They'd talk about being settled; well, he was decidedly unsettled. After all the dramas, perhaps the true challenge was to live life anonymously, as an ordinary individual. He carried on eating.

"I wouldn't allow the scandal of your affair to sabotage an excellent career," said a concerned Kay.

"What scandal?" asked Duncan, licking his finger and looking uncertainly around the room. The other three were astonished.

"The...eh..." The revelation struck Kay that he didn't even know about the newspapers.

"With Evelyn? No one's really bothered with that. Except Rose, and her friends. That type of thing happens all the time."

"But you had to leave the university..."

"Mostly because of my views."

"Your *views*?"

"Yes. The past is always divisive, don't you think? One can perceive that division from the last war: the fair-minded Brits torturing prisoners in the glass prison of Kensington, or conveniently neglecting Polish pilots after the war, Americans refusing to honour the 333rd battalion of black soldiers..."

"Everyone has some dirt on their walking stick," Heinrich observed.

"That isn't history so much as human shortcomings," Naomi objected sweetly.

"That's exactly my point," he said, going on to another scone. "There has to be something better, a more inclusive perspective."

The audience's bafflement was interrupted by the sound of the car on the gravel outside, then George entering the house hurriedly. He clattered about briefly in the hall then came in to the sitting room.

"The tea and scones are still warm," said Kay, "and you're just in time to hear about Duncan's radical new shift in historical perspectives."

"Yes, I mentioned to Dave that your next book focuses on an incident in the Middle Ages," George said, sitting down on the couch next to his wife. "I hope that's okay."

"Of course." Duncan shrugged, more focused on the scone.

"He's kind of obsessed with that era. I had no idea. He seems to have that what they call Golden Age thinking going on."

"Is he well?" queried Kay.

"He was annoying me, truth be told." When George had suggested Kay was reacting to wireless signals, the ex-GP had guffawed. "But I got what I needed to see him about." He nodded mysteriously at his brother. "Look, I know your birthday isn't until next week but Duncan's leaving and.... Well, come."

He stood, held his hand out to Kay and escorted her into the hallway where there was a large black 1940s style phone on the table alongside a vase of fresh wild flowers. Underneath the table was an open cardboard box with the old cordless phone thrown in.

"Let's go the whole hog and slow things down a bit. It was actually Duncan's idea, and it's from both of us. Now you can take the time to sit down, make yourself comfortable and talk as long as you like."

"Was this what you were seeing Dave about?" she asked wondrously, amused.

197

"Yes. I had them deliver it to his place to keep it a secret. Stupid really, unnecessary, as in the end I couldn't wait. Hope that's all right, Dunc."

The others, having followed, were standing by the door, enjoying the scene.

"Of course," Duncan shrugged again before returning to the tea and scones.

"It's actually digital," George said as Kay lifted the receiver and listened to the dialling tone. "Best of both worlds."

"I'm going to love this," she said.

As Kay was going on to her macramé class later, she volunteered to take Duncan to the station. At the last minute he was due for a panic about the lack of food in his pockets. She brought him into the kitchen and placed a packet of oatcakes in his hand.

"Whenever you feel a hypoglycaemic attack coming on, eat some of these. The oats give a sustained sugar release, whereas refined sugar simply makes matters worse."

Duncan smiled fondly at her. "May you always block my objections with your suggestions, Kay."

The other three crowded into the kitchen. George presented him with a bottle of Islay malt.

"This is from all of us," he said, "to wish you good luck in your journey."

"I...um..."

"You don't have room in your luggage? Naomi's already taken care of that." Duncan could see she was holding his wax coat and hat. "Between you and me," George proclaimed loudly, "I suspect she was a secret agent in a past life."

"George said they'll bring the coat along with all your books when they visit in two weeks," Naomi said demurely.

"I doubt you'll need it for several weeks at least," said George. "You look much smarter in your charity shop sports jacket anyhow."

After a moment's reflection and gratitude that he hadn't attempted to pack his confidante, the rock, Duncan looked at them all in turn, aglow.

"Thank you. Thank you all so much."

At the station Kay insisted on accompanying him into the forecourt, as he bought his ticket. "This could be a new start for you," she said, before he went through the barrier. "Cornwall is different, not at all like England in some ways. Apparently there's even a VAT-registered witch down there."

Duncan laughed, kissed her on the cheek and left. He was only a few paces on when he turned without knowing why. Kay had gone swiftly. In another part of the forecourt, a young woman, tall and slim, with long dark hair, marched across from the café. He couldn't rely on his vision, but his heart responded how it had always done.

He squinted. She was wearing a red top and jean-shorts. She stepped out through the doors and vanished in a blaze of sunshine. His heart quickly saddened, at all his lost causes past and future, he proceeded wearily to the correct platform.

He sat alone and disconsolate on a wooden bench in the shade. In the ten minutes it took for the train to arrive he managed to create all manner of tangles within himself. He teased the threads, he undid them, then tied them up again in more complex arrangements without meaning to. As was the case for so many, he was stuck in a logic loop – but what was it? His parting from his friends had been gracious enough, so what unsettled him?

For a start, he could argue that he had no real friends. The university lot had shown their true colours. Admittedly, he got on well with women in general without being particularly close to one. Perhaps Kay and Naomi eventually, it was hard to tell.

Then the male friends, they were even worse. There was no brotherhood, no camaraderie. The one thing a man did was watch your woman, looking for chinks in the armour of love. For all his many faults, Duncan could safely say that that was one thing he had never done even when he had been in the playing field.

He sighed. There was also the fact that beyond friendship he did miss romance, no matter how illusory. He seemed destined to appreciate the subtle sexlessness of people as he grew older. He had always believed that once you gave up on women you gave up on life. His resentment of that transcendence echoed a hard core of darkness within him. He sighed again. It was probably just as well he no longer had much to do. Everyone had their role to play, no matter if that role were minor and lacked glamour. Anyway, to be centre stage all the time was exhausting.

The train arrived. It was only two carriages and looked as if it had been made by sticking two buses together. Passengers got off, and passengers got on, including Duncan. The interior was different from what he was used to, more chaotic, the seats at unexpected right angles to each other.

He managed to get his cases into an overhead rack, puffing heavily with the exertion, then found a seat in the far corner. The little train was filling up rapidly but the seats in front and next to him remained empty. He took a bottle of water from one jacket pocket, and a paperback copy of a Conrad novel out of the other. He didn't open the book, merely taking a sip from the water as the train rattled across the Severn Bridge. The view was glorious, and quite a few of the passengers exclaimed, delighted by the rolling, glistening waters beneath. Duncan couldn't help noticing most of those thus moved were tourists, particularly an ebullient family a few seats away. Yet some of the locals were also taking in the scene in quiet appreciation.

They were in Cornwall and rumbled to a halt in Saltash. Only one person was getting out from the carriage, a young diminutive woman with shoulder-length dark hair and a backpack. It was something beyond her appearance that was admirable, a strength, a courage. She was travelling alone. Admittedly, England wasn't yet so devoid of law and order that she was in mortal danger. Still, something about the girl struck Duncan as courageous, far-sighted. She got out, alone on the platform. To where? What had drawn her to this remote spot?

The train lurched on and his attention was taken by the moving landscape, and the noisy family's appreciation of it. A field of cows couldn't be passed without comment and yells of delight. They were loud, but it was a benign noise, one couldn't help but be drawn in. After ten miles most of the carriage knew numerous details of the family's life back in London, and was sharing their ecstatic holiday adventure.

As they approached Liskeard any melodious impressions Duncan had of his environment began to waver. The harbinger of this weather change was a woman who started talking loudly on her phone, more loudly and persistently than the London family. Duncan could see her near the door, focused entirely on the invisible person at the other end of the call, subjecting everyone around to her inexorable monologue. Her signal was cut off frequently at various places along the track. Each time she would panic, yelling at and hitting the phone until connection was regained. It was puzzling, as the content of the conversation sounded banal and trivial. To Duncan it was akin to watching a baby on a teat.

The second harbinger was purely visual, a young man across the aisle, diagonally opposite from Duncan, the only other passenger in the immediate area. Having noticed him, Duncan tried ignoring him, which shouldn't have been difficult as the man wasn't actually doing anything. It was the fact he wasn't doing anything that was the problem. He was simply sitting there, staring at the wall, chewing gum, mouth open, his metal-framed glasses reflecting the light and contributing to his glazed expression. The blank remorselessness of existence was too much to bear. Duncan found it profoundly unsettling.

A sudden shout diverted his attention, and a new player entered the scene. It was a young woman again, emaciated and with short red hair. At first she appeared to be having a fit, shouting and waving her arms in the air wildly, easily trumping the other woman for spectacle. Duncan was about to get up and see if he could help, when the surrealism of nobody around reacting in any way whatsoever, stayed him; at which point, he realised she was on the phone and using an earpiece.

His journey started entering its crescendo when they got to Liskeard and the seats around him filled up. The three opposite were occupied by a man in a black suit listening to music, staring out the window, unconcerned with his fellow passengers – and two strapping youths with khaki shorts and shirts, neat fair hair and golden-brown skin. The teenage girl who had come with the boys took the seat across the aisle from Duncan and started reading a book. By this time, in his journey from admiration to repulsion, he was already considerably wound up, viewing those around with suspicion. An explosion of some sort was definitely due.

Surrounded by this day's representation of youth, Duncan was resolved not to be involved, despite his wont. As far as he was concerned, modern teenagers were a lot like thick wooden boxes, hollow but making a lot of bothersome noise when you struck them with well-aimed words. He opened his book and started to read. At least none of the newcomers were using phones, so he wasn't about to be immersed further into a barrage of electronic soup, invention being the mother of necessity. In the background, he could still hear the two women, joined now by a male baritone also indulging in banalities, about filing systems on his computer at home.

Any false security was soon belied by the youths' lack of restraint in volume and subject matter. After a cursory look at the squat podgy man with a pencil-moustache in front of them, they started talking about pornography, and it was all they talked about. More specifically, it concerned what they had watched that morning.

Duncan's mounting distaste for what he was hearing defied analysis. It probably wasn't one thing that nauseated him. It wasn't just their educated, middle-class voices swollen with arrogance and privilege. It wasn't the details of what they were describing, he had read old texts that would make Chaucer blush. Nor was it their facile misogyny disguised as frankness, boys being boys, who one day would become men being boys. It was probably all these things combined. The tipping point, however, was almost definitely the sight of the petite girl across the aisle, disappearing more and more into her book, black hair masking her face.

"Excuse me, miss," he leant across to her.

She looked up, surprised. She had porcelain skin, a few freckles and a small sharp nose, giving him the impression of someone both sensitive and perceptive.

"Are you connected in any way to the two gentlemen here?"

"Yes," she said tentatively, indicating the one furthest away, the smaller of the two. "That's my brother."

The gentlemen in question, alert that something different was occurring, fell silent, muscles tensing with anticipation.

"Well, I have to ask, are you in any way uncomfortable with what they are discussing?"

"I...eh..." Her eyes flickered from her brother to his friend then back to Duncan, as she smiled unconvincingly.

"I'm just curious how you *feel* about their attitude."

"Hey, old man," said the friend, "keep your fat arse out of this. It's nothing to do with you."

"Ahh but it is. For I am present. Anyway..." He turned back to the girl.

"I...eh...well, they don't talk about me that way," she ventured.

"Of course not!" protested the brother. The businessman next to him, uncomfortably aware something was occurring, shot wary glances at the group before turning back to the window. It was dawning upon him that he might have chosen the wrong place to sit.

"So, in your opinion, do you believe it is all right to talk about women generally that way?" continued the inexorable force that was Duncan.

"Hey, old man," the bigger boy kicked Duncan's shoe. "I bet you watch porn, you dirty old git."

"Loads of it," said the girl's brother, grinning.

"So don't start getting all high-and-mighty with us."

"Please desist from kicking my shoe in future," said Duncan calmly, eager for the discussion to continue. "And pornography is not the issue here. That is a subject for another day. I am calling into question your attitude, young man."

"What do you know? You probably don't even have a phone. The world's moved on, you know. People aren't as uptight as they used to be."

"Yeah, stupid old fool," echoed the brother, his healthy face leering contemptuously. "I bet you're on benefits or something too."

All three had by now forgotten the girl, who had at least in part been the silent catalyst. She watched the drama unfold with tremulous interest. The raised voices were now drawing attention from further afield, as the degree of menace became palpable. Even the woman having the phone fit had paused in her gyrations to pay attention. Only the businessman by the window was still pretending not to hear as they entered the forest in Fowey Valley, and he suddenly found the lines of trees to be of unparalleled interest.

The last insult was well-aimed, and hit Duncan where it hurt.

"I will have you know, I am a reputable historian," he declared.

"So, what?" glared the larger boy. "Are you on a quest for the Charter of Runnymede or something? I hate to tell you, mate, but you're on the wrong train."

"You pompous little whipper-snapper," came the explosion finally. "You think you know everything, and can do whatsoever you want?" Duncan stood up to his full height, much to the boys' amusement. "You are simply the product of a privileged, smug and chauvinistic economy. You haven't an original thought in your head. Your moral compass is set by the vacuousness of the media, and your insipid arts reflect that with agonising accuracy. Your assessment of genius is inspired by that performing monkey school you call 'Britain's Got Sex Factor'. Your ethics are governed by pure hedonism at any cost or sacrifice, as long as it's that of others…"

"Oh shut up you old fool!"

"What's going on back there?" a new voice piped up.

This belonged to a small man who looked like a police inspector on holiday. He was seated by the door and had got up to investigate.

Duncan wandered over to plead his case.

"Do you not think, sir, that the youth of today lack proper guidance?"

"What I think is that it is you causing all this hullabaloo." The man was perhaps a good ten years younger, but with his thin clean-shaven jaw and rigid gaze acted much older, and with more certainty, than Duncan.

"Hear hear," said someone else.

The two boys had now also got to their feet.

"I think there might be something wrong with him," said the brother loudly, pointing their way.

"We'd better call the guard," a woman suggested.

But the guard was busy at the far end of the other carriage, announcing their imminent arrival at Bodmin Parkway, an announcement lost in the roar of the train's wheels, the rattling of the carriage, and the aggregate commotion.

"There's nothing wrong with me!" Duncan was protesting. "There's something wrong with all of you! That is my point!"

As more people stood up, some to intercede or observe, others to leave, the train came to a stop. The doors opened, greeting those waiting on the platform with shouting and confusion. As it seemed no one was leaving from that particular door, people started to get on apprehensively, only to bump into those finally daring to exit. Duncan found himself caught in the mêlée – very much of his own making, exacerbated once he had insisted in a stentorian manner, this was all merely 'sapiential dissension!'. He was ejected backwards, still clutching his book, onto the platform and his backside just as the doors were closing.

There were looks of amusement, and looks of concern, from the carriage as it pulled away from the station.

He sat up, dusting himself down.

"Are you all right, sir?" the station guard called out, rushing to help.

"Yes, I'm fine," he said, looking up at her as she extended a hand. "I just want to read my book for a while. Would you be so good as to tell me, when is the next train to Penzance?"

He found himself perfectly happy for a time, seated on the bench against the old signal box, reading in the soft sunlight, glancing up occasionally at the conifers surrounding the station. There was a branch line that accommodated steam trains, which he would like to check out one day. This wasn't such a bad place to be stranded. Parkway stations normally lacked soul and that wasn't the case here. His delight increased even further once he discovered that the signal box was actually a café. It was while in there, sipping tea and munching a flapjack, that he realised his luggage was still on the train, hurtling towards Penzance without him.

"'It's a beautiful, tranquil place so give us your sick, your wealthy, your stress, your litter, your barking yelping dogs, and crap all over it. Talk loudly on your mobile at two a.m. because somewhere, somewhere else, is more important than here, no matter those trying to sleep because they have work in the morning. The music of the wind and the sea is not enough, so give us your own and play it at full volume. Watch TV, and get drunk, really drunk – as if Porthengrous needs any help with that. Give us lots of narcotics while you're at it, because life is not sufficiently intoxicating. Walk around with the other ice-cream lickers, the huddled masses staring glassy-eyed at anything because it's nicer than that destroyed with all the other numbskulls back home. Come on, come on, the village can take it all, even if it results in miles of metal bile spewing out of every orifice, when you and others wish to leave with your BMWs and Audis clogging the town arteries. Maybe you'll like it so much you'll buy a second home, and leave it empty for most of the year, in the desolate heart of what was once a vibrant village.'

"It's like that song you used to play, Dad, when we were little ('Come inside, come inside.'), people flocking to see 'the greatest show on Earth,' a single blade of grass growing in the centre of a huge marquee. These people, instead of making their own places beautiful, will destroy the planet and then travel hundreds, thousands, of miles just to see the show. And it's not as if they want the *real* show. 'Look at the country people doing country things.' But they *don't want* the real country, they want Marie

205

Antoinette farms, Marie Antoinette villages, and complain about the televisions being too small, about the sound of hens, the smell of fish, the dirty clothes we wear, the horse shit on the roads..."

The speaker was a young woman in her twenties with rosy cheeks and a handsome mane of thick black hair. She was standing by the open south-facing door of a small shambolic kitchen, dangling an unlit cigarette in her hand. She would never light up, the ritual was purely symbolic, one which she still enjoyed even without fire. The Aga too was cold, shade being more requisite in the summer months than light and heat, of which there was plenty.

Her listener sat quietly in the corner, a baby of just a few months' old cradled in his arms. He seemed deeply content with what he was holding, and by listening fondly to his daughter's inspired ranting.

Jasmine fell quiet, gazing at her father and son together. Enjoying the moment, she nonetheless couldn't help thinking once more how much help Duncan could provide as a babysitter, and generally.

At Penzance station she hadn't been too surprised, nor disappointed as the crowd of arrivals thinned, revealing the absence of her father. It was to be expected. She remembered the trouble he had caused in a Quiet Carriage once, objecting to the noise a couple made whilst inflating their neck-vests, then again when they ate their crisps too loudly. When a baby started crying, he made more noise than the infant.

She had gone calmly this time to the enquiry office, to be informed yes, they had received a call from Bodmin station where her father had disembarked, and they were in the process of retrieving his luggage. Would she like it? Charmed by this old-style trust – there had been no demand for identification, just a quick look and assessment of her features, the baby asleep on her shoulder – she declined. "One child at a time," she had laughed, as had they. He could sort out his own mess when he arrived, was the tacit agreement. She left just as the porter arrived with audaciously pink and blue suitcases on a trolley. With less than an hour to wait, she sat in the little café, reading a newspaper. The child remained asleep, and she enjoyed the respite as, hopefully, a sign of things to come. She had her hands full with being a mother, her husband at work every day, and the land in which they had invested requiring constant attention.

"You're not so cynical," Duncan observed now, looking up from his charge. "That's my role. Especially with teenagers apparently."

"Yes, Dad, honest – you should relax." He had told her his version of events on the train. His account was lacklustre, but she knew how to read him. "Rowan and I both saw all kinds of stuff online we never told you and Mum about, and we're all right. Well, I am. He's a prig who thinks being rich will make him happy. I'm sure he's a Tory convinced that better roads and wi-fi is the solution to everybody's problems. Eventually he'll buy extra homes in Cornwall. I pity his kids if he ever has any, which I'm sure he will. They'll be brought up by screens, watching those food programmes aimed at people wealthy enough to buy the ingredients. I'd pity Elaine if she weren't as bad. But you can't blame the internet for either of *them*. And, hey, *I'm* all right," she repeated.

"Yes, you *are* all right," murmured her father appreciatively.

They were both smiling. She replaced the cigarette in its box with the six others, leaving them on the shelf by the door, then sat down at the wooden table, stained and marked by decades of unknown history.

"Remember when Matt and I lived on the north coast," she said, "in Porthmeed? We kept complaining about the drunks gathering and rasping outside the Legion. We did try discussing it with them, but they were only interested in getting more drunk, more selfish and more mean. We laughed at this legacy of the Empire. You were the one who pointed out past battles were won by belligerent drunks; the 'raw fuel of British history', I recall you saying."

"Yes, I am always keen to draw attention to the unsung. Like at Bletchley, where the brilliant were glorified, but so much had been accomplished by the thousands of junior ranks listening for hours, capable of recognising individual senders. Who knows who we don't know in history."

"Exactly! Tra la! You're proving my point: *I* am the cynic in the family."

Although she fell silent triumphantly, it was hard to consider someone with such rosy cheeks, and such a warm smile of gleaming white teeth, as truly cynical in anything. She had too much capacity to laugh at herself. Her own opinions were therefore risible. She looked at her father, wondering why he too had become silent; not knowing that he was thinking how *he* had become one of the little people, reduced in circumstances, unsung by the lies of history.

"How did you like Porthengrous?" she asked. It was still hard to accept he had been but three miles away on the coast for a week, without her knowledge.

"I liked it," he said, casting his mind back. "I would have liked it more if it weren't for all the other tourists."

"Oh you weren't a tourist, Dad. You were on a mission even if you didn't manage to complete it then."

"I see you won't ever let that go, will you," he chuckled.

"Not as long as it gets a rise out of you, no."

"As you know, I am also interested in its history…"

"A coincidence, huh?"

"Perhaps. It must have been a busy place in the Middle Ages, and it's a busy place now despite its size. Sometimes it felt like a village of angle-grinders and strimmers. Everywhere I went people were fixing up properties, which I suppose is a good thing on one level. Then on change-over days industrial cleaning units added to the symphony. The walls of the village became a bewildering echo-chamber. I didn't know where I was, what I was meant to be doing half the time. Delivery men could often be seen, wandering, lost, confused by streets that weren't on any map, and others that were, weren't."

"Apart from not coming to see us, you were supposed to be writing, weren't you?"

"Indeed. That was difficult however because of all the noise."

"You'll have plenty of quiet in the barn here."

"I've already started another section."

"I predict you'll stay with us for a long time, your book will be a roaring success and you'll pay to finish renovating the barn, as you'll be so deliriously happy living here with us."

Duncan's eyes twinkled. "And when your mother visits?"

"Oh no running away from that one, Dad. You'll have to keep it civil. Both you and Mum are building new lives, and it's got to be as good as, if not better, than what existed before. You don't want to end up with Plymouth. But we'll cross that bridge when we come to it." She nodded at her son, still asleep. "You know you will have to give him back to me eventually."

"Yes," Duncan smiled back at her, self-consciously, as if he were emerging from his own long sleep.

"I thought you were going for a swim."

"Indeed." He rose and carefully passed the child over to her. "I'll throw some salad together while you're gone."

"Thanks," he said, as he stepped out into the hot day, grabbing his towel and baseball cap from the table as he went. "I'll do the dishes after."

"The machete's in the shed where you left it!" she called out.

The shed was past the front door and by the little road which saw little traffic. He picked up the machete that was leaning against the door with peeling, muddy green paint. Going past the crumbling stone pillars at the entrance, he paused a moment to consider the fallen White Caunce Farm sign lying propped up in a bed of nettles and gorse. Matt said he'd attend to it that weekend but Duncan wondered if it weren't within his own abilities. The post was still there. Some paint, a hammer and nails, should do the job.

Duncan's son-in-law had sunk his inheritance into the property, and Jasmine added to it with a trust fund that had been set up by Rose's father – that is, from the wealthier side of the family. The abandoned farm had been seriously dilapidated yet had a few acres to it, including the old quarry, now their secret swimming pool. It was fortunate the owner, a Cornishman, had held out for what he considered 'the right type'. Unlike so many in the vicinity, he wasn't prepared to allow another centuries-old dwelling to become a sterile holiday home for extra cash. Jasmine and Matt had felt put out initially by his probing questions, till they realised they were all on the same page.

Duncan took a deep breath and exhaled slowly. He felt good here. Porthengrous had been beautiful, but weighted down by too much history. Here they were remote from traffic on all levels, the past itself being so distant. There were relics such as standing stones, and many old tracks, all so scattered and infrequent, the land was allowed to breathe. A good place from which to build again.

Gazing at the farm, he thought of Jasmine and his renewed connection with her. Strange that this was where she had ended up. After obtaining a degree in architecture, and practising for a short time, she had surrendered, declaring nothing could be achieved until councils and politicians developed a sense of aesthetics and imagination. Her mind remained as active and inquiring as ever. Consumerism depended largely on not questioning the source; and she and Matt questioned everything, even the validity of the Fair

Trade products that lined their shelves. Thus Jasmine also questioned her own natural source, her mother, in no small way, providing Duncan with sanctuary.

At breakfast she had mentioned something about optic fibres. What was that now? Duncan rubbed the stubble of his chin pensively. He knew of the telegraph museum at Porthcurno, he should visit it sometime. Ahh yes. Jasmine and Matt knew someone who worked at the location from where all the cross-Atlantic cables emanated. A handful of cables, each no thicker than a hair, handling millions of communications every second, it was extraordinary. Technology may have mostly ended up in the hands of morons, or so he often argued, but it was still extraordinary. What was even more astonishing was that this optic fibre station was an unguarded secret here in Cornwall. The locals all knew about it. In a time of global paranoia and suspicion, it was refreshing to find an isolated, balanced perspective.

The sound of a distant tractor brought Duncan to his senses. He had been truly lost in thought. Not much traffic ever came by, but enough for him to be knocked over if he remained too long in the middle of the road. The five minutes or so he'd been there in the full force of the sun were also sufficient to cause him to sweat profusely.

He wiped his brow with his forearm then proceeded down the little track opposite the farm entrance, and headed in the easterly direction of Porthengrous. Passers-by would not notice the path. It wasn't public and was shielded from view by a mass of blackthorn. You had to crouch down to get through. They were going to keep the entrance that way for privacy.

Once through the secret entrance, he took off his shirt and left it hanging on a branch of hawthorn. It was sticky with sweat and he didn't need it.

He surged forward, swinging the machete where more growth fell on top of the branches he had felled the day before. Soon, the family and visitors would be able to enjoy unhindered passage to the quarry. He was wearing shorts, and nettles he had missed previously now stung his legs, whereas his torso was scratched continuously by brambles and wayward thorns. There were numerous insects buzzing about in the heat, damp from the marsh-like surroundings and enclosed canopy of green. As Duncan approached one particular stretch he was ready for the proliferation of horseflies, swatting them off his wounded skin as soon as he felt them touch. They gathered mostly in that place for some reason, and soon he left them behind, swinging his blade rhythmically. Despite the sweat almost blinding him he remembered the little bridge of planks across the trickling stream, and stepped cautiously along its rotting wood. He should replace it at some point. Finally he emerged victoriously from the undergrowth, to stand beneath the quarry walls. A buzzard soared across the patch of blue sky above, and butterflies danced between the clumps of nettles.

The walls were about the width and height of a large two-storey house and, with trees of many types crowning them, towered above mere human beings; their horse-shoe shape holding the still shadowy waters, nourished by a hidden stream. There were white lilies stretching across from near the entrance, covering about a quarter of the artificial sun-dappled lake, over which hovered sparkling blue dragon- and damselflies, on wings of blurred shimmering light.

There were a few discarded boulders by the entrance. Duncan sat on one, leaving his towel, hat and machete upon another. He grabbed a dock leaf and rubbed it over the nettle stings on his legs. He was also prepared this time for the other wounds, and pulled a small bottle of aloe vera sanitiser out of his shorts pocket, rubbing some of the gel onto any cuts and grazes he could reach. There didn't appear to be much actual bleeding so he considered the risk of infection unlikely. He then stripped down completely.

As the ground was littered with sharp stones and discarded foliage, he had to step carefully in his bare feet. There was a gradual descent into the water due to slabs of rock leading in, whether from natural or human design it was hard to tell.

The pads of lilies on his left, he launched into the pool. First sound waves, then those of the water, rebounded from the quarry walls. The water had been warming for weeks and was pleasant to be in. Doing breast stroke, Duncan headed for one of the patches of sunlight gleaming on the dusky brown surface.

Turning over, he floated content for a while, the sunlight filtered by the trees above, gentle on his closed eyes. His life would be complete now, he mused, if a woman were by his side. He couldn't help fantasising a bit, how Charlotte in Devon would discover what had happened the day of the unfortunate date. She would then be directed to Kerris by Kay, to be informed by Jasmine where he was at the present moment, then follow his trail of creative destruction. Lying still upon the quarry waters, he would hear someone approach, a skirt brushing against nettles, sandals tapping dry broken twigs. His eyes would half-open to see her, a quietly lit vision, by the water's edge. She wouldn't say anything, would kick off her sandals, let her skirt drop to the ground with the rest of her clothes, and she would step in gingerly to join him. His life would be complete.

He waited awhile. Nobody came. It was only a fantasy, he reminded himself. Besides, was he really troubled by its unfulfillment, any more than he was by that of others? He was meant to want things, every character in a story did, so he was told by everyone; but he no longer truly wanted anything. Desire itself was an artificial separation manufactured by Time, a way of denying the present. He didn't want to be so dependent on outer circumstances, he didn't *want*.

He opened his eyes, the scene bereft of company except for damselflies darting around. Strange, they were called such when they were both male and female. One copulating couple in flight caught his attention. A single one came particularly close, hovering. When suddenly it veered off in the direction of the lilies, Duncan decided to follow. He was curious to hear what the wings of these glamorous insects sounded like. So far he had heard nothing, as if they floated on silence. Horseflies, the guards of a secret treasure, soon dispelled any hopes he had of discovery, their noisy clatter drowning out all else.

As he drew closer to the lilies, he wondered what they smelt like. He pushed delicately amongst the pads, as they swayed on their stalks protruding delicately and firmly from unknown depths, till reaching a flower. Thrusting his head close to it, he inhaled deeply. It was divine. It was... How could he describe it? The scent was both subtle and powerful, totally unique. He could think of nothing with which to compare it. He took several more inhalations, then pulled back towards the centre of the pool.

It mildly bothered him. He was supposedly a writer of sorts. He had been commended for his ability to recreate past events vividly, yet no matter how much he advanced as a communicator he would never be able to portray with any degree of accuracy, the scent of a lily.

The damselfly – he assumed it to be the same one – glided over him back to from wherever it had come. He lay on his back in the dappled sunlight, listening to the chatter of birds, and the occasional murmur of wings. He was soon deeply content, even his shortcomings as a writer no longer troubling him.

Except his tooth now made its presence felt. For almost a week he had been avoiding eating on the left side of his jaw, also taking painkillers with every meal or snack. The strategy seemed to have worked, in that no pain had manifested in all this time. Now suddenly the amnesty was over.

He felt with his tongue that something was loose. It could have been the tooth the dentist was keen to extract, he wasn't sure. It would make sense. He played some more with it, using his tongue, then started pushing more aggressively.

He was about to reach in with his fingers when the whole tooth came loose. Instinctively, as his mouth filled up with blood, he spat it out.

It had been with him for most of his life, he realised plaintively, catching a glimpse of it as it sank beneath the waters. He turned on his side to eject more bloody spittle, then returned to floating on his back. There was a dull pain in his jaw which, oddly, felt good. Something had been completed. Heck, he really was going to become a toothless old man. He turned briefly to spit out more blood. One of his cuts seemed to have opened too.

Thus, naked, corpulent, floating amidst the hollow echoes of the unassailable quarry walls, haunted by the indescribable scent of a lily, surrounded by iridescent insects, unknown fish and eels beneath, a crow calling far above; he relaxed in deep contentment and a benign fusion of water and blood.

He knew now with absolute certainty that the world was full of love, romances merely contained by that love, as wonderful as each may be.

Corporal King was waiting for him near the end of Runway One, as close as he could get to the hut without going on the grass. He was leaning against the staff car, smoking. On seeing Donnel approach he dropped his cigarette, snapped to attention and saluted.

"Do you remember me, sir?" he asked as he came to relieve Donnel of his bags.

"Of course I do, Corporal."

"Weather's not much better than when I picked you up then," he said, putting the luggage in the boot.

The air was damp and with a trace of mist.

"Not quite as bad," Donnel commented, getting in to the back.

King got in, started the ignition and they headed towards the main entrance.

"The group captain wanted to extend you this courtesy, sir."

"So I understand. That's very considerate of him." Not wishing to encourage further conversation, Donnel didn't add the humorous speculation that the station commander merely wished to make sure he was actually leaving.

The first Bellman hangar was indistinct in the haze. Donnel felt Smith was probably at work there on a Walrus that needed extra attention, so he had heard; not from Smith, who hadn't returned to the hut the previous night. Nobody had, except for Hawker who crashed in during the wee hours. He was snoring heavily just ten minutes earlier, and was unwakeable. Donnel had left a note.

They crawled past the squadron office. He looked in vain for a sign, of life, of anything. The door remained closed. He sighed inwardly. He felt he had done what he could, which was nothing. There were two women in his life, whether he liked it or not, whether he saw either one of them again or not. By accepting the responsibility of the world, through the Ford Lauderdale posting, he had effortlessly managed to evade personal responsibility.

King was talking about the movie he had recently seen. Donnel leaned forward.

"Corporal?"

"Yes, sir?"

"I would appreciate it if we didn't talk. I'm still paying for last night."

"Of course, sir," said the jocular Englishman.

In truth, only Donnel's jaw hurt. He rubbed it now. Despite being a semi-invalid, Smith still packed a mighty punch.

So this was how his British tour ended, his only souvenir a US Navy Colt given him by Maggie, saying she never wished to touch a gun again. He wondered what her line of work was, that she had the luxury of such choice.

She was there now, outside Ravenscroft about to get into the Hillman, talking with Spiffy. Donnel turned as they went past, watching as they saluted each other and she got into her car in order to return to Station X, whatever the heck, wherever the heck, that was.

He sank back into his seat, this penultimate chapter of his life over.

Joyce left Sandra in the office, saying she needed a twenty minutes break. Squadron Leader Francis also understood the occasion and told her to take as much time off as she required that afternoon. Since the girls had agreed to go to Malta, he was generally more relaxed, having a team he could rely on. He knew of Joyce's engagement, so was surprised and relieved that she agreed to the posting; for he wasn't going to insist on their accompanying him, it was more a favour granted by his superiors. He wasn't to know that Sandra's heart was perilously close to breaking, that she was eager for a new sky fresh of associations, and with more challenges to distract. Nor was he to know that Joyce's loyalty to her friend still superseded that to her future husband, particularly when he was doing so well.

She walked towards the Bellman nearest the hut now occupied by the American Navy, her time there already a distant memory. How could so much of significance occur in so small a space, in so limited a time? And how fragile it had been. Maggie gone, David Proudon disappeared under mysterious circumstances, and Jackie Donnel gone, taking with him a precious part of Sandra. Ben Hawker she had only caught glimpses of these past five days, once cycling to Yelverton with a brace of pheasant swinging from the handle-bars, another time gathering serim and sphagnum moss by the roadside. He never seemed to notice her, being too far away, or too busy. His uniform was becoming subtly shambolic once more, she had noticed, another sign of Maggie's absence.

"You're too late, Sergeant." A voice startled her out of reverie.

"What?"

One of the airmen Smith worked with was standing in front of her in filthy overalls, his thin, amiable face smeared with grease and sweat in the baking heat. He was carrying a glim lamp. "Trev's over there, Sergeant," he said uncertainly, pointing. The team were on first-name terms with each other, yet nobody knew if that familiarity extended to fiancées. "They're about to take off."

She followed his gaze south-east to where a Walrus was taxiing in their direction, building up speed. She hadn't heard it for the sound of a Typhoon's engine being tested in the hangar by the office.

"That's him?" she asked, thrilled.

"Yes," said the young man, coming to stand alongside.

"He said he might get to fly it," she commented.

215

"Well, he did think as he fixed it, he oughta have a go."

They found themselves walking past the watchtower in order to get closer to the runway.

"Is he alone?" she asked, shielding her eyes against the sun blazing fiercely from a pristine sky.

"No, Steve wanted to go too. He's never been up before. It's only a short test flight, but he'll enjoy it. Something to write home about."

"Have you been up...Mark, is it?"

"Yes, Sergeant."

"'Joyce', please. We're alone here."

"Joyce... There he goes."

The Walrus gathered speed, risible by the standards of its more glamorous peers. Nonetheless, Joyce felt an increased thrill as it lifted from the ground, knowing how important it was to her lover.

She smiled broadly, finding it hard to contain her enthusiasm, and not wishing to.

Her companion smiled also, watching with her as the plane started a gentle circuit. As it turned over the moor, he said to Joyce, "I'll be going now. Got to get this back to Stores."

"Yes, thank you, Mark. See you again."

He lingered a bit, reluctant to leave. He liked Smith and he liked her, they each brought an interesting, refined air to his world, without being snotty.

When he did get going, Joyce didn't notice his departure, being too enraptured by the tiny dot in the sky to the south, growing bigger, coming back home. She walked forward to where the two runways met, as if to greet it.

In its two years of existence, RAF Clearbrooke had had its share of nasty accidents and fatalities, tasters of what others elsewhere were facing on a far greater scale and intensity. It had not been attacked once.

Fittingly enough, as the skies above the airfield were mostly a cobalt blue, laced with a few wisps of fan-shaped cloud, conditions were not so clear over the channel. Even above Plymouth a gradual thickening was in evidence.

If this abundance of cloud-cover towards France proved fortunate for a group of four Focke-Wulfe 190s, it was their first taste of good fortune in some time. Earlier that year many of their squadron had been lost due to ill-advised night-raids over the east coast of England, de Havilland Mosquitoes making short work of them. Ridiculously, some of their number had been so lost they had ended up landing in England itself.

This lone raid on Plymouth docks could therefore be viewed as an attempt at regaining their self-confidence. However, that particular dish is rarely served cold, and the old channel fears resurfaced in the blood of the two pilots who had survived the 1940 raids. Both of them were looking anxiously at their panels, the fear – now perennial – of that red light indicating an empty tank was not rational, but was insistent. Fear of discovery also kept them so low beneath the radar, one pilot lost a wing tip to the waves early on.

Their fear may have seemed prescient when a patrol of Spitfires spotted them. On being informed, Operations immediately alerted a training patrol nearby of Hurricanes. The Czechoslovakian pilots took this not as a warning but an invitation.

The Germans realised very quickly they were outgunned, the 1000 lb bombs each of them carrying now being nothing but a hindrance. So they did the only thing they could. They climbed desperately until lost in the clouds.

In the chaos that followed, shapes being followed, shouts over the airwaves in at least three different languages, one German fighter emerged eventually over Cornwall. The pilot had no idea where he was, only that it had to be England he could see beneath, and he knew he had to bear south. The chatter on his radio had faded into incoherence. He was on his own.

Being the youngest of his squadron, he had no irrational terror of the red light and was confident he had enough fuel to get back. As he turned east, he was further reassured by the fact nobody was shooting at him and he prolonged the trajectory, somewhat mesmerised by the rolling grandeur beneath despite the restricted vision of the cockpit. This was a country he might enjoy visiting one day.

He came to his senses at glimpsing Egloston ahead. He had to get rid of the bomb and here was an opportunity. Despite his years, a ruthlessness had been cultivated over the past months, with so many fallen comrades whose promising friendships with him had hardly begun. This ruthlessness gained extra fuel from the merciless destruction of German cities by the Allies. He had no qualms about releasing one bomb on an English town.

The bomb was powerful enough to level a three-generations old department store built from local granite, ripping apart two mothers and their children, several American GIs and all the staff. Scarcity had proven fortuitous in that there weren't more people present, due to the meagre supplies and little money with which to purchase them. After the war, eventually, the site would become a multi-storey car park.

Soon the pilot did regret having dropped the bomb, because he now saw Clearbrooke airfield when bearing south, and felt he had missed an opportunity. Determined to make more of the day count, he dropped altitude swiftly. There was a kind of fate in how all this was turning out, he thought, the ease with which he was dispensing destruction whilst simply going home.

Joyce became aware of an ominous drone turning to a throaty roar.

The Walrus had not yet touched ground, but was about to when she turned to see the German plane descend.

Two machine guns blazed unnecessarily, for the pilot's aim was true and the ferociously shaking cannons were all that were needed. Doing justice to the German love for explosive shells, the Walrus erupted in flame, blood and horror within seconds. Flesh blended with steel and canvas. If there were any screams they were swallowed by the merciless sounds of machine attacking machine, heads and limbs scattered with other flying debris.

Joyce ran, spent shell cases falling like hot rain.

The plane was so close. Her fiancé was so close.

She ran, screaming, the heat of the blazing shambles upon her face.

She would have gone on, leapt in, an unwitting suttee, but Mark was rushing towards her. He threw her to the ground and held her back. She fought against him uselessly, howling, disbelieving.

The lone Focke-Wulfe was a diminishing dot in the sky by the time the airfield started to react.

Joyce, collapsing, knew the war was truly over for her, as something broke inside.

Like a cruel joke, or a lament, the siren started wailing. People and vehicles converged on the scene, with blood buckets and green goddesses.

Angels zero.

The band played and the couples swayed elegantly, not least Donnel and Sandra. She had proven a quick learner.

Through its fusion of different styles, America had taken over the dance hall that evening and provided it with joy and ebullience. As Sandra turned in a gyre, mirroring lightly, Donnel felt any sense of time disappearing. They were always here, they were always in love. The song ended on a triumphant note, only for another to take its place immediately, slower, gentler. They danced a few inches away from each other, hands entwined and on each other's waists, eyes meeting on the softening edge of an ecstatic terror.

The sense of completion was overwhelming – or so he would have thought, if he had had any room for thought. All he knew was that everything ended and began here, where time no longer existed. The feeling of annihilation was inexorable and indescribable; here while the world took leave of its senses, here was all sense, in her yielding warm body, delicate steps reflecting his, her deer-like eyes, and dress a shimmering, diamond-white, iridescent waterfall.

Acknowledgements

There were several adaptations of stories that ended up on the cutting room floor. One of them was from a book by Hugh MacBride, and told how he attended a talk soon after the war by an RAF pilot who had been shot down and taken prisoner in Germany. As I recall, the pilot was treated to beer and sausages by the local authority, then the conviviality was brought to an abrupt end by the news that the intelligence officer from the Luftwaffe was approaching. The Germans quickly tidied everything up to make the room look official and by-the-book. When the officer arrived, he exclaimed, 'What are you idiots doing?! Don't you know this man is a hero of his people? Where is the beer and sausages?' The pilot told the story honestly, but the RAF officials were obviously uncomfortable with this portrayal of the enemy.

I am being defiant here and including this story as a 'deleted scene', in a sort of quiet resentment that I couldn't fit in adaptations of it and others. Though they won't ever be included in the Director's Cut, their existence does touch on the fact that innumerable sources led to the novel's creation, not all of which can be given the credit they deserve. The numbers are too formidable.

Certainly, a growing awareness as I wrote this was that some of the elderly people I saw around me in the twenty-first century were the young men and women I was attempting to depict on the airfield. I spoke to most of them only in passing, as I sat next to them on a bus, or bumped into them in a café. Others, with whom I was fortunate enough to be granted lengthy interviews, often iterated variations of a sentence that formed a background theme in this book, that 'We didn't fight life like they do now.'

This is a story about stories, from different eras and perspectives, some of which are based on fact. The stories I learned from those named here, those unnamed, including from the internet and from the (very) select bibliography, played a major part. Whatever the merits of this particular tale, I can only hope I have done some justice to the emotional and spiritual magnitude of each of its sources.

221

My current home Mousehole in Cornwall appears in various guises, in different centuries, so I feel it appropriate to thank three of its residents directly. First, Jack Guard for his time and memories, particularly regarding his experiences on 'K' sites. It was certainly serendipitous, that a decoy airfield would feature strongly in the plot, and that one of my neighbours actually spent a lot of time serving on one. Any deviations from the truth regarding decoys, are entirely mine. Sylvia Pender Johns also shared her experiences of Mousehole during the war; which, along with her book about her brother Jack Pender, helped form some of the background colour. Another neighbour, David Hearle, had insights and anecdotes from his experiences in the Navy that were consistently helpful.

Angela Stead and her brother the aforementioned Hugh MacBride gave generously of their time, lending me manuscripts from their books, thus providing me with details and nuances of life during wartime, particularly as seen through the eyes of children. Their book 'Siblings' Haven' is still available, and Hugh's own book mentioned above, 'On Her Majesty's National Service: My Time in the RAF', may well be in print by now.

My father cast a helpfully critical eye over a couple of passages related to flying, and provided valuable insights into the chain of command in the Royal Air Force, terms of address, and technical information.

My mother provided important details about music and the use of gramophones.

To those who know that area of Devon, the airfield is clearly based on RAF Harrowbeer. Despite keeping as close to its geography and history as I could, I had to make just too many changes for the sake of the story, and thus decided to alter its name – rather cheekily as local historians may note.

Many of those devoted to studying the airfield and to putting on the annual 1940s event – such as the RAF Harrowbeer Interest Group – were extremely helpful.

Michael Hayes of the RAF Harrowbeer Archives was particularly supportive through his dedicated research and understanding of the airfield. He filled in many gaps and managed to put me right on the smallest details. Again, any deviations from the truth are entirely mine.

Sarah of 'Boudoir' in Penzance helped extensively with advice about 1940s clothing.

Penzance Public Library when it was in Morrab Road had an impressive range of books on the Second World War, some of which are listed in the bibliography. To have such a resource close to hand was a blessing I never took for granted. The internet – as to be expected in the twenty-first century – was invaluable. There are too many sites to mention, but the Imperial War Museum (physically as well as online), Wikipedia and the BBC Archives certainly stand out.

Online sources were essential also for the medieval research; as was Jennifer Harpur who deserves special thanks for changing my mind about Chaucer.

Mike and Kei have never met actually or even virtually but at time of writing are managing to bring together their wonderful design skills and aesthetic sensibilities to work on the cover. Silvia Pastore also deserves thanks for bringing my attention to the genius of Eric Ravilious.

Premgit and Sandhya, among other things, introduced me to Emmylou's version of the Neil Young song which haunts these pages. I mention their names specifically here last, but they should really be the first. Without their light on the moor, none of this would have been possible.

Some of those who supported this publishing endeavour through Kickstarter expressed a wish to remain anonymous, and I will respect that whilst acknowledging that the twenty-three individuals who made pledges ensured that publication happened. Quite a few also gave essential creative advice. In a novel that in part examines collective will, it is entirely fitting that making it into print is due in no small way to a group effort.

Thank you everyone, named and unnamed, for your part to play in the creation of this novel.

Select Bibliography

Listening to Britain: Home Intelligence Reports of Britain's Finest Hour – ed. Paul Addison and Jeremy A. Craig

The Stories of Flying Officer X – H. E. Bates

The Knights Templars and The Key of Solomon the King – A. Bothwell-Gosse and S. Liddell MacGregor Mathers

Fighter: The True Story of the Battle of Britain – Len Deighton

Humanity: A Moral History of the Twentieth Century – Jonathan Glover

The Few: July-October 1940 – Alex Kershaw

I Only Joined for the Hat – Christian Lamb

The Secret Life of Bletchley Park – Sinclair McKay

Got Any Gum Chum? – Helen D. Millgate

Millions Like Us: Women's Lives During the Second World War – ed. Virginia Nicholson

Typhoon Pilot – Desmond Scott

First Light – Geoffrey Wellum

Lightning Source UK Ltd.
Milton Keynes UK
UKOW02f0255150916

282979UK00003B/34/P

9 781787 190467